TEN THIRTEEN

"Harry, turn around and have a good look. There's a black sedan that was with us up First Avenue."

I twisted around. "Black Buick, I think." The Buick was in the access lane. We were in the middle and now Fran was kneeling on the backseat next to me. "Move to the fast lane," I told Finelli, and as he swung over, the Buick shifted into the middle lane.

"He's following," I said to Finelli. The Buick roared ahead, sat beside us for a moment, and then the left rear window moved down. I just had time to push Fran to the floor. Finelli shoved Paula down. I was clawing for my gun when the shot from the Buick passed me and smashed a hole in the left rear window. A second shot came so close I swear I felt the breath of the bullet across my face. . . .

Also by E. V. Cunningham:

The
Wabash Factor

E.V. CUNNINGHAM

A DELL BOOK

Published by
Dell Publishing Co., Inc.
1 Dag Hammarskjold Plaza
New York, New York 10017

Dell ® TM 681510, Dell Publishing Co., Inc.

ISBN: 0-440-19390-7

Reprinted by arrangement with Delacorte Press

Printed in the United States of America

December 1986

10 9 8 7 6 5 4 3 2 1

WFH

For Julie, Brother and Friend

Chapter 1

"WHO WAS THAT?" I asked my wife, Fran, after she had answered the telephone and had finished talking.

"That was Professor Oscar Golding, advisor to presidents, and Stillman Professor of Sociology at New York University—" And seeing my face, "Come on, come on, Harry. I'm only trying to lighten things up. You've been on edge all day. Enough."

"You know what I dislike most about intellectuals, about people like you and my brother? I'll tell you—"

"Harry, you're more of an intellectual than either of us. You're better read—"

"I'm a high school graduate and I'm a cop, so don't give me that and don't patronize me."

"I'm not going to let us have a fight about this," Fran said.

"What did Oscar say?"

She stared at me with that half smile of hers, and I considered the luck that had brought me to a tough little Irish kid who happened to grow into an amazing woman. We had a good marriage. We had two kids who were in college. We had a nice place to live. Fran was a teacher at Columbia, only an instructor in the English department, but still at

7

Columbia. We had a lot of things going for us, and if we had an occasional battle—well, we were only human.

"What did Oscar say?" I asked her again. Oscar was my brother, a college professor who had used the media and his own talent for publicity to give himself a national reputation. He had been called down to Washington as an advisor to former President Ford—who certainly needed all the advice he could get—and he had been interviewed at least fifty times on various talk shows. We had a pretty good relationship as such things go. Oscar liked the notion of a brother who was a police detective. It added color to his life. He liked color.

"He said that interest was very high, and that they've scheduled it in a larger lecture hall. That means at least five hundred students, maybe more. He feels that you must answer questions."

"No."

I had been fool enough to let Oscar talk me into giving a lecture on "Homicide in an Urban Setting" for one of his sociology classes. It was the last thing in the world that I should have done.

"No," I repeated. "You call Oscar back and tell him to forget it. I've been working all day on this miserable speech. I'm willing to stand up there like a dumbbell and read it. I am not willing to answer questions. So just call Oscar back."

"He's your brother," Fran said. "You call him."

"He'll talk me into it."

"Then you have no backbone, which is something I can do nothing about. For God's sake, Harry, you're an intelligent man. You're a lieutenant of police in New York City. You didn't need me to call in sick and take a day off to write a speech for a bunch of college kids. I know that you'll never forgive yourself for not going to college and you'll live your life in awe of the idiot kids who do. But if you just stand up there and speak for an hour on some aspect of real police work, you'll be giving them something they never got from people like Oscar. I know. My life at work is filled with Oscars."

"How about the speech I have here?"

"Great."

"You're not putting me on?"

"Cross my heart. Look, it's four o'clock already. You pour some vodka, and I'll get crackers and cheese. We'll have a late dinner after your talk."

Then as I began to pour the vodka, the telephone rang, and that was the beginning of a very crowded and curious evening. After that evening, nothing was the same again.

The telephone call was from Frederick Lawrence, curator of seventeenth- and eighteenth-century paintings at the museum. He had been close to out of his mind these past three days because the museum's most precious Vermeer had been stolen. For those who find this confusing, let me note that Jan Vermeer was a Dutch painter, born in 1632 and dead forty-three years later. In this short time, Vermeer managed to produce a body of paintings that rank with the best the world has known. This according to Lawrence. Having looked at the Vermeers that were not stolen, I found them very beautiful; I am not competent to make any further judgments.

But according to Lawrence, Vermeers were valuable beyond belief, every single painting noted, catalogued, and verified; so to steal a Vermeer made no sense whatsoever, since it could never be sold. Lawrence's mind danced with images of mad collectors who would keep such a painting in a locked room, images which, as a practical policeman, I rejected. As far as I was concerned, the painting had not been stolen but kidnapped.

"What is it worth?" I asked Lawrence at the time our investigation first began. He had already shown me a print of the picture, a lovely young woman in a blue and white dress, her skin a translucent milky white touched with pink.

"You're kidding," he said.

"Kidding? Why should I be kidding? I asked you what the picture is worth."

"Painting, painting, please call it a painting, Lieutenant."

"Painting."

"Yes, oh, yes. You were asking me how much it is worth?"

"That's what I'd like to find out, Mr. Lawrence."

"Yes, of course," he said. "It's really impossible to say."

"Why? Why is it impossible?"

"Well, suppose it were to be put up for auction at Sotheby's. I mean, that's out of the question, of course, but suppose the museum were in such desperate straits that we had to put it up for auction. Today they're all in the collecting game, Japan, Germany, France, and the Arabs, of course, and even a few Americans in the same league, not to mention Fort Worth and Los Angeles and Houston—city museums—and well—well, I'd set a floor for the bidding at ten million dollars. But that's not what it would sell for."

"What would it sell for?"

"I really can't say, but over the floor."

"Guess," I pressed him.

"For this Vermeer, twelve to fifteen million."

"And that's real, twelve to fifteen million for that little painting? Is that a fact?"

"Absolutely."

"I've read stories and seen movies about crazy collectors who hid stolen treasures so that they could feast their eyes on them when they desired to, but I don't buy that kind of thing. A man owns something important, he wants people to know about it. From what you tell me, I gather this painting could not be offered anywhere for sale?"

"It's a Vermeer, Lieutenant. A Vermeer offered for sale today would be an international event."

"Then the painting was kidnapped, and it will be held for ransom."

Mr. Lawrence did not like the idea of a police lieutenant telling him flat out that one of New York City's most valuable paintings had been kidnapped, but then he would not have appreciated a person of my intellectual level telling him anything at all. For some reason, he preferred the notion of a mad collector, and perhaps in spite of his lecture on price and value, he was licking his lips at the thought of the four million dollars that would be paid by the insurance company. Conceivably, he was not as passionately in love with Vermeer as he made out. So I was not too surprised on this afternoon to detect a note of disappointment in his voice when he told me that the museum had received a ransom note.

"Your Captain Courtny gave me your number, Lieutenant. Otherwise I would not have dreamed of disturbing you at home."

"That's all right. Tell me about the ransom note."

"It was mailed to the museum yesterday, special delivery."

"I presume Captain Courtny told you to copy it and send him the original for the police lab."

"Yes."

"What does it ask for?"

"Five million. Tomorrow. In cash. Which is why I must see you immediately."

"That's impossible. An hour from now I have to address a class of New York University students."

"I don't believe you, Lieutenant!" Lawrence shouted. "Here we're dealing with the survival or the destruction of one of the most valuable paintings on earth, and you tell me you have to address a class of college students?"

"It won't alter the odds for survival, I promise you, Mr. Lawrence. We should be finished no later than seven-thirty, and then my wife and I will have a bite to eat and we can meet you at the museum at nine-thirty."

"That's no good. The museum will be closed."

"Open it."

"Open it? Open it? Do you know what it means to open the museum after the alarms are set?"

"I think I do. I still want the museum opened, and I'd like the director and the president to be there with you."

"That's out of the question," Lawrence said.

"Considering that we're dealing with five million dollars, I should think they'd both want to be there. Tell them I might just recover the picture"—I used the word deliberately—"tonight."

"I'll tell them no such thing. I'm sorry, Lieutenant, but you're making a poor joke out of a very important matter."

"My wife and I will be at the museum at nine-thirty. I suggest that you be there."

I put the telephone down and turned to Fran, who was observing me with interest. "I don't think Mr. Lawrence is very fond of you," she said.

"I'm a Philistine."

"Yes. Of course you are, and Philistines become very irritating when they turn out to be right. Why aren't you more interested in the ransom note? I'm not a witch. I heard you mention it."

"Sure you're a witch. The hell with his ransom note and his damn Vermeer. The thing is, if I agree to this question-and-answer thing tonight—I mean, where do I draw the line? Oscar gives me a lousy subject like 'Homicide in an Urban Setting.' The last thing in the world any cop wants to talk about."

"Why didn't you tell him that?"

"He always intimidates me. You know that. Now suppose these kids ask questions about those crazy Hollywood crimes that you read about? I don't want to speculate."

"That's outside of your purview, Harry. But there are just as many crazy crimes in New York. You just have to be firm. You can talk about something, or you can tell the student that you have no wish to discuss it."

All of which I knew, but everyone has his own terrors, and one of mine was public speaking. How my wife did it every day, standing up before a class of smartass kids, I do not know. She pointed out that I had no problems talking to the detective squad over at the precinct. She had walked in once when I'd blown my top completely and was letting them have it from both barrels; but that was another matter entirely. A New York City policeman—and I have no hesitation in stating that they are the best in the world—has his own problems of existence, very unlike those in civilian life, and being a Jewish cop complicates them even further. I remained sane because this lovely woman I had married kept a balance in my life and saw me through my bouts of cop-depression.

My brother, Oscar, on the other hand, always faced me with a mixture of wonder and affection, still unable to believe that the same genetic factors had given rise to both of us. The Stillman Chair of Sociology at New York University paid one hundred thousand dollars a year, which enabled Oscar, in spite of inflation, to live on Park Avenue in a four-bedroom apartment. What with speaking dates and television appearances, his income was twice that; but Oscar was

12

openhanded. He found it hard to believe that Fran and I could live on East 89th Street without my being on the pad. The fact was that we had bought the apartment sixteen years ago for twenty-two thousand, borrowing the money and paying it off slowly and painfully. Today, the apartment is worth ten times what we had paid for it, but that was luck, not brains and not dishonesty. Oscar's wife, Shelly, always seemed a bit miffed that our apartment was as pleasant as it was, mostly I suppose because Fran had done a better job than Shelly's professional decorator. Shelly had gone to Wellesley and it hurt that a streetwise Irish kid who had a public education at Hunter College should have both taste and brains. On the other hand, it may be that I'm leaning too heavily on Oscar and his wife. Certainly, on this evening, Oscar was cordial and appeared genuinely delighted to see Fran and me. Even Shelly was being her nicest. I'm sure Oscar convinced her that I needed all the moral support that could be provided.

"You're both having dinner with me after the lecture," Oscar decided.

"As long as we break loose at nine or so."

"Nine? Why nine?"

"The case of the stolen Vermeer," Fran said. "Harry has a meeting at the museum at nine-thirty."

"The stolen Vermeer. Of course, that's in your bailiwick, Harry, isn't it? Every so often, a thief steals something as utterly outrageous as this, and of course it's entertainment for everyone."

"Except me," I said shortly.

"I just don't believe it's worth ten million dollars," Shelly said.

"Why not?" Fran asked. "One large missile costs twice that."

"Come on, Fran. We're not going to argue about the freeze."

"Not tonight," Oscar agreed. "Let's get over to the lecture hall. We start in five minutes."

We were still at Washington Square, and now we picked up our pace. There was no line of stragglers drifting into the lecture hall when we got there. Every seat, except two at the front being held for Shelly and Fran, was taken and there were kids standing two-deep at the back of the room. Oscar whispered to me that this was a tribute to me; but the plain truth was that they didn't know me from Adam. While there might have been an added measure of interest on the basis of a lieutenant of police scheduled to talk about murder, it was Oscar who drew them with his reputation of walking, so to speak, where no other professor dared to tread, dealing with delicate subjects without a shred of delicacy.

Oscar, fifty pounds heavier than I and four inches over my five foot eleven, introduced me as his brother and possibly one of the very best cops on the New York City police force. He also mentioned my commendations and a particular medal that I keep in a drawer and never talk about.

That was all I needed, and even with Fran smiling encouragement from the front row, the first two or three sentences lay dead in my throat. But then my voice picked up, and when I realized that the young men and women who packed the hall were listening openmouthed to what I was saying, I began to feel more at ease.

I had structured my remarks to rebut the notion of New York City as the homicide capital of the nation, reminding them that in terms of population, Miami, Los Angeles, Detroit, and a number of other cities could put New York well out of the running.

"As a city, we are very special, very unique," I said. "We have over fifty different nationalities living here in this city, and for the most part, they live in peace with each other. Of course there is murder, but most of these murders are murders of passion, a great many where family members kill within the family. Then we have mob execution, drug-related to a very large extent. And burglaries, of course, burglaries that turn into homicides, muggings that turn into homicides, and even random killing. But the notion that so many out-of-towners have that the streets of New York are unsafe to walk is simply not true."

Fran nodded. "Go on doing exactly what you are doing," her nod stated.

"Tonight," I went on, "I'll try to explain how we deal

14

with a specific homicide. And when I finish, you can ask questions that might fill in the empty holes."

Well, it was not exactly the best construction and it didn't have the neat phrasing that one of Oscar's lectures might have had, but it held my audience and possibly gave them a better notion of how a city precinct goes about dealing with a homicide. When I finished, a dozen hands went up, and I began to answer questions. I discovered what every teacher knows, that the best kind of instruction comes out of the question-and-answer process.

After I had answered half a dozen questions, Oscar, who was dealing with the students, pointed to a tall, skinny young man with glasses.

"I'm not one of Professor Golding's students," the young man said, rising. "I'm a medical student, and my name is James Oshun. I hope that still gives me the right to ask a question?"

"I think so," I said.

"You work in Bellevue, that gives you a vested interest in homicide. Wouldn't you say so, Lieutenant?"

"Not exactly as you put it, Mr. Oshun, but I get your point. What is your question?"

"Well, isn't it true, Lieutenant Golding, that these homicides you are so proud of solving are committed by very stupid people?"

I hesitated. Fran had warned me that there's frequently a student with a game to play, with a noose, a trap, a neat net to drop over the head of the unsuspecting lecturer.

"Stupid people," I said slowly. "Perhaps. Some are stupid, some are neurotic, some are victims of uncontrollable passions—and most of course are pathological."

"But isn't it true," Oshun went on before I could stop him, "that if a really smart guy set out to do a murder, you characters wouldn't even know that a murder had been done —much less solve it?"

Now Oscar rose to take care of Oshun, but I waved him back. Something about the boy intrigued me. I had the feeling that he wasn't trying to provoke me, that something bottled up in him was exploding.

15

"That's possible," I acknowledged. "Do you have something specific in mind?"

"You bet I do, Lieutenant." He was scared but he couldn't stop now. "Stanley Curtis. That's what I have in mind. They murdered Stanley Curtis and then walked away grinning. There wasn't even an investigation."

There was a buzz of voices all over the audience now, and once more Oscar got up to silence Mr. Oshun. "No," I whispered to Oscar. "I want to hear what this kid has to say."

I guess others did too, because now the whispers died away and every head in the room was turned toward Oshun. Stanley Curtis, you may recall, was one of the Democratic candidates for the presidency. To many people, especially the young, he was the only candidate. Fran, who feared that the world would end very soon in an atomic holocaust unless something was done to halt the proliferation of atomic weapons, considered Curtis to be a cross between Abraham Lincoln and Franklin Delano Roosevelt. For myself, I had been a cop too long to believe in good men in politics, yet I must admit that the simple, straightforward decency of Stanley Curtis was somewhat wonderful in our times. It was only ten days since he had died of a stroke while eating dinner one evening at Restaurant La Siene on 51st Street.

"That's a serious charge, Mr. Oshun," I said. "That's a very serious charge. As far as the news reports were concerned, Stanley Curtis died of a stroke. His family doctor was in attendance and concurred with that. I can understand the kind of feeling you would have for Curtis, but what good does it do to claim that he was murdered?"

The boy started to speak—then shook his head, stood for a moment, and dropped back into his seat.

Wisely, Oscar put an end to the questions at that point. Anything now would have been an anticlimax to Oshun's wild charge. The students trickled out of the hall.

Oscar congratulated me. "Absolutely professional, Harry. You'd make a damn good teacher."

I felt exhausted. "If I had to do this kind of thing every day all day, I'd be an invalid in a year. I'll stay a cop."

"You'd get used to it," Fran said, coming up to reward me with a kiss. "Anyway, you were super."

"Harry, you amazed me," Shelly said.

Fran looked at me and shook her head hopelessly, and Oscar said, "Coats on. Time for the payoff. I intend to buy you both a superb dinner. How about the La Siene?"

Fran shivered. "Oh, no. No. I couldn't."

"Come on, Fran," I said, "you're not going to pay attention to that wild charge the kid made. If Oscar wants to buy us a fifty-dollar dinner, we should jump at the chance. He'll never loosen up like that again."

"No. Please."

"I can understand that," Oscar said. "It gets spooky. Suppose we do the Four Seasons."

In the restaurant, dinner ordered, sipping our drinks, Fran said, "I don't want to give you the impression that I'm one of those crazy conspiracy buffs. It's just that Stanley Curtis meant something very special to me. Harry here can be as cynical as he pleases about politicians, but there are good men in politics as well as anywhere else. I just couldn't face the thought of eating in the place where Stanley Curtis died."

"Right on," Shelly said. "I'm with you, Fran. I am sick and tired of those truth-about-the-Kennedy-assassination books that come out every month. I wasn't as crazy as you about Stanley Curtis, but I'm sorry he's dead. Still, people die of strokes. It happens all the time."

"Can't we talk about something else?" Fran asked.

I was looking at my watch.

"Plenty of time," Oscar said. "When do you have to be at the museum?"

"Nine-thirty."

"It wouldn't do any good to ask you what's going to happen there?"

"None."

"Come on, Harry, I'm your brother. I'm buying you food and drink. I love you. I'm nourishing you. This Vermeer thing could be the biggest conversation piece that ever dropped into my lap, and you're being as closemouthed as some CIA lunkhead. Come on—have you found it?"

"Lunkhead," Fran said. "Really, Oscar, I've never known

you to be that flippant with a heavy piece of the establishment."

My brother grinned and pointed out that he had tenure now.

"You had it twenty years ago," Shelly said apropos of nothing that made sense. But this was Shelly. Oscar slept around, but it was Fran's opinion that a man married to a Shelly had to sleep around. Otherwise, he'd strangle his wife. However, I had a feeling that Oscar was fond of Shelly, who was very pretty if not very bright.

"I wish I could, but I can't," I told Oscar.

"Keeping his mouth shut is an integral part of Harry's religion," Fran told Oscar. "*You* lose a conversation piece, but *I* am driven absolutely crazy. I live with the man. I've had to learn to read his face and be content with that."

"Read about the Vermeer, then," Shelly said.

"All right. Either he knows who took it or he knows where it is or he found it or something like that."

"Bravo!" from Oscar. "But you know, Harry," he went on, "Vermeer is something special in man's history. When the whole European world still wallowed in ignorance, prejudice, and hatred, those thrifty burghers of Holland had created a civilization of tolerance and cleanliness and proper beauty. When you look at a Vermeer, you see it, everything proper, clean, quiet, orderly. Now, according to the *New York Post*—"

"Really, Oscar," Fran interrupted. "You read the *Post?*"

"It's yet another side of this throbbing city. After all, I am a sociologist, my dear Fran. And as I was saying, according to the *New York Post,* the Vermeer was stolen by some criminal-minded collector so that he might lock it in a room where he alone could savor its pleasure and beauty. Do you buy that, Harry?"

"No."

"Neither do I. And do you know why? Because if such an art-collecting psychopath existed, he'd have his minions steal something truly overwhelming, as for example 'Aristotle Contemplating the Bust of Homer.' "

"I believe the museum paid less than two million for that."

"That was preinflation, Harry. Anyway, the point is that I simply don't believe a quiet little gem like the Vermeer would suit a loony collector."

I nodded.

"No more than that? Harry, Harry, you disappoint me."

Riding uptown in a cab, Fran said, "It was such a good dinner. You could have given Oscar a hint about the Vermeer."

"How do you know I had a hint to give him?"

"Going to the museum at nine-thirty—of course you have a hint, and a lot more."

"I'll drop you off at the apartment."

"You will not. If you think I'm going to miss the fun of whatever you have scheduled to happen tonight, you are absolutely out of your mind, Harry. And I heard you telling Mr. Lawrence in your most arrogant manner that he was to have the director and the president there and that you might even turn up the painting."

"You don't really believe that?"

"I think I do."

"All right, then come along." And as a matter of fact, I was quite pleased that she had insisted. I would have suggested it in any case. Nothing a man likes better than to be a hero in front of his wife.

"You're a dear. You really are," Fran said. "I just can't imagine how spooky and strange a museum is at this hour. When you retire, ten years from now, we're going to England—first shot, aren't we?"

"So you say. Absolutely."

"You know why I thought about that, Harry? Spooky stuff, empty museums, and Madame Tissaud's Waxworks—it is Madame Tissaud, isn't it?"

"Something like that, I think."

We were at the museum now, and I paid the driver. Fran and I walked to the lower-level entrance, where a guard was waiting.

"Are you Lieutenant Golding?" he asked me. I nodded, and then he pointed to Fran and asked, "Who's she?"

"She's my wife."

"Could you show me your identification?" He looked at

my badge, and then informed me that he had instructions to allow me to enter, but no one else.

"Then suppose you go inside and get new instructions."

"Yes, I suppose I can. What did you say her name was?"

"Golding," Fran said. "Fran Golding, Mrs. Lieutenant Golding, the lieutenant's wife."

He nodded without moving a muscle in his face, and then he went inside. I waited with Fran for about five minutes until he returned and said that we could follow him. We went into the museum through the coatroom to the elevator, and then back past the Greek votaries and vases to the great central gallery. They were waiting for me, Lawrence, and with him Willard Stevens, the director, and Joseph Lubbler, the president.

"I told you my wife would be with me," I said to Lawrence, not kindly. "Why all that nonsense at the door?"

Fran looked at me strangely. Lawrence sighed and cast a glance at the guard, as if to indicate that the guard's stupidity was to blame. "I'm sorry, Lieutenant."

"I suppose you have a good reason for calling us here tonight, Lieutenant. I don't know why we agreed to it. Neither you nor the New York City police appear to comprehend what is at stake." This from Lubbler, not one to accept arguments or instructions from an underling. "I spoke to the police commissioner today, and he promised a whole new approach to the theft. Also, both Stevens and I left dinner parties this evening. So suppose you get right down to whatever you have in mind."

"And explain why it had to be this evening, like some ridiculous charade," Stevens added.

"I don't want the guard with us," I said. "I want us to be alone."

For a moment, this took them aback. Then Stevens said to the guard, "Go downstairs to the door, Maguire, and stay there until we all have gone. It shouldn't be too long." Then, when the guard had left, Stevens turned to me. "Now what, Lieutenant?"

"Let me explain," I said, as gently as I could manage, considering my irritation. "When Mr. Lawrence told me about the ransom note, with instructions to make the drop tomorrow, I realized that I had to see you all tonight. I was scheduled to address a group of students at New York University, and I felt that was an important obligation. In any case, we would have met here after the museum closed. By the way, did the instructions for the drop arrive?"

"Just before the museum closed," Lawrence said. "I turned them over to Captain Courtny at your precinct. I have a Xerox copy with me."

Stevens rustled around in his pocket. "Do you want to see it now?"

"Later. By the way," I said to Lubbler, "are you thinking of paying out five million dollars?"

"It's worth twice that."

"A child is worth more than any price, and a small painting is easier to get rid of than a child's body."

Later, Fran asked me why I'd said that. I suppose it was sheer petulance. There is a peculiar thing in New York City, an upper class as real as anything that may exist in Europe; it consists of the rich, the political, and the people who run the artistic institutions, the theaters, the concert halls, the museums, not the working actors and writers and painters, but the managers. And these three men were completely of that upper class. All of them were in evening clothes, and all of them exhibited contempt for the intelligence of a cop. This, I admit, provoked me to the point where my own behavior was rather childish.

"Then you would not pay the ransom, Lieutenant?"

"Can we discuss that later? I want to go to the gallery now."

With nods and shrugs that indicated their willingness to go along with me and get it over with, whatever it was, they led the way up the broad staircase to the galleries. There were over thirty large rooms that housed the work of the masters, room after room of paintings whose worth was beyond calculation, wealth that ran to billions of dollars, protected with every modern burglar alarm and device imaginable, yet not worth stealing. Thievery is a practical business. What you can't fence is not worth taking. That was my immediate reaction when I'd heard that one of the most

21

valuable paintings in the world had been taken from the museum.

The rooms were lit. There were five rooms that housed the Dutch masters. The Vermeer had been taken from the last room, taken out of the frame, which had been subsequently removed. Nevertheless, there was a shadow on the wall where the painting had been.

"Here we are, gentlemen," I said. "Now I would like to see the ransom note."

Lawrence handed me the bit of paper. It read: *If you want the Vermeer back, put five million in a knapsack and wait on the platform seventy-second station centrel pk west one to three tomoro. no cops or no pikshure.*

"You see," Lawrence said, "he spelled four words wrong."

"Indicating what?" I asked. The words were made out of letters cut from magazines. "He also spelled *knapsack* and *station* correctly. He decided that we should think of him as an ignorant man. How ignorant he is, I don't know, but he's very stupid. His plan for the drop indicates an IQ of one hundred or so."

"Is that why you brought us here?" Stevens asked with considerable irritation. "To give us a psychological profile of the thief? You can spare us that."

"No, gentlemen. I brought you here because you received that ridiculous note. I wanted us alone here because this was an inside job, and I did not want to be overheard. The painting is here."

"What?"

"What the devil are you talking about?"

Even Fran was regarding me with doubt and a little bit of alarm.

"Listen now," I said. "It's a small painting but it's in a large, ornate frame. Four bolts had to be unscrewed before the painting could be removed from its frame. The thief would have to know about the bolts. He would have to have a small pliers, and he might have to return several times before he had them all unscrewed. That suggests an inside job, but let's put that on the shelf for the moment and stick to the problem of the painting. I'm a cop and maybe not the brightest, but I got a lot of years on the force and in all that time I never heard of one of those loony collectors who steal valuable objects and sit and look at them in some secret room. I don't believe it. A thief steals to sell what he steals and there's no way he could sell that Vermeer. I heard that it's worth ten million dollars. That information came from Mr. Lawrence—"

"It certainly is worth that," Lubbler said.

"Possibly, but I like a second opinion. So I spoke to a dealer friend of mine on Madison Avenue, and he said that it might bring ten million at auction, or five million, or two million, depending on who attended the auction and who was bidding. But the crook who pasted up that ransom note must have heard the ten million figure to make his own figure so preposterous. And a knapsack. Can you imagine getting five million in bills into a knapsack?"

"Damn it, Lieutenant!" Stevens snapped. "Is the painting here or isn't it?"

"I knew it was here the day of the robbery. Wouldn't the thief have been a total horse's ass to try to get it out of the museum? The only intelligence he displayed was to leave it here."

"Where, for heaven's sake?"

I pointed to a large, stuffed leather bench in the center of the room. "Taped under that bench."

After a properly long moment of astonishment, the three men leapt at the bench. It fell to Lawrence to get down on his stomach, for the bench was quite low, and then to wriggle under it. By all rights, they should have instructed me to crawl under the bench, but they were so excited at the thought of retrieving the Vermeer that for a moment they forgot I existed. Then Lawrence remembered and called out, "Please pull me out, Lieutenant!"

I grabbed his ankles and pulled him out, dusty but triumphant, the stolen Vermeer in his hands, long strips of adhesive tape still attached to the back of the painting. At least the thief had shown enough sense to tape it with the paint side up. Lawrence sat on the floor, holding the painting as if it were an adored child, his two colleagues crowding close to look at it. I had not realized that three grown, intelligent men could adore a small picture painted hundreds of years

23

ago, to a point where they were practically drooling over it. Lawrence even took his handkerchief from his breast pocket and dusted the face of the painting gently. I went to Fran and kissed her cheek. It was reward for being very silent and never telling me to stop before they took me away to the booby hatch.

Stevens finally tore himself away from the painting and asked me, "When did you discover that the painting was there?"

"The day you discovered the theft."

"And you kept the information to yourself? How did you dare to? I think it the most presumptuous act on the part of a city employee that I have ever encountered, not to mention that it made fools of all of us."

Now he hit me where it hurt, and Fran recognized my anger and reached out and squeezed my arm in a manner which said, "Take it easy, Harry, nice and easy. These are very powerful people, and this museum is the most important part of your precinct and maybe the most important museum in the world, so please darling take it easy." I know she was telling me that because I was thinking exactly the same thing, and I controlled myself enough to say, "I've recovered your damn painting, and I let it sit there until the ransom note came, because if I told any one of you where it was, you would have blabbed, and since I'm pretty damn sure the thief works here, I had to leave it where it was until now, because that's our only chance of picking up the crook. And believe me, it was a lot safer under the bench than on your wall!" I kept my voice down, so what I said was not quite as nasty as it looks in print. With proper police procedure, I should have taken the stolen property over to the station house with me, but I knew that if I even suggested such a thing, these three men would have fought me like tigers before they'd have let the Vermeer out of the building.

Instead, I sort of apologized and said to them, "I'm sorry we had some words, but you have the painting and that's what matters."

"Yes, that's what matters," Stevens agreed.

"I'll make arrangements about the pickup tomorrow morning. Good night."

As I walked through the galleries with Fran, Lawrence called after me, "Thank you, Lieutenant. We're really very grateful."

Chapter 2

WE WALKED BACK to our apartment, and all the way Fran never said a word. It was only ten-thirty.

When we got into the apartment, Fran said, "I'll make some tea." She was looking at me very strangely. I sat down in the kitchen and smiled at her.

"Don't grin at me," she said.

"You don't enjoy having a brilliant husband, do you?"

"You're smart enough for me, but we've lived together a long time. How did you know the painting was under the bench?"

"Brilliance. Intuitive comprehension."

"Harry!"

"All right, but I wasn't going to let those three snobs know that I wasn't some kind of police genius. Do you know who Edgar Wallace was?"

"Should I?"

"No, you don't read detective stories. I do. Always have, ever since I was a kid. But Edgar Wallace was before our time. Most of his stuff appeared during the twenties and the thirties, and I used to pick them up as used paperbacks for a dime mostly when I was a kid. He wasn't much of a writer, but damned ingenious, and in one of his stories he had a gal steal a picture from a London museum and hold the picture for ransom. She cut it out of its frame, pinned it to a window shade, and then rolled up the shade. A pretty unlikely job, but in the story it worked. Well, that stuck in my mind. They don't have window shades in the museum, but first thing I walked into that gallery the day the Vermeer was stolen, I remembered the Wallace story. I looked around, and there was the bench. It had to be the bench. So I sat down there to tie a shoelace, reached under and felt the picture."

"Incredible," Fran whispered.

"I'm incredible. The kettle's boiling."

"But how could you be sure it was the Vermeer?"

"What else could it be?"

"You said the thief was stupid. That's not stupid, taping it under the bench."

"If it was a guard who'd stood in that room five years, figuring out how to steal that picture, then it was stupid, believe me."

"Harry," Fran said to me, "do me a favor, please. Don't tell anyone about the Wallace story."

"You want to keep me in the genius class?"

"Don't ever apologize to me about that," Fran said. "We both know how smart you are, damn smart. But if the boys over at the precinct feel that it all came out of your bright little head, it will do you no end of good."

She was right. I walked into the precinct house like a conquering hero. Sergeant McGruder at the desk bowed and saluted. Evidently, Lawrence—who, I learned, had reported to the precinct—spared nothing in praise of my acumen. When I walked into the detective room, I was met with cheers and the clapping of hands and three reporters waiting to get my personal story. A few minutes later, Captain Courtny beckoned me into his inner sanctum.

Courtny was an overweight, cigar-smoking cop who made up with a lifetime of experience what he might have lacked in intelligence. He had a deep, hoarse voice and a constantly troubled frown, but today he greeted me with a bone-crushing handshake.

"Harry, you pulled off something good. It's the kind of thing that's worth more to the department than even solving a tough homicide. You got to believe me. It shows brains.

27

People say to themselves, could it happen in L.A.? No way. They got stiffs in L.A. Could it happen in Detroit? Never. They got bums in Detroit who only know brass knuckles. Chicago, Atlanta, Philly—never. It's a New York thing. It gives the department class, and nobody ever died from too much class. Only one thing, Harry, keeps it from being perfect."

"Oh?"

"You should have told me at the beginning."

I nodded and sighed.

"Pride, Harry. You wanted it for yourself. Well, I got to admit it was the most peculiar collar ever came our way, if you could call it a collar. What the hell! You deserve it. Let's talk about the drop this afternoon."

"The drop's off, Captain. There are three reporters in the squad room. I should have sworn those dumb bastards at the museum to silence, but it wouldn't have helped. They were all bound for dinner parties, and not one of those important characters could have resisted telling the story of the Vermeer. How did those reporters get here?"

"Come on, Harry. It won't be in the papers until tomorrow. Lawrence called me an hour ago and told me. The reporters were here for the Snelling case and they latched on to something they still don't know what it is. The TV crowd isn't on to it."

"I'll bet it's all over the museum."

"Harry, we got to go through the motions, whether you're right or wrong. These are big taxpayers we're dealing with."

We went through the motions. I had a detective cutting up newspapers and putting them into cashlike packs. I sent another detective out to buy two knapsacks and I put every uniform I could detach into civilian clothes. It still wasn't enough, and I had to borrow a dozen more from Manhattan South over the sour comments of their captain, who stated that with all our smarts, we didn't need bodies. Since the kidnapper had not been thoughtful enough to tell us whether he would be on a downtown train or an uptown train, we had to cover both. Since about four trains an hour came by on each side of the tracks, I had the devil's own time putting a man in every car, even though the uptown crowd got out

28

at 86th Street and the downtown crowd at 59th Street, where they continued their circular motion. It was an exercise in futility, as I'd known it would be. No kidnapper appeared to grab a knapsack of cut newspapers. When I returned to the station later that afternoon, the media were present, ABC, CBS, NBC, not to mention channels 5, 9, and 11, and a fancier group of reporters than usually hang around a precinct house. Toby Horowitz, the art critic of the *Times,* was there jumping with excitement. He wanted to find out how much I knew of Vermeer and whether I was aware that my brilliant piece of deduction was a boon to mankind. If some poor kid had been kidnapped, there might have been one or two reporters waiting to get the facts, but kids are more easily produced than Vermeers. If not, we wouldn't have wars.

They threw questions at me as if I were important. I wasn't important. I was a police lieutenant in a midtown precinct, a cop in a city that had more than thirty thousand cops, and if I had learned anything about a situation like this, it was not to talk to the media in words of more than one syllable. But it was very plain by now, if it had not been this morning, why the kidnapper had not appeared to collect his boodle. I am sure that even as far away as Tokyo, they knew that the Vermeer had been recovered.

When I got home that evening, Fran was watching the crowd scene at the precinct on our television. "You're good-looking enough," she observed, "but not very amiable. In fact, you're downright surly. But it's interesting. The tough-cop image."

"Save your sarcasm, lady. I am damned disgusted by the whole thing."

"Why? Why?" Fran wanted to know. Then she held up her hand for silence. I was delivering my one-syllable answers, and she was hanging on to every word I said. She flicked off the television and demanded, "Why on earth should you be disgusted? My goodness, Harry, you come off like a wizard in shining armor. For the next twenty-four hours, you're the hottest name in town, and since I'm your wife, I also sizzle a bit."

"I'll tell you why I'm disgusted. I know I'm a benighted

Philistine, but as far as I'm concerned, a painting is a piece of canvas with some paint on it. I don't give a damn whether it's the Mona Lisa or a Vermeer, it's cloth with paint. Since I've been a cop in this city, I've seen children kidnapped, babies raped, people hacked to pieces, and men who kill for hire walking free on these streets—and no one ever made much of a fuss about it. But here's a painting stolen, and the whole city goes crazy."

"Because it's unusual, Harry. You know that. We have murder and violence every day, but how often is a great painting stolen? It takes our minds off the horror of every-day crime. It's a sort of deluxe crime. And by the way," she added, "you'll be interested to know that the kid at your lecture called about an hour ago."

"What kid?"

"The tall, skinny kid—don't you remember? The one who was convinced that Stanley Curtis was murdered? I think his name was Oshun. I wrote it down somewhere."

"How did he get our number here? If he wanted to speak to me, why didn't he call the precinct?"

"I asked him that. He's a bright kid, Harry. He figured that with all the fuss and bother over the Vermeer, he'd never get to you."

"How did he get our number?"

"I asked him that too. He knew your name, and he called every Harry Golding in the book until he got to us. He left a telephone number," Fran added tentatively. "Are you going to call him?"

"No. He's a nut. This city is full of nuts, and I've had enough of them today."

It was two days later when Oscar telephoned and invited us to the dinner party. When I speculate on where it began, I am unable to choose among three events: the stolen Vermeer, the lecture at New York University, or the dinner party. The dinner party was in honor of Asher Alan, who, according to those who knew, would be the next prime minister of Israel. From everything I had heard, Alan was upright, honest, and highly intelligent, the one man in the Israeli leadership who had the respect of even his Arab enemies. Since Oscar was in large part responsible for the creation in Tel Aviv of the

Sociological Institute, raising several million dollars toward its construction, and since he had lectured there on several occasions, it was understandable that Asher Alan should be his guest. It was less understandable, to me at least, why he asked Fran and me to be there. Oscar and I were close, but we functioned in different worlds.

"He asked that you be there," Oscar explained. "I don't want you to be hurt, Harry. I would have invited you in any case"—hardly likely—"but when Alan heard that you were my brother, he was absolutely delighted. You know, this Vermeer gambit that you pulled off was in the press all over the world, and Alan loves the thought of a Jewish detective doing it. So will you come?"

"Of course I'll come. I don't get an invitation like that every day, Oscar. Fran and I will be there."

When I told Fran about it, her face lit up. "I know you don't give a tinker's damn about politics, Harry, but this man Asher Alan is absolutely unique. I think he's going to change history a bit. But good God, what can I wear to one of Oscar's fancy affairs?"

She called Oscar back to find out whether it was formal, and then she and Shelly had a long discussion, the upshot of which was that Fran put out two hundred and fifty dollars at Bonwit's for a new dress. We had a few words about it, but she convinced me that considering inflation, two hundred and fifty dollars was not an exorbitant price.

I must admit she looked good in it. She was the prettiest woman in the room that evening at Oscar's apartment. She was forty-three years old but she could have passed for thirty, and that's not the stacked statement of a man who loves her. Every head in the place turned toward her as she walked in.

There were two other couples there that evening, aside from Oscar and Shelly, myself and Fran, and Asher Alan and his wife, a lean, deeply tanned woman with sun-streaked hair and flashing blue eyes. Alan was a tall, barrel-chested man in his mid-fifties, almost bald, with a warm, open smile. The rest of the party consisted of Frank Bessington, under secretary of state in the Reagan government, his wife, Sally, Delver Glenn, head of the department of sociology at New

York University, and his wife. Bessington was a sharp, narrow-nosed product of Stanford and the California Establishment, one of those whom Oscar had gathered into his eclectic circle of friends. Delver Glenn was a stout, amiable academic, technically Oscar's boss. Both their wives were thin, self-effacing women, made to be seen and not heard, except that they appeared more pleased to meet me than our guest of honor. But then, they had been meeting guests of honor all of their married lives, while a real, live city police detective was something they had never encountered before —certainly not at a dinner party. I was embarrassed that here, at a dinner party which boasted the next likely prime minister of Israel and a real working member of Reagan's government, attention should focus on a cop.

"But you are not just a policeman," Delver Glenn said. "You have plunged head over heels into an Agatha Christie mystery, and with more aplomb than her Hercule Poirot."

"Just luck."

Watching me, Fran's face said, "Don't you dare mention Edgar Wallace or I'll never speak to you again."

"Of course," Asher Alan said, "as an Israeli, I'm taken by the notion of a Jewish policeman. In Israel, our whole police force is Jewish—"

"We must have several thousand Jewish policemen," Fran said. "We've even had a Jewish chief of detectives, and right now we have a black police commissioner. Don't ever sell New York short."

"Heaven forbid!" His English was excellent, tinged with a slight British accent.

"Where did you learn your English, if I may ask?" Oscar said. "It's extraordinary."

"You know, it's the second language in all our schools. And in the Foreign Service, I did a three-year hitch in London. My wife, Deborah, is better than I am at languages. She speaks nine of them fluently. I wish I had the gift. When you live in a very small country, you must have language. But is it true that you have thousands of Jewish policemen?"

"I haven't seen the statistics," I said, "but we have a very large police department. I'm sure it comes to several thousand."

"And do you think your very large police department will ever catch the man who stole the Vermeer?"

"I doubt it. As you should know, Mr. Alan, size alone does not solve problems."

"Touché. If that were not true, we would not exist."

I was relieved, when we finally sat down to dinner, that the talk turned away from me and the ridiculous business of the Vermeer. Fran loved dinner at Oscar's house because, as she put it, Shelly was totally dedicated to *Architectural Digest*. Her table always looked like an advertisement for British china or Tiffany glass, and though Fran would never admit it, she would have loved to set up similar situations. She was seated across the table from me now, settled between the State Department and the department of sociology, while I was flanked on either side by the silent wives of Fran's table partners. Just as well. I wanted to listen, not to contribute.

There was some polite exchange of light conversation that took us through the crabmeat and the main course, and then Bessington said, "I do suppose that anything said here could be privileged, so to speak. I mean, there's so much we all want to ask you, Mr. Alan, but I'm sure you would only talk off the record. Oscar is an old friend, and he can tell you that I can be trusted. If it's off the record, none of it goes back to Washington."

"Why should it be off the record?" Asher Alan asked. "I've come here to make my views known."

"Hear! Hear!" Glenn said.

"In any case," Oscar told us, never one not to drop a name when the right moment came, "Asher meets with President Reagan in a few days." And to Bessington, "Do you think it's proper, you being with the State Department, for Asher to talk here about things he might be saving for the Oval Office?"

"Why not?" Asher demanded. "I have no secrets. I'm sure the President has on his desk a memorandum of absolutely everything I stand for—from the return of most of the West Bank to the Palestinians to the complete withdrawal of Israeli troops from any foot of foreign soil. I have screamed loud enough my anguish over what has happened to Israel. I

33

was born on a kibbutz. I've fought in every war since forty-eight, and I will not keep silent and see my homeland turned into a mindless garrison state by those who have taken over from Mr. Begin."

"Then you believe Israel can live in peace in an Arab world?"

"Yes—because the Arabs need Israel as much as the Jews do. We will talk to them, persuade them, and learn to live with them. And they need us. We have the best hospitals outside of this country. We have medical schools, doctors. We manufacture the most advanced medical products in the world. We have factories for electronics, for computers, for agricultural equipment. We have the finest agronomists in the world. Together with us, the Arabs can take a giant step. But enough of that. I want to hear about the Vermeer. There's real storybook drama."

"Just one last question," Fran begged him. "I'm not Jewish, but my husband is and we've been married a long time. So I feel it as a Jew would, and one thing that makes me utterly heartsick is the sale of munitions made in Israel. The utterly corrupt Santa Marina government has equipped a whole army with your Uzi guns."

"I know that," Asher Alan replied bitterly. "Bought with money your government gives them. It will stop. We will sell no munitions. There are other ways to survive."

After that, the table conversation turned to the Vermeer and to the life led by a cop in New York, as opposed to a policeman's life in Israel. "Of course," I said to Alan, "even with your growing problems of crime and enforcement in Jerusalem and Tel Aviv, it just cannot be compared to our situation. When Fran and I were in Israel three years ago—we were in Jerusalem—we found our way to the police station. I think there are two of them there."

"Yes, two."

"Well, we walked in and I told them I was a New York cop, and they invited us to have tea with them and look around. Can you imagine—tea at three in the afternoon. The cells were open and empty. The male cops were sitting around and flirting with the lady cops, and during the hour or so we remained there, not one arrest was made."

34

"I suppose everything's a matter of contrast."

"Thank heavens," Oscar said. "Can you imagine how dull it might be otherwise?"

Shelly moved us into the living room for coffee. It had turned out to be a very pleasant evening indeed. But the party broke up early. Deborah Alan explained to Shelly that her husband was very tired. They had been across the country and had spent a week in Los Angeles before returning to the East. It was too much. His blood pressure was high, and the physician who had seen him in Los Angeles had advised a slower pace and more rest.

As Fran and I walked home, she told me of the conversation between Shelly and Deborah Alan. "He looks healthy enough," Fran said. "I do hope it's nothing serious."

"You were impressed with him?"

"I'm not easily impressed with politicians, but yes, I think he is something. I certainly do."

Chapter 3

THE FOLLOWING EVENING, Fran and I went to the movies to see Woody Allen's new film, *Broadway Danny Rose*. We found ourselves doubled up with laughter and wet-eyed with nostalgia. Fran and I are both New York City products, street smart and at home nowhere else than among the dirty shadowed canyons that go to make up this most remarkable of all cities; and to journey back to the Carnegie Delicatessen, not as it is now but as it was twenty years ago, made for an evening of sheer joy. We were still talking about the film when I unlocked the door to our apartment and heard the telephone ringing. It was then about twenty minutes to eleven.

The voice on the telephone was Oscar's. "Harry, something terrible has happened."

"What? It's not Shelly, is it?"

"Harry, Asher Alan is dead."

"What!"

At my elbow, Fran cried, "For God's sake, Harry, what happened?"

"Is this some damn dumb joke?" I asked Oscar.

"No, no, Harry. No."

"What happened?"

"This evening, Harry, Asher, Deborah, and two men from

36

the Israeli Consulate were having dinner at La Revier, and Asher fell ill. They called an ambulance and took him to Bellevue. Deborah went with him. He died in the ambulance. It was a massive stroke. Deborah telephoned me. I'm at the hospital, and I'll bring her back to my apartment."

"How is she taking this?"

"You can imagine. God Almighty, what a tragedy—what a rotten tragedy! Harry, will you meet me there, at my apartment?"

"Now?"

"Yes, now. We'll leave here in a few minutes."

"All right. Sure. But there isn't anything that makes you feel this is a police matter, is there, Oscar?"

"No, nothing like that."

"Because if it is, I can get Joe McCarthy to meet us. His squad covers that area. The restaurant is on Sixty-third, isn't it?"

"Yes, but there's no reason for police. The poor man died of a stroke. I want you at the apartment because Fran will be good with Deborah and because you keep your cool. You can control the press. I can't."

Fran had picked up the telephone in the bedroom. She was shaking after she put it down. Then she began to cry.

"Darling, we hardly knew him."

"Did I know Jesus any better?" she whispered through her tears.

Ah, well! You can take a Catholic out of the Church, but you can't take the Church out of the Catholic. I had no notion of how one might relate Asher Alan to Jesus and I considered Fran's question farfetched at best, but shared her sense of loss, not only for his tiny country but for the whole world. I put an arm around her and held her close, and then I helped her on with her coat and we started downtown toward Oscar's apartment at 78th and Park. After we had walked a block or two, Fran dabbing at her eyes, she turned to me and said, "Of course. There's the connection."

"What connection?"

"Don't you see? Damn it, Harry, nothing stinks to you unless there're two men knifing each other, or some hit man rubbing out dopers or some moron torching buildings." She had stopped walking and now stood facing me, bristling. "Well, this stinks to me!"

"What?" I almost shouted.

"I will tell you what. Stanley Curtis dies of a stroke. Asher Alan dies of a stroke. Two beautiful human beings. Curtis was having dinner at La Siene. Alan was eating at the Revier—two of the classiest restaurants in New York. Harry, did you ever study statistics?"

"Fran, you know damn well I did. Where is all this going? Oscar begged us to get over to his place as soon as possible, and instead we're standing here on the street, yelling at each other."

"Is it statistically possible that two of the most well-known, well-loved, open-minded men on earth should die the same way in two New York restaurants within a few weeks of each other? Come on, Harry, you remember that kid at NYU as well as I do, and you're a cop."

I drew a deep breath and said, "All right, I'll think about it. Now let's go on to Oscar's."

"I'm not letting you off the hook. You can talk me out of anything. You don't talk me out of this."

"If I knew what *this* was."

I knew, of course. I knew what she was driving at, but it was not my discipline, as Fran and other academics say. It was a writer's discipline, a particular point of view that flourished apart from the real world, in a world of books where the traditions were different, where the schematic was different and where life was shaped as a puzzle and where crime was an intelligent process. I read the books myself; I loved them because they had absolutely no connection with the filthy, unspeakable criminal world of a New York City cop. Fran was wrong. Homicide was stupid, senseless murders, mob executions, knife fights in bars, crazed lunatics who raped and killed little children and old women, killers who robbed stores and wiped out the men behind the counters, degenerates, morons. Smart? I never met a criminal who wasn't stupid and most that I met were morons, but I've only been a cop for seventeen years.

The one evening they had spent together had created something between Fran and Deborah Alan that I was wholly unaware of; but I had been too absorbed with Alan himself and Bessington and Glenn to have paid much attention to what the women were saying to each other. I spend my days with the police department, where the woman's roll is a little less than it might be. Now Deborah and Fran fell into each other's arms. Shelly was fussing with food and wiping her eyes. Having opened the door for us, she tried to speak, but burst into tears and fled back into the kitchen. Fran led Deborah to a couch and eased her into it. Oscar pulled away from three men he had been speaking to, and took me aside to whisper into my ear.

"That one, the tall one, he's the consul-general. His name is Hashim. The other one is the Israeli ambassador to the UN, Bleckhem. They wanted to take her to the consul-general's home, but she wouldn't go with them. They're both Begin appointees. The third feller—"

"I know him, Frank Levy, one of Koch's assistants."

"Koch tried to get here. Evidently, he's the final speaker at some important function that's running late. He may be here later. I don't know why she wouldn't go with the consulate people. They're nice enough."

Oscar took me over to the men and introduced me. Levy remembered meeting me. The two Israelis were glad to find a Jewish police officer present. They were going over the details of what had happened, when the doorbell rang again. This time it was two of the top men from the United Jewish Appeal. Anyone who has witnessed the process of news spreading knows how mysteriously it happens and how hard it is to explain. The reporters began to show up and then the media cameramen. I blocked them at the door, and said, "There will be no statement from Mrs. Deborah Alan. She will answer no questions. Tomorrow perhaps, but not tonight."

"How did he die? At Bellevue they said a stroke."

"As far as I know."

"Where did it happen?"

"I can't say now."

"Come on, come on."

"The Israeli consul-general is preparing a statement. Perhaps in an hour."

"And what are you doing here, Lieutenant? What's your connection?"

"This is my brother's apartment, Professor Oscar Golding."

"Then how is your brother connected? Is he related to Alan?"

"Is he the same Oscar Golding who was with President Ford?"

Two more Israelis pushed through the media crowd. The apartment was filling up, and I had to call the Israeli UN delegate to identify the newcomers.

"They're from the consulate," he told me. "They'll take care of the door if you wish, Lieutenant."

I thanked him. I pushed through to the living room couch, where Deborah Alan still sat, Fran on one side of her, Shelly on the other; even in that very bitter moment I couldn't help noticing how beautiful this woman was. People came over to mention condolences, but then they drew away. The bereaved frighten people. I bent over Fran and whispered, "I'm going to slip away. They don't need me here." The mayor had just come in, his tall figure looming over everyone else. "They keep wondering what a cop is doing here."

"Where are you going?"

"Bellevue."

"Why?"

"Because I respect your brains as well as your body. Do you remember what he said his name was?"

"The kid?"

"Yes."

"Oshun, I think. James Oshun. Thank you, Harry. Be careful."

I rose now, and Deborah Alan looked up at me. I took her hand, thinking, What do you say? What can you say? Then I left.

Downstairs at the curb, a line of chauffeur-cars were parked, and one of the drivers, recognizing me, said, "Want a lift, Lieutenant? I got twenty minutes to kill."

"Can you make it to Bellevue in that time?"

"Lead-pipe cinch—with a cop in the car."

40

"Just drive easy. I can't fix tickets. This is Honest City, America."

"Yeah?"

"Yeah."

"As long as you say so."

He dropped me off at Bellevue and turned back uptown. The small perks of being a cop. The lady sitting at night reception was an old acquaintance, a black woman, Lil Dutton by name. I had done her a small favor years ago, and she remembered. I asked her if she'd seen James Oshun.

"Maybe you come to the wrong place, Lieutenant. He'd be at the school. And right now he'd be sound asleep, if he was a good boy, and maybe even if he wasn't, because two things a medical student don't get enough of is food and sleep. But what did you say his name was?"

"I think James Oshun."

"Fourth-year student?"

"I don't know."

"Hey, what about this? Is he a tall, skinny kid, maybe almost six and a half feet, pasty white skin, and great big horn-rim glasses?"

"Good description."

"Jimmy O. That's what they call him. You are in luck, Lieutenant. Absolutely. I know this kid because he come in one day and he hands me a bag of gumdrops. Sweets for the sweet, he says. Now ain't that nice or not? He comes from a place in Ohio called Findley. He say, we going to be friends, we got to know origins. I tell him I'm from One Hundred Seventeenth Street and St. Nicholas Avenue and he tells me he's from Findley, Ohio."

"Lil—please, how can I find him?"

"I said you were in luck. He's working this shift in the trauma section."

For Bellevue, it was a very quiet night in the emergency section. The admitting nurse sent me down the corridor where the small treatment rooms open off each side. Oshun was sitting in a swivel chair at one of the plastic desks, his feet up, his eyes closed, snoring lightly. His long, dirty blond hair had drifted over his face, where it swayed back and forth in time with his breathing.

"Oshun?"

He awoke with a start from his guilt-ridden sleep, mumbling, "Sorry. I must have dozed off." Then he took a closer look at me. "Do I know you?" he asked.

"Lieutenant Harry Golding. I spoke to Professor Golding's class at NYU. Remember—about Stanley Curtis?"

"Yeah—oh, yes. Sure. The cop."

"Can we talk somewhere? About Curtis."

"Sure. I can get away for half an hour. I'll get someone to cover for me. But wait a minute—I don't want you to think I'm crapping out. It's a light night, so I caught a few winks. You get awfully tired. They take seven years of your young life and beat the shit out of you, and then you're a doctor. Maybe that's why we get so greedy."

In the cafeteria, Oshun sat opposite me, two pieces of apple pie and two balls of vanilla in front of him. His attack on his food was direct and determined, and he talked while he ate.

"How come?" he wanted to know.

"How come what?"

"How come the other night you figured I was something the chipmunks overlooked and tonight you pay me a midnight call—except"—looking at his watch—"that now it's almost one in the morning. That's got to be big stuff. You figure I know something after all?"

"I want to know why you think Stanley Curtis was murdered."

"The word's around the hospital that they brought in a DOA who was pretty hot stuff. They put their best team on him, but it was no good. He was DOA absolutely. An Israeli or something of like nature. Does that figure?"

"Maybe. Back to my question."

He was finishing off his first wedge of pie and ice cream. He swallowed and said, "Why do I think Curtis was murdered? Because I'm smart and I'm a damn good doctor. Yes. Already. Now, in my final year. I spent four years working after school, high school, in Doc Kennedy's office in Findley. I watched, I listened, I helped, I learned. All I ever wanted to do was to be a doctor." He was into his second piece of pie now, and he paused to jab at me with his fork.

"Why wouldn't they give him an autopsy? There are more stinking closed doors in this profession than you can shake a stick at. Who was I to ask for an autopsy? Well, I watched Curtis and listened to him on the telly plenty of times. He was a healthy man. His color was good. His movements were well controlled. I can watch someone on the telly and tell you a hell of a lot about his physical condition. Not only that. I spoke to his wife after he died, made up some cock-and-bull story, but it got me into her apartment. Curtis was in good health. A little high blood pressure, but nothing to account for a stroke—"

"Wait a minute, Oshun, hold it. Suppose you tell me why you lied your way into her apartment."

"Come off it, Lieutenant. Don't go holy on me. I guessed that he was on some kind of medication and I had to find out what."

"Wouldn't they publish that?"

"A candidate's illness? Are you kidding?" He paused in his eating. "I'm not trying to be some kind of smartass, Lieutenant. But you know that no candidate admits to illness, physical or otherwise."

"All right. What did you find?"

"I found that his physician had put him on a drug called pargyline. When I say his physician, that's stretching it. No, twisting it. I called his physician, a Dr. Stephan Hyde, and he wouldn't even talk to me. He said it was none of my damn business."

"Then his wife told you, Curtis's wife?"

"No. She showed me the bottle. So there it was, pargyline. I'll tell you something, Lieutenant, it is sure as hell nothing I'd prescribe for a modest high blood pressure. And maybe his blood pressure was not so modest. That's something you can't tell looking at someone. I don't think I'd prescribe pargyline for any high blood pressure. Don't tell me I'm not a doctor. I'm as smart as most. And the label on that bottle called for too high a dosage—double what it should have been."

"How high was his blood pressure?" I asked him.

"Of course, I couldn't be sure. I had to rely on her memory, and she thought it was like one ninety over one hundred. Well for a man under his strain, campaigning and all that, and loading his stomach with oversalted food in bad restaurants—well, I wouldn't give him any drug. I'd take him off salt and slow him down and have him eat a lot of asparagus as a diuretic."

"But you can't be sure of what his blood pressure was—not without speaking to his physician."

"No. That's right. But let me tell you something about this stuff called pargyline. I don't like it. I don't like any drug that sets up the user to accidental disaster. It's what we call a MAO inhibitor, or specifically a monoamine oxidase inhibitor. Aside from its use for high blood pressure, it functions as an antidepressant. But in its side effects, it has just too damn many life-threatening possibilities. In terms of drugs, an amphetamine interacting with it could cause death, or tricyclic, or guanethidine, but those are other prescription drugs and they can be avoided. The tyramine foods are something else."

"What are they?" It was a strange jungle I had never set foot in before.

"Not they. Tyramine is one of the chemical components of the body, perfectly normal, and in a healthy body tyramine helps to sustain blood pressure. They used to think of the body as a simple mechanical machine, Lieutenant. No way. The human body is complex beyond belief, and we are only beginning to scrape at some understanding of what it really is. Now you put a patient on pargyline, and this harmless tyramine can become a deadly killer, so the patient must avoid foods that have large amounts of tyramine. The combination of the food and pargyline can shoot up the blood pressure and induce stroke."

"What foods?"

"A great many; cheese, yeast, red wine, beer, vermouth, avocados, liver, salami—I can't call them all off from memory. But the point is, as far as Mrs. Curtis knew, Stanley Curtis ate whatever was put in front of him. He did try to avoid salty food and he didn't use the saltshaker. I tried to find out what he ate the night he died, but at that point she clammed up. I guess she realized that she was talking to some kid she didn't know from Adam, and she wouldn't even let me look at the bottle again, so I couldn't get the address of the druggist. All I can remember is that it was someplace on Madison Avenue."

I noted the words in my notebook, *pargyline, tyramine,* while Oshun went back to the counter for another piece of pie and ice cream.

"Why all this interest?" he asked when he returned. "And don't brush me off like you did before. I want to know why you're here picking my brains."

"Why do you think they'd murder Stanley Curtis?"

"You're serious? He's a good guy. The bad guys don't go to church." He finished chewing a mouthful of pie, and then shrugged. "The hell with it. You don't believe a word I said. God help us if we can only look to the cops."

"If this man whose body they brought in today had been taking pargyline, would there be any way to detect it short of an autopsy?"

"In the first place, Lieutenant, this was a man with diplomatic status according to the scuttlebutt. He was some kind of Israeli government figure, wasn't he?"

"Yes, but not necessarily with diplomatic status."

"Anyway, a VIP. They've probably picked up the body already and taken it to the funeral home."

"Back to my question."

"Yeah." He frowned and closed his eyes. "Israel—a lot of sun there?"

"He wasn't coming from Israel. He had spent a week in California."

"More sun." Oshun opened his eyes and nodded. "It might cause a rash or a heavy sunburn if he had been on pargyline. But that wouldn't prove anything. You knew the man, Lieutenant?"

"Slightly."

"But you saw him. Did he have a rash, reddish spots here and there on his face, possibly on his hands?"

"I don't remember. Give me the name of the doctor again."

Stephan Hyde, the doctor's name. I jotted it down. Then I suggested to Oshun that he should not make this a subject of conversation among his friends.

"Afraid I'll undercut you, Lieutenant?"

"No. I'm afraid of other things."

When I got back to our apartment, Fran was still awake, waiting for me, more disturbed than I could remember her being in a long time. "It's two o'clock in the morning," she said. "I was so worried, Harry."

I took her in my arms and reminded her of an old, old agreement. She was married to a cop. That precluded worry, otherwise we'd both go crazy.

"Did you find him, Harry?"

"Put up a pot of tea and I'll tell you the whole story. It leaves us nowhere, but it's sure as hell interesting."

When I had finished, Fran stared at me for a while—just sat there silent, staring.

"Well?"

"Suppose this kid is right."

I shrugged. "I don't know. I never handled anything like this before. Things don't come packaged this way. My inclination is to forget the whole damn thing. Life is full of coincidences."

"Why did you tell the kid not to talk about it to his friends?"

"I don't know—just a feeling."

"My heart breaks for Deborah. She's a wonderful woman. Oh, I'm terribly tired, Harry. Let's go to bed." Then she added, "What kind of a feeling, Harry?"

I dodged that and asked her whether she knew what kind of plans Mrs. Alan had made.

"As far as I know, the body is being flown back to Israel, on the evening El Al flight, I think. Deborah will go with it. She's staying with Oscar. Did you know that when Shelly spent a summer in Israel on a kibbutz, it was the kibbutz where Deborah was born? That's how they know each other so well—poor dear."

"I didn't know that, no. Tell me, Fran, did you notice that Asher Alan had a rash?"

"What?"

"Did you?"

"No. For heaven's sake, Harry, let's go to bed."

Before I left for the precinct in the morning, I told Fran

46

that I wanted to talk to Deborah Alan, not as a person with condolences but as a cop. At first Fran protested that Mrs. Alan deserved the privacy of her grief, but when I mentioned that I was moving along Fran's own line of thought, she said she'd try to arrange it with Shelly. "But I'll be at school, Harry, so I'm not sure when or how."

"Whenever. Just leave word at the precinct."

Sergeant Toomey was double-parked in front of the building, and he mentioned an argument with a meter maid. "Snotty kid, says she's coming back in half an hour, and if I'm still here, I get a ticket, cop or not."

"That's what you call integrity. How does it look for today?"

"Not very heavy. A couple of cases."

At the precinct, I gave out the squad assignments and took Bolansky and Keene aside. I told Bolansky that I wanted him to start on Madison Avenue and 96th Street and hit every drugstore down to Madison Square. I told him that I did not for a moment believe that he would have to work his way down to the Twenties, but that was the scope of it. He was to find a drugstore that had filled a prescription for Stanley Curtis. The doctor's name on the prescription would be Stephan Hyde. The prescription should be on file, and he would ask the pharmacist to let him have the prescription long enough to make a Xerox copy of it. I supposed that legally the pharmacist would not have to surrender the prescription or even reveal it, but I could anticipate no reason why he should not show it to Bolansky. I suggested that the prescription might be between three and four weeks old.

Keene's job was to visit the two restaurants, Revier on 63rd and La Siene on 51st Street. I told him to check the newspaper files for the exact date of Curtis's death and then to find a copy of the restaurant check for Curtis's table. If the commotion was such that no check had been presented, then he was to try to find out exactly what Curtis had eaten. With Asher Alan, it might be less difficult. He had eaten at Revier only the day before.

"I'll do my best," Keene said, "but you know, Lieutenant, I can't imagine a restaurant owner who's such a callous son of a bitch that he'd try to collect a bill after a diner dropped dead. The more likely thing would be to tear it up and never even put it on the books."

"That's true and very likely, but then you could possibly find a waiter or a floor captain who might try to piece something together."

"I'll certainly give it a shot."

The telephone rang, and it was Oscar, but I could barely make out what he was saying. Downstairs, the uniforms had brought in a gang of eighteen kids who had been terrorizing subway riders. They were all underage and would be back on the streets within hours, and they were taking advantage of the juvenile status by screaming their heads off. The door to my office had a wire vent, so I could hear all the noise and I shouted for Oscar to speak loud. What I pieced together was that Mrs. Alan would talk to me if I came right over.

I told Toomey to take over, then I poked my head into Captain Courtny's office and told him I was leaving to have a talk with Mrs. Alan.

"Who?"

"The widow of the Israeli who died yesterday."

"Should I ask you why?"

"I don't like it."

"I don't like anyone's death," Courtny said unfeelingly, "but on the city's time, I don't make condolence calls."

"It's the way he died."

"I hear he had a stroke. But if you want to make something out of it, go ahead."

"You're a generous man."

"Butter up if you want to, but don't get snotty with me, Harry. And if you think you got something, I want to hear what you got before I go home to my wife and kids."

He had no wife and kids. He was a strange, sour, lonely man, and like as not, come midnight, he'd still be in his office, feet up on his desk, drinking beer and reading the arrest reports.

Having no desire for a driver tagging along with me all day, I took the car myself and double-parked in front of Oscar's apartment house. Shelly opened the door for me, and when I asked how Deborah was, Shelly shook her head. "She was all right last night with that crowd here, but then it struck home. She didn't sleep much. She fell asleep about four. She's inside taking a bath now, and the people from the consulate are due to pick her up in about an hour."

"Was she reluctant to talk to me, Shelly?"

"Oh, no. She knows you're here as a cop. She's not only heartbroken over her husband's death. She's bitter."

"Oscar? Is he here?"

"He had to leave for school. Would you like a cup of coffee?"

Wrapped in a long flannel robe, Deborah Alan joined us in the dining room. Her hair was tied in back of her head, and her bloodshot eyes were encased in dark hollows.

"If you'd care not to talk," I began to say, "I'd just—"

"No!" she interrupted sharply. "You're a policeman, Mr. Golding. You are not here to offer condolences or to tell me how sorry you are that my husband is dead. There isn't any sorrow, except in a wife's heart. That's the world we live in. You're here because you think there's been a crime. You think my husband was murdered. Yes?"

"I think there's at least a serious question."

"I think he was murdered!" she said flatly.

"Why?" I asked gently.

"Because I knew him. Why should he have a stroke? There was no reason for him to have a stroke. He was a strong, healthy man."

"Tell me something, please, Mrs. Alan. Did he have a rash on his face and hands."

"That doesn't mean anything. You eat something doesn't agree with you, you have a rash."

"But did he have a rash?"

"A slight rash, yes, on his face. Just a few red spots. I covered them with some pancake."

"And was he taking any medicine?"

"Yes, some pills. Three a day. He got them in California."

"And where are they now? Do you have them?"

"No. They were in the medicine cabinet in the hotel."

"What hotel?"

"The Regency," she said. "We were in room 1908, but people from the consulate were there this morning, and they packed my things."

"Excuse me for a moment," I said. "I'll use the phone in the study," I explained to Shelly, who was sitting with us, hanging on to every word. In the study, I called the precinct and told Toomey to get over to the Regency and find that bottle of medicine. If it wasn't there, he was to question the chambermaid, if the room had been cleaned. If he still could not turn it up, he was to go down to the Israeli Consulate and try to find out whether the medicine was in her luggage. "And with charm, Toomey. Charm. They're diplomats. *Please,* charm with everything."

Back in the dining room, I said to Mrs. Alan, "California —was that where the medicine came from? I mean, you got it there?"

"Yes."

Then she told me a story which, under different circumstances, would have been perfectly reasonable—but then, everything I touched in this case was reasonable until you scratched at the surface. During the Alans' stay in Los Angeles, a number of fund-raising parties were given, at which the Alans were the guests of honor, the main drawing card. I knew from my own experience that this was a usual procedure. The Israeli need for foreign exchange was so desperate that regardless of what diplomatic circumstances brought an important Israeli to our shore, the diplomat was also used as a magnet for fund raising. At one of these fund-raising parties, in a large Beverly Hills mansion, Deborah had fallen into conversation with a man who told her his name was Dr. Herbert Green, a very ordinary name that might or might not be Jewish. She had mentioned her husband's exhausting schedule, and she thought she had said something about her husband's high blood pressure.

"Not that it was ever high enough to require medication," she assured me. "But when you are eating restaurant food morning, noon, and night, you load your body with salt."

He was very sympathetic, this Dr. Green, and he thought it might be a good thing for Asher Alan to stop by at his office. He told Mrs. Alan that she should put aside stories she had heard about the exorbitant fees American doctors charged. He would consider the examination as his small contribution to Israel. This question of the fee was more important than it might sound, considering the international attention that had been paid to Asher Alan. If not exactly a poor country, Israel was nevertheless a place always short of cash, and its people traveling abroad counted every dollar. Deborah's statement about her husband's blood pressure not being high enough to require medication is also open to question, since she did mention a fainting incident, which may well have been the result of very high blood pressure. As I said earlier, Asher Alan was a robust, heavily muscled, high-colored man whose physical strength and well-being belied the notion of illness, but possibly the fainting incident helped him to agree to visit Dr. Green. When he returned from the visit, he told Deborah that he had been given a clean bill of health, except for a warning about his blood pressure. Dr. Green had given him a prescription for pills he was to take, two pills, three times a day. She also mentioned that during this Los Angeles interval, Alan had been relatively depressed. By the second day after taking the pills Green prescribed, Alan's mood had changed. The depression had lifted and physically he felt better.

"Did he see Dr. Green again?" I asked Deborah.

"No."

"Did you ask any of the people you met there about Green?"

"No—he was so engaging." She stared at me hopelessly, and then she began to cry, whispering through her tears, "What am I going to do? What can I do?"

Shelly sat down beside her and put her arms around her.

"One more question?" I said.

"What good are the questions? You only make her more miserable," Shelly said.

"Please," Deborah said, nodding.

"Where did you have the prescription filled? Or did your husband have it filled?"

"I did."

"Where?"

"In Beverly Hills."

"But where in Beverly Hills? Can you remember where?"

"I don't know Beverly Hills that well, Lieutenant. It was a corner store. That's all I can tell you."

51

Toomey was back at the precinct when I arrived, and he told me he had failed in his search for the medicine bottle. The baggage had been removed and whatever remained in the room had gone into the trash compactor. Toomey had then called the Israeli legation and had spoken to the attaché who had done the packing. No, he had not packed any medicine bottles.

"Sorry, Lieutenant," Toomey said.

"There are ways, Toomey."

I put through a call to the Beverly Hills police, where I found myself talking to a Sergeant McNulty. I gave him the doctor's name and Alan's name.

"You know, Lieutenant," he said to me, "we got a lot of drugstores."

"Corner stores." And then I added, "McNulty, I'll write your name in gold. Anything you're looking for in New York, you got a whole precinct working for you."

"I'll see what I can do."

It was less than an hour before he called back. The prescription was for pargyline.

"Do you have the address—the doctor's?"

"Yeah—It's an empty office."

Chapter 4

"THE PHARMACY?" Dr. Stephan Hyde said. "Of course I know what pharmacy he used. Bromstein's, between Sixty-fifth and Sixty-sixth on Madison. An excellent chemist—and very careful."

Dr. Hyde was an elegant man, in an elegant office. I noticed two well-equipped examining rooms, which appeared, granting my quick glance, to have every instrument known to modern medicine. An exaggeration, of course, but the rooms were well and expensively equipped. His office bespoke money and taste, and since Fran had trained me through the years to recognize antiques and to know something of stuff such as rugs and hand-blocked wallpaper, I could do what the Internal Revenue people call an outside search. The "partner's desk" would fetch at least thirty thousand at auction, and each of the Queen Anne chairs would go for at least five thousand. Behind the desk and facing it were two Chippendale armchairs that would have made Fran weep with envy and the curator at the Met salivate with greed. I hesitate to put a price on them. On the floor was a silk Kirman that was unquestionably real, even to my untutored eye.

The doctor himself was equally elegant, silk shirt, silk tie, embroidered vest, blue cashmere jacket, gray trousers, and natty Italian shoes. He had a long, narrow face, thin black mustache, and a combed but not polished head of hair. And he was most cooperative when I told him that I was looking into a few puzzling facts relative to the death of Stanley Curtis.

"Delighted to be of some help. I'm very uncomfortable about Stanley's death," Hyde said. "Of course, a decent physician is always devastated when one of his patients dies, even if the patient suffers from some incurable ailment. But Stanley was not a sick man, which makes it all the more a cause of anguish."

"Might I ask you the nature of the prescription you gave him, and why you prescribed it?"

"It was a placebo."

"What!"

"Oh, yes, simply a sugar pill. Oh, Stanley had a bit of high blood pressure, but nothing to worry about. But he was a man with great faith in medicine and, if I may say so, considerable faith in myself. The public figure was one thing, the inner man another. The inner man was dependent, the perfect candidate for placebos."

"Isn't that something of a swindle, the use of placebos?"

"Oh, no, not at all," taking no umbrage at my suggestion. "It's a legitimate and frequently miraculous part of medicine, and very old, too—a path for the body to follow to cure itself. And you know, Lieutenant, for the most part, the body cures itself, not the physician. It's incredible what belief can do."

"Did you see him again after that? Did you take his blood pressure to note the effect of your placebo?"

"A placebo would never work with you, Lieutenant. You doubt everything. No"—the first trace of acerbity in his voice—"I did not examine him again. He was killed a week later. Damn it, Lieutenant, the man was a dear friend!"

"Then you shouldn't object to my lack of belief in terms of his death. I am trying to find out what killed him."

"We know what killed him. He died of a massive stroke."

"Was it indicated?" I asked sharply. "You are his physician. You examined him a week before."

"A stroke is rarely indicated, as you put it. If it were, perhaps we could prevent it."

"What would you say if I told you that the drug delivered to Curtis's home was not a placebo but pargyline?"

"I would say your statement is ridiculous. All we have to do is to call the pharmacist. Shall I?"

"I'd rather you wouldn't. Not at this moment."

"What on earth ever gave you such a notion, Lieutenant?"

"I had reason."

"I would like to know what your reason was!" he said angrily. "Do you realize what you are doing, accusing me of prescribing a drug that was not indicated? I've been decently open and fair with you, and this is what it leads to. Well, get the hell out of here! I am through with you and your questions!"

When I told it to Fran afterward, she pointed out that he was quite right. He had answered my questions openly and fairly, and as Fran put it, I had responded not to the words of the man, but to his somewhat sinister appearance, his long face and thin mustache and dark, steady eyes. "Nonsense framed by film and television," Fran said. Perhaps she was right.

I have often longed for an occasion to wander around my precinct on foot, but when a lieutenant of New York City's police moves, he moves in a car, linked by radio phone to his precinct house. Occasionally, I've struck out on a very limited mission on foot, but not without temerity. It was only a few blocks from the doctor's office to L. D. BRONSTEIN, CHEMIST, on Madison Avenue. On the West Side, a drugstore is frequently called a drugstore and infrequently a pharmacy, but never a chemist. On the East Side, a drugstore is frequently called a pharmacy, infrequently a chemist, but never a drugstore. Pharmacies carried everything from tunafish sandwiches to nuts; chemists, self-consciously occupying a higher level, sold only drugs and toiletries. Such was Bronstein's, established in 1915. The white-haired Mr. Bronstein was evidently a son of the founder, and he greeted me courteously if not warmly. When he discovered my errand, he froze up.

"My prescriptions are very confidential."

"You know I can get a court order to unfreeze your prescription file. Come on, Mr. Bronstein. It will be much simpler if you dig up that single prescription—and it'll be a sort of public service."

"What are you after?" Bronstein asked me. "I've known Dr. Hyde for years. He's an excellent and responsible physician."

"I'm not sure what I'm after, and I'm not sure it reflects in any way on Dr. Hyde. Please believe me, Mr. Bronstein, I'll try to keep this confidential."

Bronstein stared at me a long moment, and then he went into his back room and returned with the prescription. "There it is. Placebo. A little sugar pill, in case you don't know what a placebo is, and the prescription was phoned in by the doctor."

He showed it to me, and it was exactly as he said. *Placebo*, and under it, *By phone*.

"Wouldn't he have to mail a confirmation?"

"Not for a placebo, Lieutenant. That's not a prescription drug, although you can rest assured that it has its place in medical practice."

"Is this your handwriting?"

"No. The prescription was taken by my assistant."

I nodded at a young man behind the counter. "Him?"

"No. Fellow named Richard Bell."

"Did you check the prescription, I mean the filled bottle?"

Bronstein smiled tolerantly. "I had other things to do. The placebos are bright vermilion, marked with a *p*, unmistakable. Bell was quite capable of counting out fifty pills. In fact, Bell is a very capable man."

"Where is he?"

"He called in sick this morning. He'll be here tomorrow."

"I'd like his address and phone, and if a detective called Bolansky comes after the same thing, tell him I have the information and that I'll see him at the precinct."

Sighing deeply, Mr. Bronstein produced what I'd requested. Bell had an apartment on 88th Street between West End Avenue and Riverside Drive. It was a shabby, depressed street, crime-ridden but not excessively so for the West Side, and the corners held splendid if somewhat unkempt old apartment houses. Bell lived not in one of the fine old buildings but in a converted brownstone. I found his name in the hallway listing, and I pushed the button several times. No answer. Then a departing tenant conveniently opened the hall door for me and I went inside. Bell's apartment was listed as 4B, which meant climbing four flights of stairs. At the door to 4B I pressed the button again. No answer, although I heard the ring clearly. I tried the knob and the door opened. The living room, which faced the street, was about sixteen feet square, furnished with inexpensive but not tasteless Scandinavian furniture, and in one of the severely designed chairs, Mr. Bell was sprawled. He was not sick; he was quite dead, a bullet hole in his head and a trickle of dried blood across his forehead and face. He was a tall man, middle thirties, with one of those good-looking, characterless faces that you see in network shows. His hair was blond, his wide-open, staring eyes blue, and he wore gray flannels and an old turtleneck sweater. His hand was cold, and on the floor, apparently dropped from his hand, was a copy of *Sports Illustrated*.

West 88th Street is covered by the West Side precinct, where Lieutenant Joe Finelli runs the detective squad. I knew Finelli well enough to know that he was tough, rigid, and generically suspicious, so it was no surprise that he greeted me with "What the hell are you doing on my turf, Golding?"

"Just take it easy, Joe. The city's the city. I didn't know a crime had been committed. I had an address on Eighty-eighth Street. I went there. I rang a bell and got no answer, so I turned a knob and went in. The occupant is dead. His name is Richard Bell, he's a pharmacist. When you get here, I'll tell you more."

Finelli had cooled down when he arrived with a convoy of uniforms, detectives, fingerprint, and forensic. He took me aside, and after I had given him as much information as I thought wise to give him, he sort of apologized. He was a big man with sloping shoulders, a very dark beard, and a sour, unlit cigar that lived in his mouth.

"All right, Harry. I'm sorry I blew at you. Let's have

dinner some night. We'll bring the wives and tell each other how rotten the profession is."

"Soon as I can free a night."

I stayed until forensic came up with a surmise. Mr. Bell had been shot through the head with a large-caliber revolver or automatic, sometime between nine-thirty and eleven. He was dead and the back of his skull was on the chair behind him. All of which I had guessed. Forensic did not bother to comment on his hypo tracks, assuming that I knew a doper when I saw one. I softened Finelli a bit more by remarking that as much as Fran and I loved Italian food, we'd never hit a really good restaurant.

"Then you got a surprise coming to you, Harry. I know the best goddamn restaurant in this city, Italian, but up in the Bronx. You don't mind coming up to the Bronx?"

"Not at all."

"Only at this place, I take the check. I'm hot shit there, and no way do I let them see someone sitting with me grab the check. On me. Don't argue. I'll pick up you and Fran. When?"

"As soon as I consult with Fran."

Fran was not crazy about Italian food, but she would, I hoped, serve the cause, and I made a note in my book to select the date. There were enough notes there now to be confusing. I was tempted to write, Don't offend the Finellis of this world. You will need them.

It was almost five o'clock when I got back to the precinct, and things had lagged. Toomey, left alone and in command, never pushed things, even though he was smarter than most cops and reasonably responsible. Anyway, there was not much to grab at as he ran through the day's doings. As for Keene, he had been to both restaurants, and both of them had destroyed the checks. "Common decency," they told Keene. In Curtis's case, the waiter could not remember anything he had ordered, except that he was fairly certain one of the men at the table had downed well over an entire bottle of red wine. The waiter recalled that it was a modestly priced California Zinfandel, a heavy red peasant wine. The waiter recalled some remarks by others at the table when Curtis insisted on the California Zinfandel, and the waiter also remarked on the odd fact that no one skimped on the dishes, the restaurant being a very expensive one. He did not recall what the dishes were, but he did remember the contradiction in the quality of wine and food.

"I could talk to his wife," Keene said. "She'd remember."

I shook my head. "Not yet. I'll get around to talking to her myself."

As for Asher Alan, the waiter's memory was much better. Alan had started with one of their specialties, a large plate of mushrooms vinaigrette, followed by broiled liver with Spanish sausage, and then a very odd dessert, not on the menu but specifically ordered, sliced bananas with sour cream and sugar. The waiter sliced two bananas into a bowl—he did this himself because the pastry chef was miffed at the inelegant nature of the dish—and then he added a large gob of sour cream and two tablespoons of brown sugar.

"You got name, address, and telephone of the waiter?"

"Absolutely."

"All right, start a file. Type a full report, names and addresses where we have them, and remind me to give you the stuff on Dr. Hyde, Oshun—"

"Oshun, Lieutenant?"

"James O-s-h-u-n, Bronstein, and Richard Bell. Bell is a dead junkie, a homicide over on the West Side. So you remind me and I'll fill you in on all of them before I go home. Also, tomorrow, you go over to the West Side and lick Finelli's ass, because they don't like to share. But get everything they have on Richard Bell. Also, get a full, formal statement from each waiter."

"I got it."

I looked at Keene thoughtfully, and then I nodded. He was good, and that was all the praise he needed.

"And your wife called."

"Thanks." I called Fran then, telling her that I would be home in about an hour, and then I went into Alex Courtny's office.

It was Courtny's boast that he paid two dollars each for his cigars, that the leaf was grown in the Canary Islands from the finest Cuban seed, that they were better than the Cuban originals, and that they smelled as sweet as a summer evening. Myself, an ex-smoker these past fifteen years, rigid as only a convert can be—well, for myself the fumes in Courtny's office were unbearable and to sit there was a mild form of torture. But sit there I did until I had spelled out every detail of my investigation.

When I had finished, Courtny sat silent for a while, puffing on his cigar; then he pushed the cigar at me and asked whether I saw this as some sort of conspiracy.

"Maybe. I don't know yet."

"You want to know what I see, Harry?"

"That's why I'm here."

"I see a junkie who got a bullet in his head, which is a destination that a lot of junkies in this town are headed for, and then I see a couple of coincidences, and then I see—you got to forgive me on this one, Harry—then I see two guys who are maybe first-rate public guys, but who also pig out every chance they get. As for that medicine, Harry—what do you call it?"

"Pargyline."

"Yeah, pargyline. Well, a thing like that can be confusion. I never been to Beverly Hills. You know, funny thing, I never had any big urge to go back to Europe. I was there as a kid in W. W. Two, and they can shove it if they can find an asshole big enough, but America is something else, Grand Canyon, Yellowstone, San Francisco and the cable cars, and Hollywood. Never been to any of them. My army training was in a shithole state called Georgia, and since then I been a cop, and Washington, D.C., been my travels. But Hollywood, that's something I want to see. Beverly Hills—stuff it. It's a little bugass town that almost don't exist, so I am not impressed by what any Beverly Hills cop tells you over the telephone, not impressed one damn bit."

I ignored the fact that he had wandered all over the map, and said, "I could send Keene or Toomey. They'd be back the same day."

"Beverly Hills?"

"Yes, sir."

"No way."

"All right. But can I continue the investigation?"

"How many troops?"

"Just Keene. And myself."

"You were out on the town all day, Harry. Was it this business?"

"Yes."

"Harry, you're an old pro, a down-to-earth cop. You got brains and talent for the job, and I think the world of you. But there's nothing in this, and the doper's misfortune belongs to Finelli, not to us."

"Alex," I said to him, "do this for me. I only met Asher Alan once, but he was one of the good guys and Fran thinks he was Jesus Christ returned to earth. I don't like the thought that a man like that comes into our city and is murdered—"

"You don't know that!" he interrupted sharply.

"No, but damn it, let me find out. I'll pay for a trip to Beverly Hills and do it on my own time. But let me run this a few days."

"I'm weeping for you. If you pay for a trip to Beverly Hills, the smartasses will think you're on the pad. Do you know what airfare is today? Ah, the hell with it! Put in a tab and the city will pick it up." Then he added, "If you're right, Harry, he died here, but he was murdered in L.A."

Courtny was no fool. A bigot, yes, a man still controlled by all the hates of his childhood, but no fool. "Harry," he said, "you buy all this conspiracy crap, and it is bullshit, pure unadulterated bullshit. The dagos, the Russians, the Arabs—they go in for this conspiracy shit, but it is not American. No way. Those jugbunnies in Hollywood fill the TV screens with it, but that is pure, unadulterated bullshit. It is not the American way."

"No, and Kennedy was killed by one brilliant marksman with a rifle that couldn't possibly hit the target, and his brother was murdered as an interesting coincidence, and Martin Luther King was zapped by one nut who hated blacks—"

"And you're going to tell me that the kid who shot Reagan was part of some conspiracy? No, sir. I read all the books on Kennedy, and I reject all of them. Jack Kennedy, God rest his soul, was killed by a nut named Oswald, and that's it, and don't get me pissed off any more than I am,

Harry. I gave you the trip to California and you can put Keene on it for three days tops."

"I'm leaving the house," I said to him. "I've had a long day." That's the word for the precinct. Mostly, a cop talking to another cop calls it the "house."

I left my car parked in front of the precinct, one place where I would be spared a ticket, and I walked home. It was one of those splendid March evenings, a wind not too cold to be uncomfortable whipping through the city, the last of a good sunset muted by the twilight in the canyons, the street-lights going on, the home-bound citizens brisk and alive, as they always are on an evening like this. There was an electric current in the air that New Yorkers understand, part of what makes this city what it is.

Outside my door, I smelled Normandy chicken and scalloped potatoes, both done at the hand of a master. But after I had acknowledged that to Fran, I told her that she worked as hard as I did, and once in a while it wouldn't hurt to let me do the cooking.

"Two reasons I don't do that. Firstly, I get home before you do."

"We don't eat much before eight."

"Second reason . . ." She hesitated.

"Well?"

"You're a lousy cook, Harry."

"That's a real nice, positive thing to say. What about my ham and eggs?"

"I do believe you're hurt. We haven't had ham or bacon for ten years. We're on a low salt diet. Harry, darling, no one expects you to be a good cook. You're a Jewish American Prince."

"What!"

"Oh, Harry, come on. I don't mean anything nasty. But your parents, God bless them, were as poor as church mice. Your mother—and you know I adored her—well, she worked her fingers to the bone, scrubbing, cleaning, knitting sweaters for her kids, and your father worked himself to death and borrowed money he couldn't pay back, all to raise their two sons as if they really were of royal blood and send them to college—"

62

"Oscar," I interrupted. "I never went to college. I grew up to marry a shanty-Irish kid who went to college—"

"Hunter! Free! No tuition, and I waited tables."

"I never got there. I was working and paying Oscar's tuition. And furthermore, you're an anti-Semite."

"Me? Me with two beautiful Jewish kids who tore me apart birthing them, and you have the *chutzpah* to call me an anti-Semite!"

She always fell into that phony brogue when she wanted to impress someone with her ancestry. *Chutzpah* was one of a dozen Yiddish words she knew, and she used them to death. The insertion in the midst of the brogue was an indication that she was truly angry. In a moment, she would deliver her pedigree.

"You bastard," she said to me. "I am Francesca O'Brian O'Brannigan Murphy, and with the blood of kings on both sides, and you dare to call me an anti-Semite!"

"I take it back, I apologize, and I love you, and if you don't cool down, I'm not taking you to Beverly Hills with me."

"It's a joke."

"No joke. And if you're nice and sweet and get dinner on the table, and if you can work a couple of days' sick leave from the college, I'll let you sit next to me on the airplane. The city pays my fare and we can afford yours. Providing you can get the two days. We can leave on Sunday, have Monday and Tuesday working days in L.A., and be back on the late plane Wednesday morning."

"You have me," Fran said. "Don't worry about the two days. I'm on the plane with you. And I take back all the terrible things I said."

During dinner, I brought her up-to-date on the day's developments and asked her what she thought.

"I don't know, Harry. There's a way to agree with everything Courtny said. He was talking from a lot of experience. We all expect doctors to be smart, but smart is not a requirement for being a doctor. A retentive memory is much more important. Doctors are not trained in logic, in the art of reason—if indeed anyone can be trained in those disciplines.

So it could very well be that your Dr. Green—by the way, does he have a first name?"

"Herbert."

"Well, it could well be that your Dr. Green is simply a very inept and stupid doctor. They exist. My grandmother Maureen was killed in a hospital when they pumped her full of penicillin without finding out whether she could tolerate it. Doctors give stupid and dangerous prescriptions sometimes, and it may well be that your Dr. Green did that. Tragedy but no crime."

"That could be, yes."

"As for the junkie—what was his name?"

"Richard Bell."

"Well, he might have been high," Fran suggested. "Switched bottles with no evil intent."

"That could happen."

"Then from that point of view the case comes apart at the seams, and Courtny was right."

"Is that what you think, Fran?"

She took a moment or two before she said, "No. No, I'm on your side. I think there's something awful here. I think there's something here that kills without thought or conscience. It terrifies me."

"Why," I persisted, "when you gave such a logical explanation?"

"Because there's nothing logical here. By the way, did you call information in Los Angeles or Beverly Hills? They might have a Dr. Green listed."

"They might, but it won't be our man. The Beverly Hills cops are not idealists."

"You're convinced?"

"Pretty much. But suppose there were five Dr. Greens out there? What could I learn over the telephone?"

"Well, what will you learn when we go there?"

"I'll find one of the women or men at the party who saw him talking to Asher Alan. When a man like Asher Alan is at an affair, he becomes the center of attention. People gather around him, not necessarily to talk to him but to hear what he is saying to someone else."

"Yes, of course."

"One more thing," I said slowly. "You owe me one. Instead of getting down on your knees and apologizing for calling me a Jewish American Prince, you just passed over it."

"That's right," she admitted. "Maybe I owe you one, but I'm not getting down on my knees. If I owe you one, let's go to bed."

"Your students should hear you talk like that. No, I want payment in kind. I told Lieutenant Joe Finelli that we'd join him for dinner at an Italian restaurant in the Bronx, and it has to be tomorrow night because the next day we're going to Los Angeles."

"Oh, no. I'll get down on my knees and apologize."

"It's too late."

"Harry, do you know what an evening with Joe Finelli and his idiot wife is like? It happened to us already; why does it have to happen again? I didn't mean to cut your heart out when I called you a Jewish American Prince. I meant it as a kind of compliment."

"Why can't you take your punishment with grace and honor—as for example, Kevin Barry?"

"Who is Kevin Barry?"

"You don't know, you with the blood of kings on both sides?"

"You're skating on thin ice, Harry."

"Kevin Barry, the boy hero of the Irish Rebellion, hanged by the Brits in 1920, and on the gallows, he shouted, 'Shoot me like an Irish soldier, do not hang me like a dog!'"

"Did he? Good for him. But he didn't have to spend an evening with Joe Finelli."

"A coward dies a thousand times, the brave man only tastes of death but once."

"What's that?"

"Shakespeare or something. And it's important. I need the good graces of Joe Finelli. You might even enjoy it."

"That will be the day."

The following morning, I called Mrs. Stanley Curtis, and she agreed to see me at two o'clock. Then I called Oshun and tracked him down in the pathology lab of New York University medical school. My interest at that moment was fixed on the pill bottle that Mrs. Curtis had shown. If the murdered pharmacist-junkie had deliberately switched the placebos, why put the name of the dangerous drug on the bottle? Was it to cover his own action? Would he then claim that the prescription was for pargyline and that he was innocent of any wrongdoing? I put it to Oshun once he was on the telephone. "This time, Oshun, I want the facts, not any of your damn surmises. Did you clearly see the medicine bottle at the Curtis place, and did you read the name plainly?"

"I'm not sure," he replied after a long pause.

"You're not sure? Damn you, you're not sure?"

"Hold on, Lieutenant. You said 'clearly.' I'm not in a position to say I saw it clearly. I'm trying to be honest with you. She showed it to me and then she snatched it back. I only had a glimpse of it."

Beautiful, I thought, beautiful, beautiful. He only had a glimpse of it. What had been a house of cards began to shiver. I called Mr. L. D. Bronstein at his drugstore. "If you make up a placebo, what do you put on it?"

"What? What? What on earth are you talking about, Lieutenant?"

I explained by pointing out that a bottle of medicine had to have a label and that something had to be put on that label.

"I see. We put a code mark on it and in my case, I use the name *plebo*. That is related to no known drug, just in case the patient should try to renew it somewhere else."

"No chance that you would put pargyline on the label?"

"Good heavens, no!"

"Could Richard Bell have done that?"

"Why, Lieutenant? Why would he? Anyway, poor soul, he can't answer that question, can he? He was a decent man, a quiet man."

"Does he have any relatives that you know about?"

"None. And I'm not sure that was his real name. He had some kind of accent, maybe Hispanic."

So there I was. Oshun unsure of what he saw, Bronstein telling me that the label said *plebo,* and the whole thin fabric of conspiracy ready to dissolve into thin air. One more loose end, and then I would drop the whole thing and forget it. The loose end was Mrs. Curtis. I had made the appointment and I might as well go through with it.

The Curtis apartment was on Madison Avenue between 66th and 67th streets, in one of those wonderful old buildings that have somehow survived New York's maniacal urge to tear down and replace anything more than ten years old. The elevator was still an open cage, and the apartment was huge, with ceilings twelve feet high, all of it furnished in gold-leaf Italian and French baroque, the last thing in the world one would expect from a man like Stanley Curtis. You might expect it from his wife. Curtis was fifty-four when he died; his wife was three years older. He had met her when he was a freshman at Harvard and she was a senior at Wellesley, and he had fallen madly in love with her. At age twenty-two, Felicity Curtis, according to what I read, had been a very beautiful young woman. Now she was fat and not very attractive, her hair badly bleached and showing gray at the roots. She was dressed in a diaphanous gown that suited her poorly, and she wore too much harsh makeup for a woman of her age. The gown was pink, and she waved the color away, telling me, "Lieutenant, I hope you didn't expect me to appear in widow's weeds. I am not mourning the saintly Stanley Curtis. There are four little amateur whores in this town who will mourn him sufficiently, and if I am not upgrading his memory, I am no longer bound by his need to be elected. A political wife is a doozy, Mr. Lieutenant, and I'll bet Mary Todd Lincoln could have told a story or two if anyone had listened to her."

I didn't know how to reply to all this, whether to defend Stanley Curtis, which was certainly not my obligation, or to join in her denunciation, which I considered a nasty price for her cooperation. The result was that I listened and waited.

"As a matter of fact," she went on, "you are fortunate to catch me here today, Lieutenant. Tomorrow I'll be on the *Queen Elizabeth,* embarked on a marvelous ninety-day cruise around the world. Stanley had a tidy little insurance policy of three hundred thousand dollars, and I'm selling the apartment because I am absolutely nauseated by this baroque junk which was my taste twenty years ago and which I clung to because Stanley hated it so. The apartment goes up for sale at a selling price that is positively indecent, a million two. Of course, we have twelve rooms and you could play tennis in some of them, but still the price is preposterous. Yet the real estate folk tell me we'll sell it within two months. Dear old suffering, noble Stanley has made me a millionaire. What do you think of that?"

"Very nice," I agreed. "I gather you were not fond of your husband?"

"Only the people were fond of Stanley." She stared at me thoughtfully out of two large, baby-blue eyes. Time had ravaged the rest of the face, but the eyes were young and clear. Finally, she said, "I am going to open my heart to you, Lieutenant. I am not making any public statements about Stanley, but if you want to whisper this around, why whisper away. About a month before he died, he received a large sum of money. Fifty thousand dollars. I know how large it was because after he died, I found the money, in cash in one hundred dollar bills in a locked drawer in his desk. My attorneys have paid the proper amount to the tax people and the rest I have. But think of it—Mr. Clean picking up fifty grand so dirty he couldn't deposit it or even trust his safe deposit box. No." She smiled. "I was not fond of Stanley. Now, what are you here for? Have you found out whose fifty thousand that was, and do you want to grab it?"

"As far as I can see, the fifty thousand is yours, and since the feds have taken their bit, there's probably not too much left."

"Bless your heart. You know, Stanley did not leave me without debts."

"I'm sure of that."

"And what are you here for, young man?"

The flattery was going both ways. When you call a beat-up city detective "young man," you are either totally near-sighted or cozening. I quickly put an end to her modest flirtation by telling her that I was interested in seeing the medicine bottle containing the pills that Dr. Hyde had prescribed for her husband.

"Oh!" she exclaimed. "Oh, no, not the bottle again."

"What do you mean by not the bottle again?"

"My dear Lieutenant, I am thoroughly exasperated by that business of the bottle. First a snotty kid from some medical school—"

"Did you show him the bottle? Did you put it in his hands?"

"I started to, and then I said to myself, what business is it of his or anyone's? So I snatched it away."

"Did he look at it?"

"I don't know. What does it matter?"

"It matters, believe me, dear lady."

"You're very charming for a policeman," she said, smiling. "And very polite."

"We try."

"Well, he may have caught a glimpse of it. Then, a week later, Dr. Hyde called and asked whether I still had the medicine bottle."

"When was that, exactly?"

"I'm such a rattlebrain—two weeks ago?"

"Can you pin it down?"

"I'm afraid not."

"What happened?" I asked, unable to conceal my eagerness. "I mean, after Dr. Hyde called you? Did he have someone pick up the pill bottle?"

"Well, that's certainly what he intended. But after the incident with the young man, I was thoroughly annoyed. It was one thing for Stanley to treat me like garbage during our married life, to refuse me the joy of having children and to stay married only because his career could not endure a divorce; it was another thing to have me pestered and pestered after his death. So when the young man left, I threw the bottle in the refuse can."

"What!"

"Of course. I got rid of it. What good was it? Stanley was dead."

For a long moment, I sat facing her with my eyes closed.

"Lieutenant, did I do something awful? It won't interfere with my cruise, will it?"

"No, it won't interfere with your cruise. What did Dr.

Hyde say when you told him you had thrown the bottle away?"

"He was very provoked. I don't care. I never liked him anyway. He kept pressing that I be absolutely sure I had thrown it away. I finally convinced him. He wasn't my doctor. I wouldn't trust him as far as I could throw him. But Stanley had faith in him. Stanley thought he was such a great judge of character. But I think Stanley was a total dud in that department."

"Yes." I started to rise.

"Lieutenant. That was not the end of it. Yesterday, Mr. Bronstein, our pharmacist, called, and he said he would like to look at the bottle, if I would permit it. He's a very nice little man, and I said I would be delighted, but that I had thrown the bottle away. He sounded so disappointed. I told him that if it was to complete a bill, he could put down any reasonable price and I would be glad to pay it. You know what medicine costs these days, and I didn't want the poor man stuck with the bill. But he said no, it was not that. He sounded so upset."

"Mrs. Curtis," I said to her, "you are a sensible, attractive, and bright woman—"

"Flattery will get you everywhere."

"—and therefore, you must remember what was written on the label of that bottle."

"No. I never bothered to look at the label. I'm a very vain woman, Lieutenant. I seem to be confessing everything to you, and I never put on my reading glasses unless I intend to do some reading. So the words on the bottle were simply a blur to me. Do you understand?"

"Yes." I sighed. "I think I do."

Chapter 5

I GOT HOME EARLY and took a bath and changed my clothes. I owed that much to Finelli, and I have found that whenever I put down someone, even in my own mind, my Jewish guilts begin to work me over until I have placed myself among the worst anti-ethnic bastards. Fran came in and remarked that she had read in the Sunday *Times* that most men prefer showers. "I don't," I told her. "The only time I shower is over at the precinct house, and I hate it, and what I would do if I had my druthers would be a whole day in a nice hot tub."

"It would play havoc with your skin. What are you so depressed about?"

"Being a cop."

"Tell me about it outside. It's too hot in here."

I sat in the bedroom later and watched her dress and told her about the day. She had a good figure, not very different from the figure on the girl I married. She would go out of the house at seven-thirty, winter, spring, or summer, and jog for half an hour—something I would not do if my life depended on it.

"So what do you think, Harry? Is the case blown?"

"I don't know. What's left except our guesswork?"

"Los Angeles."

"And tonight Finelli's sure to tell me that Bell was a simple, ordinary Mafia job, same as you get four times a week."

"I said Los Angeles. Beverly Hills. Our trip. Being together and maybe getting to the bottom of this."

I shook my head. "It's just not enough."

"Harry," she said, "I will absolutely kill you. I already lied my way out of three days at the university and I've spent a hundred and thirty dollars for two new summer dresses and thirty-one dollars for a pair of sandals, and I've never been to that peculiar place, and if we don't go with the city paying half our fare, we'll never go; you know that."

"I suppose not. I can't think of any reason why we should go to Beverly Hills."

"Exactly," Fran agreed. "But we made up our minds about it, and we have the tickets, and I'm as excited as a kid about it because it's been two years since we've gone anywhere except to the old shack up on the lake, and it has to be a real kitsch thing, like that fat lady's apartment you were telling me about—and please, Harry."

"Let me think about it."

"Please, Harry," she begged.

"Let me think about it."

Finelli arrived at seven-thirty, and Fran and I got into his big four-door Olds after the necessary hugs and kisses with his wife, Paula, who was not quite the idiot Fran held her to be. She was a round, warm woman, marvelously put together and with a devastating effect on most men, black hair, black eyes, and a delicious smile—nothing to entice an Irish lady in her early forties with small breasts and red hair. Fran suspected that I would like nothing better than to jump into bed with Paula Finelli, and I will admit that the notion had crossed my mind; but I'm sure it crossed the mind of every man who laid eyes on Paula. The "idiot" reputation came from the fact that Paula hardly ever said anything, but as I told Fran, that was hardly proof that she was an idiot and Finelli's two hundred and forty pounds of truculent muscle was enough to dissuade any sane man from thoughts of conniving at adultery.

"You know, Harry," Finelli said to me as we pulled away from the house, "I'm glad about this evening. I always looked at you as one of those guys who passed the lieutenant's test the first time. I took it three times, so I put myself down. But Jesus God, I don't enjoy hanging out with the apes. I like you and Fran, and Paula says your Fran is the most first-rate lady she's ever been with. Paula's from Tuscany, and why she ever agreed to marry a Sicilian bum like myself, I'll never know. But like I said, we'll have fun tonight. You never ate such food, never."

We had turned up First Avenue, and were driving north.

"Pasta," Finelli said. "What you get in most Italian restaurants is not pasta. Garbage. Italian junk food. You'll eat a *cozze alla marinara* like you never tasted, a *fettuccine alla romana* that will spoil you for what they call pasta, a *calamari ripieni*—you like squid, Harry?"

"Love it."

"Good. That's stuffed squid, but women don't like squid. For the ladies, they got a dish called *braciole all'oreste cianci* —not just one dish a lady can enjoy, but this is Paula's favorite, beautiful thin steak, it melts in your mouth."

Finelli, revealing a poetic bent I had never suspected, drove across the Willis Avenue Bridge, swinging left onto the Major Deegan. "Best way to the North Bronx," he explained. "It misses Apacheland. I don't like to be reminded. I spent two years there." A moment or two later, he said to me, "Harry, turn around and have a good look. There's a four-door black sedan that was with us up First Avenue. I deliberately missed a light, and he did the same thing. He stayed behind me over the bridge, and when I slowed here on the Major Deegan, he slowed too."

I twisted around. "Black Buick, I think."

"Could be a Buick."

"About fifty, sixty yards back." The Buick was in the access lane. We were in the middle, and now Fran was kneeling on the back seat next to me. "Move to the fast lane," I told Finelli, and as he swung over the Buick shifted into the middle lane.

"He's following," I said to Finelli, who then increased his speed from fifty-five to seventy miles an hour. The Buick roared ahead, sat beside us for a moment, and then the left rear window moved down. No car window moves too fast,

73

and this gave me time to push Fran to the floor and Finelli time to shove Paula down. I was trying to drop my window —fortunately Finelli drove a button car—and clawing for my gun at the same time when the shot from the Buick passed me and smashed a hole in the left rear window. A second shot came so close that I could swear I felt the breath of the bullet across my face. Then I had my gun out and began to empty it at the Buick. The black car roared away, up the Major Deegan Expressway at an increasing speed, past eighty and touching ninety, screaming from lane to lane as it shifted to pass the other cars on the road; and meanwhile there was Fran demanding to know what was happening and Paula sobbing, and Finelli yelling into his radiophone, "Did you hear me? This is Lieutenant Finelli, West Side Uptown, and I got a ten thirteen on the Major Deegan. Where? How the hell do I know where? I'm doing ninety miles an hour at night—somewhere between the George Washington exit and Yonkers—"

"Finelli," I shouted, "cut your speed."

"What in hell do you mean?"

"Finelli, we got the girls in the car! I don't want a shoot-out!"

"A black Buick, four-door—"

He heard me and sanity penetrated, and he cut his speed back to sixty. The Buick was gone.

"What happened back there?" he wanted to know. "Anybody hurt?"

He allowed the car to drift down to fifty miles an hour, edging over to the right-hand lane, and said to his wife, "You can sit up, sweetie. I never wanted anything like this to happen with you around. I'm so sorry. Jesus, believe me, I'm so sorry." She kept sobbing, and he put an arm around her, drawing her close to him. It was a side of Finelli I had never seen and it was very touching.

"Anybody hurt back there?" He had turned his car off the Major Deegan onto an access road, and now he was on the city streets in the North Bronx. He pulled over to the curb and stopped. His radio was squawking.

"So this is what you do for a living," Fran said, her voice shaky.

"Are you all right?"

"Yes. In five minutes I begin to scream."

"I gave up the chase!" Finelli was shouting into his radiophone. "I was in hot pursuit, but I gave up, and that's why I can't tell you where the goddamn car is. I have two women in my car, and I do not engage in hot pursuit with two women in my car."

Later, in Mama Pasquella's Restaurant, Finelli said, "You know, Harry, the big Jewish contribution nobody talks about? It's the word *schmuck*. Without it, what do you say? Those total schmucks wanted to know why I couldn't continue the chase, even after I tell them I got two ladies in my car. So drive carefully they tell me. At ninety miles an hour, I should drive carefully. Any wonder they got increasing crime in the city? Schmucks. The cops never got the car. Ninety miles an hour on the Major Deegan, and they never even picked up a license plate."

Finelli had introduced Fran and myself to Mama Pasquella, a tall, stout lady in an ankle-length black dress who greeted us as if she had known us all our lives and whose warm embrace enveloped Paula, still tearful. Her information service was better than the CIA, and by the time we were seated, she knew all about the two bullet holes in the window of the car, plus the fact that we had been through a horrendous incident, horrendous to her since she knew none of the details aside from Paula's tears. Finelli had opened the evening with an enormous platter of Italian hors d'oeuvres to buttress our drinks, and I must say that I had never eaten such food in an Italian restaurant before. I glanced at Fran reproachfully, and she shrugged her shoulders without interrupting her eating, but nodded to indicate that later there would be an apology.

"Eat," Finelli said. "We got to be glad we're alive. If those bums in the Buick had used shotguns, we might all be in the hospital now—or in the morgue."

"Nice way to talk," Fran said. "I don't like your profession."

"Who does? Harry, why do you suppose them bums tried to kill us?"

"You tell me. It was your car."

"Yeah, but they must have been parked outside your house, waiting."

"Then why did they wait until we got out on the highway?" Fran wanted to know.

"Easier getaway. They could get trapped on the city streets. You know, Harry," he said to me, "I been nice to everybody. I don't know why anyone should try to waste me."

I could just visualize Finelli being nice to everyone. I suggested the mob.

"Yeah," Finelli said. "They know how I hate them. I hate the goddamn Mafia more than the devil himself. They put a stink on every decent Italian in this country, and they know how I feel about them. They're looking to establish more business on the West Side, and I ordered my squad to make it difficult, really difficult. But the mob don't kill cops as a regular thing. Sometimes, but not often. They're organized, and they know that killing a cop won't bring them nothing, only make the other cops mad. Anyway, this don't look like anything the mob does. It don't smell Mafia, and I got a lot of time put into smelling Mafia. If it was the mob, we'd be dead now. No, I think it was a private job. The bums who take contract work are not much damn good. This could be private contract work."

"On you or me?"

"For heaven's sake," Fran cried, "why should they want to kill either of you? This is the craziest thing I ever heard of." And then she added, "It could be a mistake, couldn't it? They could have mistaken this for some other car?"

I looked at Finelli and he looked at me. A long moment before he nodded and said to Fran, "Sure, it could have been a mistake."

I felt a cold chill, because it was no mistake and they were not trying to kill Joe Finelli. They were not even trying to kill me. Finelli had said that the bums who take contract work are not very good, but sometimes they are very good indeed. Any professionals out to kill me would have used sawed-off shotguns or something like an Uzi gun and splashed the whole car full of bullets. They wouldn't have given two damns about killing three people who were not the

76

target, and they wouldn't have missed. This was a warning. If they had hit me, it would not have troubled them, but they would just as soon have missed me, as they did.

Finelli changed the subject, but not by jumping to what book he had recently read or what movie he had seen. Not in Finelli's world; his world was specific, and he said to me, "Hey, Harry, that Richard Bell guy, you still interested?"

"Absolutely."

"Who is he?" Paula asked softly and apologetically.

"A doper got iced in a dump on Eighty-eighth Street, but you know something, Harry," he added, turning to me, "this is a very curious doper. In the first place, he has no yellow sheet, and in the second place his name ain't Richard Bell, which maybe you suspected because he has a spic look. We wouldn't have never ID'd him at all, if not for a file on illegals they keep in Washington. Not much of a file, because we got maybe two million illegals entering the country every year, but I guess they had a reason for glomming on to him. He's from Santa Marina."

"Where's that, sweetie pie?" Paula asked, her second remark, as apologetic as the first.

"Central America."

"It's one of those countries, Paula," Fran said kindly, her conscience beginning to work, "that Reagan has gotten us involved with. We've sent them countless millions of dollars to resist a guerrilla movement against a clique of very rich people who control the country. We send them arms, aircraft and money, but very little food. The population exists at the edge of starvation. The rich own plantations where they grow sugar and bananas. Not a very big country, but a most unhappy one."

Paula gazed at Fran with wide-eyed admiration.

"All out of *The New York Times,*" Fran said, somewhat embarrassed.

"Except you left out the commies," Finelli reminded her. "That's what this guerrilla movement is, what they call Marxist, but that ain't in my precinct. In my precinct, there is something very peculiar indeed. This doper, Mr. Ricardo Sanchez, is shot in the head with a forty-five-caliber gun, shoots a bullet like this." He demonstrated the length of the bullet with his fingers. "Following the procedure with such a homicide, we send the bullet downtown to the police lab." He paused and grinned at me. "I got one for you, Harry."

I nodded.

"A beauty. I been saving it." He paused as the waiter set down an enormous platter of *uccelleti scappati,* a veal and prosciutto dish I had never tasted before, and with it a bowl of green noodles with chunks of sweet butter melting upon it. "I'll save it a little longer. First *mangiare.*"

"It's delicious," Fran said. "It's more than delicious. I've never tasted food like this before."

"Mama Pasquella, she was born in Tuscany, worked in restaurants in Milan and in Rome, so you got the best of everything. She teaches the cooks. Look at this place." The restaurant was packed, every table taken. "Just like this until midnight. So now listen to me, Harry. I could ask you to guess but you'd never guess in a million years. The bullet that killed Sanchez came from the same gun that killed Judge Charles Fitzpatrick in Washington, D.C., about two years ago. I got that from the computer."

"But how . . ." Fran's question trailed off. She sat with a forkful of food halfway to her mouth.

"The FBI puts the stuff on discs," I explained. "It's the miracle of modern times that's supposed to replace common sense. Down at the police lab, they have a computer that ties in."

"You're too cynical, Harry," Finelli said. "Anyway, suppose you tell me why the gun that killed a federal judge should come into my precinct and kill a junkie pharmacist?"

"Did you call the Washington cops?" I asked him.

"What then?"

"What did they say?"

"They said that the murder of the judge was a hit. At least, that's how they figured it. But the guy who runs the Appellate Division was afraid of some kind of scandal and he gives it to the media as a mugging."

"You got that from the Washington cops?" I shook my head. "Come on, Joe. Cops don't give out anything like that. They sit on it till death do them part."

"Huh!" Fran said. "Death do them part."

"I didn't get it from the Washington cops, Harry. Of course not. I got it from Frankie Delogio, who's Paula's cousin and who runs a precinct down there in D.C. He's a captain, so he hears things, and he tells me this in strict confidence, which is how I'm telling it to you. Of course, he wants to know all about our junkie, so it's a trade. Now Frankie tells me that this judge, a very big wheel in the Appellate Division, leaves his house in Georgetown about nine o'clock in the evening. When he and his wife eat alone, he goes out after dinner and walks to a cigar stand two blocks away and buys himself a two dollar Don Diego. He smokes it as he walks back, and sometimes he sits down on the steps of the little stone house they live in and gets a few more puffs in that way, because Frankie tells me his wife won't let him smoke a cigar in the house. Can you beat that? An appellate judge can't smoke in his own house." He put this last to Paula, who shook her head hopelessly. "Paula here would brain somebody says I can't smoke a cigar in my own house. Bring us another bottle of that beautiful white Sicilian wine," he told the waiter.

"The judge," I reminded him.

"Oh? Yeah. So the judge is walking home, smoking his cigar, when either a car pulls up next to him or maybe somebody on foot, because there were no witnesses, and drills him through the head. It just happens that a prowl car is cruising and they find the body before anyone else, so Washington homicide has control from the word go. The judge has two hundred or so in cash, a five hundred dollar watch and a gold ring, so they know it's no mugging."

"I can't believe it," Fran said. "Even the *New York Times* story had Judge Fitzpatrick killed by a mugger, and I remember an editorial about no neighborhood, not even an ultra posh place like Georgetown, being safe from crime."

"Sure *The New York Times* ran that story because it was the only story there was." Finelli paused to fill our glasses with the white Sicilian wine. "They don't do things in Washington like here. Since the Kennedy killing, they're scared to death about terrorists and conspiracies and political hits. They got a very nervous city. You know that, Harry."

"True. That's true, Fran."

"Well, right away the Washington cops know it's a hit, so they sit on it; and I guess there wasn't a word of it leaked out until this bullet is taken out of the doper's head."

I was absolutely intrigued, as if I were watching a spider spin his web, a crazy homicidal, clever spider. "Joe," I said to him, "there's got to be more. Did Delogio give you anything else? He must have."

"Harry, you must be a lousy poker player. I'm telling you this, and you're sitting there with your mouth open like you're watching one of them dumb movies about international spies. That's absolutely all that Frankie gave me, but you and me, we're old buddies so I'll call Frankie back and see what I can squeeze out of him. But it's got to be a trade-off."

"If we ever bust the guy, it's yours. It happened on your turf. I wouldn't dream of trying to claim the collar away from you."

"Come on, Harry, that ain't the trade-off I'm talking about. I want to know what you're into, what brought you to Sanchez, what have you got that makes you look like someone about to jump a beautiful broad?"

"Nothing."

"Come on, Harry. Don't diddle me."

"Is that how you look when you're about to jump a beautiful broad?" Fran asked me.

"Harry wouldn't do anything like that," Paula said firmly.

"I'll tell you what I have," I said to Finelli. "I have a case where there may or may not be a poisoning. I had to check it out in the drugstore where Sanchez worked. Sanchez was involved but off duty, so I got his home address and walked in on the body. Now you have it, Joe—all of it."

Finelli stared at me thoughtfully for a moment or two, and then he said, "I got to visit the john, Harry. Keep me company."

"No need," I protested.

"Put your self in need."

I sighed and apologized to the ladies, and as we walked away from the table, I heard Paula confiding in Fran on the strange habits of men when it came to the de-de. That's what she called it, the de-de. In the men's room, we waited for the lone user to depart, and then Finelli said, "What kind of shit are you giving me, Harry?"

"I didn't give you any shit," I replied, angrily and brilliantly. "I told you the truth."

"Bullshit!"

"All right. If that's the way you like it, leave it that way. I'm your guest tonight, so I can't say what's on my mind." I started for the door.

"Hold on!" Finelli barked. "I don't leave things that way. That lady out there means more to me than anything in my life, and you almost killed her tonight—and me and Fran, and you, too."

"What do you mean, I almost killed her?"

"I'll tell you what I mean. I may have put down the slobs who do contract work. They're the maggots in the asshole of this city, but usually they're good, and this guy with the thirty-two, he's got to be an old pro. He was after you, Harry, maybe to scare you, maybe to kill you, but he was after you, not me, and you know that as well as I do."

I nodded. "That's right. He was after me."

"Why?"

"Joe, I swear to God I don't know. Maybe because I was noodling around in this Sanchez–Bronstein affair."

"Who's Bronstein?"

"A nice old guy who owns the drugstore where Sanchez worked."

"Does he come into this?"

"I don't know that either."

"There seems to be a hell of a lot you don't know."

"You can say that again."

We were sweet-talking each other as we came back to the table. I had gathered from Finelli how excited Paula had been at the thought of dinner with us. We had little of what is special, but we were very special to Paula.

"Seminar over?" Fran asked.

"You could say that."

"I'm so happy they get along so well," Paula said.

When Finelli dropped us at our apartment house, Fran threw her arms around Paula and kissed her. It was real. A little danger can change people remarkably. I thanked Finelli for a good evening and the best dinner I had ever eaten. It was almost that.

An hour later, I sat in the bedroom with a shoe in my hand, watching Fran in a nightgown and combing her hair. Looking at me in the mirror, she nodded and smiled. "Just don't say you told me so."

"I'm not an I-told-you-so person. You know that."

"I have everything packed. I'm so excited I won't sleep a wink. I wouldn't sleep anyway, thinking about that terrible shooting spree on the highway."

"Still frightened, kid?"

"A little. I'm not sure. You've been a cop so many years. Nothing like this ever happened before."

"I've been on the force seventeen years and tonight is the first time I fired my gun off the range. Well, you can live in New York a lifetime and never be mugged, or it can happen the day you arrive."

"We have to be at Kennedy before eleven. When do we leave here?"

"Ten is plenty of time. Pretty sure we're going, aren't you?"

"When I saw that look on your face when you were listening to Joe Finelli, the look he said you have when you're ready to jump a broad—incidentally, a very interesting observation from an old buddy—when I saw that expression on your face, I knew you'd go to Los Angeles if you had to walk."

Chapter 6

THE WONDERFUL THING about my wife is that she is almost never bored or depressed. Any trip on an airliner is as exciting as a trip to the moon, and to sit on a great 747, winging our way across the continent to Los Angeles, in a window seat, should have had her in a state of modest ecstasy. Not this time. She had managed a proper show of ebullience until we boarded the plane, and then she sank into her tourist-class seat and grunted answers to my questions. After we were properly up in the sky, the wheels raised and the seat belt sign off, I reminded her that we were supposed to mix at least a measure of pleasure with the business New York City had dispatched me on.

"Yes."

"But you don't want to talk about fun, do you? You want to sit there and sulk. You don't even want to talk about that street they call Rodeo Drive, which I hear is like two blocks of Madison Avenue."

"Oh, shut up, Harry," she said.

"Great."

"I have problems," she said. "I have to think about them and sort them out."

"You want to talk about those problems?"

She was silent for the next fifteen minutes or so, which led me to suspect that she had no great desire to discuss her problems, and then she came out of her stupor or reverie and patted my hand on the armrest, and told me that she continued to have reasonable affection for me even though she had problems. "You know, Harry," she said, "how some Jewish mothers tell their daughters not to marry a butcher because a man who spends his life hacking away at dead flesh is likely to lose his consideration for living flesh?"

"Do they? First time I ever heard about it."

"Well, your sainted mother, may she rest in peace, told me that."

"Jewish mothers aren't sainted. Irish mothers are sainted."

"Well, my sainted mother, may she rest in peace, felt the same way about cops. She called them the unholy curse of the Irish, and she kept warning her daughters not to marry a cop, because he would only bring them grief and misery. She had a brother and two cousins who were cops, so she knew from experience. Then when I brought you home, she was delighted, because she said here you found a nice Jewish boy and he won't beat you up and he'll never be a cop. That's why she almost fainted when you turned up at the door one day in uniform after four years of marriage. But, you see, I didn't share her prejudice about cops. The Irish cops of her day have passed into the great wherever that cops pass into."

"There are still a lot of Irish cops," I said, thoroughly confused as to where this was leading.

"Ah, yes, and there are black cops and Italian cops and Hispanic cops and Jewish cops and Polish cops and whatever else you want to throw into the bag, and when you beat me, you don't leave welts."

"You shouldn't even say that. It's our secret."

"Right. And you know, Harry, all those years I never really worried. You loved your home and you loved me and the kids, and you never hung out until all hours of the night with the bums at Scanlon's place, down the street from the precinct, and you kept telling me that you never fired your gun and that was all very comforting, except that you came home one night from Scanlon's stinking drunk, after my sainted mother told me Jewish boys don't get drunk."

"My God," I said, "you are an instructor in English lit in the stately halls of Columbia University. Do you teach your students to write sentences like you talk?"

"That sentence of yours could use some tailoring, and I'm trying to be bright and amusing because I'm scared to death." Tears welled in her eyes now. "I'm just scared to death, Harry."

"I know."

"The way you and Finelli tried to lay off that car thing as some kind of case of mistaken identity. Well, you didn't put it to Courtny as a case of mistaken identity. I heard you talking to him on the phone when I was in the tub this morning, and to quote you, you said that those motherfucking bastards were trying to kill you. Thank God you don't talk like that at home. They were trying to kill you. You know it and I know it and Finelli knows it, and Harry, I am frightened."

"Not kill me, Fran. Frighten me, I think."

"That's crazy."

"No, not so crazy. If they wanted to kill me, they would have used sawed-off shotguns or a machine gun." I leaned over and kissed her cheek. "You're frightened, I'm frightened. In a situation like this, only a psychopath wouldn't be frightened."

"Great comfort."

"All right, so it's no damn comfort. On the other hand, we're alive and we're smart, and that's what counts."

"No more secrets, Harry. You want me to stay with you through this, then no more secrets. Otherwise, I'll walk away. I swear I will."

"Okay, no more secrets."

"Good. You say we're smart. How does that help us? I've read that if a determined assassin is out to kill someone, he cannot be stopped."

"True and not true. There are degrees of determination."

"Now tell me the truth. Are they trying to kill you?"

"I don't think so. Dead, I might stir some sleeping dogs. But we have to face the fact that we don't know who they are or what they are or what they want or what they don't want—considering that there is a *they*. We cannot dispense with the possibility that we're dealing with a series of coincidences that in no way relate to each other, and that we have put together a shaky structure that only exists because you and I both admired Asher Alan and had some childish notion that it was wrong for him to die like that here in this city, in our city."

"It was wrong," Fran insisted. "Rotten and wrong."

"Sure, and that's why we're going to Los Angeles, to find out about Dr. Green and tie this thing up. That's the only lead we have left. The business of Stanley Curtis and his wife and the drugstore is so confusing that it's meaningless. The connection with Sanchez could be a coincidence. The killing of Sanchez happens every day in this city, and the business on the Major Deegan Highway could have been a mistake."

"You said it wasn't."

"It could have been. The first thing a good cop learns is not to be sure about anything."

"And you don't think there could be someone on this plane who has been paid to kill us?"

I smiled. "No."

"Well, how do you know, Harry? I've been looking at every face. I could pick out a dozen who look like—"

"No!" I cut her off sharply. "No one looks like a hit man! No one wears his crazed mind on his sleeve! So just stop that!"

"All right," she said meekly.

"There's a pattern in such things. I've lived with such patterns a long time. If there's anything valid in our conjectures, they will wait for my next move. Then they'll make their move. It's like a game, but everything else in life is a sort of game, only this is simpler. I have never seen a criminal who was intelligent. If there was any intelligence in crime, they'd take over tomorrow. Even the big mob outfits are stupid beyond belief. You remember the *Godfather* books and films. They took in millions, but they lived like demented people, their lives full of agony and fear and suspicion, and everything they did was stupid. That's the nature of the business. If they took a few of their millions and built some legitimate enterprise, it would indicate some intelligence—"

"And if they did, Harry, would you know?"

I looked at her sharply. Then I sighed and leaned back and closed my eyes. I must have dozed. When I opened my eyes, I saw that Fran was writing in her notebook. I leaned over, and there in a neat column she had written:

Stanley Curtis

Asher Alan

Richard Bell (Sanchez)

<u>Judge Charles Fitzpatrick</u>

She had underlined the last name, and now she turned to me with a raised brow and asked, "Another coincidence?"

"The fact that the junkie and the judge were both killed by the same gun means very little in terms of the rest of it."

"Oh, no? Then why did you start panting like a hound dog when Joe Finelli told his story?"

"I was not panting like a hound dog, no, sir."

"Come on, Harry, here's Fran. I've been around you a long time. When we left the apartment to go to dinner, you had just about canceled out of the California trip."

"Yes," I agreed reluctantly, "it made a difference." At that point I wanted nothing more than to drop back into that lovely state of half sleep where time vanishes. But she wouldn't have it. She jabbed an elbow into my ribs and hissed, "Harry!"

"I must be utterly demented," I whispered. "Here I am on official New York City police business, and I have not only got a broad with me but she happens to be my wife. If she weren't my wife, it might be understandable—"

"Harry," she hissed again, "there are times when you are absolutely disgusting, and if I were not married to you, I'd have nothing to do with you. You're a male chauvinist pig, but in spite of that, instead of going to one of those nice empty seats all around us, I am going to talk and you are going to listen."

"Yes," I said weakly. "I'll listen."

"Now what do you know about Judge Fitzpatrick?"

"Federal judge and a big wheel in the Appellate Division."

"Why not mention that he was also a man?"

"I thought it was obvious."

"Clever!" she snorted. "Oh, why do I get mad at you, you're such a very nice man, but smart?" She shrugged. "The word's around that Jews are smart. Ah, well. Joe Finelli is pretty smart. I realized that listening to him last night, but like you he probably reads the crime news and the sports page and nothing else."

"Not so. I read the front page of the *Times* and I read the op-ed page most of the time too."

"The important news is always inside. Oh, I'm not trying to put anyone down, Harry, but sometimes you make me so mad. You and Finelli were so damn sure that there was no connection between Sanchez and the judge that you never even raised the possibility that there might be a connection between Judge Fitzpatrick and Santa Marina."

"Is there?"

"Think!"

"It was two years ago—yes, of course."

She nodded comfortably.

"Santa Marina, of course." I thumped my forehead with my palm, the American gesture of stupidity. "Why didn't I think of it? Do you remember?"

"More or less. Congress had finally put its back up against any more military assistance to Santa Marina. We had been pouring untold millions into Santa Marina to put down a guerrilla movement against a thoroughly vicious and corrupt government that ruled with *death squads*—murder squads."

I began to recall it. Twenty-five thousand men and women murdered by these death squads in a few years.

"Well, Congress was just fed up, even many of the Republicans were fed up, but when they refused the shipment of more arms to Santa Marina, the President went over their heads and began to move the arms. Then Congress went for an injunction to halt the shipments, and Judge Fitzpatrick gave it to them. It's more complicated, but that's the essence of it."

I thought about it for a while, and then I told her that while it made our flimsy puzzle more intriguing, it didn't make it any more reasonable.

"Well, you do remember, Harry, that at the time some stories linked the judge's death to the death-squad thing, but the FBI soon put an end to that, just as they had put an end to the incident of the ex-general hanged by terrorists, telling the world that the general had committed suicide. It's wonderful how our great free press becomes silent when the FBI tells them that their speculations are unfounded. But when you put it together with what Finelli told us last night—"

"What do you have? The same gun killed the doper and the doper worked for Bronstein, the pharmacist, and maybe the doper had some certificate of pharmacy which may or may not have been genuine, because most of the work a pharmacist does these days is count pills, and anyway he could have worked for Bronstein without any papers at all. That's what Bronstein told me—that he was just a clerk behind the counter."

"Then could he fill prescriptions?"

"He could certainly count pills with the pharmacist overseeing him, and since the labels are there, he could have typed a label with Bronstein out to lunch, or filled the bottle —hell, it would be a lead-pipe cinch with him working there in the pharmacy, but on top of that I got absolutely nothing from Mrs. Curtis, who hated her husband's guts and is happily sailing around the world on the *Queen Elizabeth.*"

"And you complain about my sentences going on and on."

"So everything is connected and everything is coincidence. You pay your money and you take your choice."

"Still, we're on our way to California."

"I needed a vacation."

"You're a dear, funny man. I don't think Jews should be cops. They're too complicated."

At the airport in Los Angeles, the sun was shining. They tell me it's almost always shining, except when there's too much smog or the occasional sprinkle of rain. But by March, the rain has practically stopped, and today there was little or no smog. We took a taxicab to the Beverly Crest Hotel, a small but fairly pleasant hotel on South Spalding Street in Beverly Hills, chosen by the New York City police travel service. The cab cost twenty-three dollars, all of it a legitimate expense, the room eighty dollars, fifty allocated to the NYPD, and thirty to Fran.

Fran walked around the room, grinning at the purple bedspread and the pink walls. She decided it was lovably horrible, but in all truth, the fact of being three thousand miles from New York City at this moment elevated her spirits. From our window, we could see the pastel and plastic city of Beverly Hills, defined by palm trees and lines of cars bumper to bumper, all of it rather hazy under a yellowish curtain that had been absent at the airfield. There, alongside the ocean, we had noticed no smog, but we were told that the beach was a refuge from the smog. We were not travelers. When the kids were with us, we spent our vacations at a lake in the mountains, and being here in Beverly Hills almost balanced being in Europe for two streetwise New York products. After a good look at the room, Fran threw her arms around me and said, "Harry, let's not be killed by some nut. This is such fun."

"I'll keep trying," I assured her.

After we unpacked, I called Sergeant Thomas McNulty at the Beverly Hills police force. He happened to be day sergeant at the desk, and I got through to him immediately, and he sounded pleased as punch that the one New York cop he knew was here in Beverly Hills. He asked me how I liked his city, and I said that all I had seen of it was out of our fourth-floor hotel window, but it was certainly different. He said that it grows on one, and I answered that I was happily ready to let it do just that, and that I had three days to encourage its growth.

"I owe you one, McNulty," I said to him. "I want to take you and your wife to dinner—you are married?"

"You can count on that."

"What's a good place?"

"Any place will cost you a bundle."

"Let the City of New York worry about that," which was a lie, because Courtny would put his back up at even the thought of taking another cop and his wife to dinner and charging the city. But I figured it was worth whatever I put out.

"Okay. I know a place downtown where we can eat good and talk without putting a down payment on the place. Do you have wheels?"

"No. I don't know my way around. I'll use cabs." That the city would pay for.

"Then I'll pick you up. How long will you be here?"

"Three days."

"Then we'd better make it tonight. I'll pick you up at six. Where?"

"Beverly Crest."

"Yeah. My wife's name is Hanna."

"Francesca—Fran."

You talk to someone on the telephone and you try to make a picture of them; usually the picture doesn't define the person very well. My picture of McNulty after talking to a deep, strong voice was a sort of Clint Eastwood type, but the sergeant was something else entirely, average height, red hair, freckled round face, good-natured blue eyes, and a bit plump from eating too much of the good food we had that night.

"I hope you like Japanese food," he said. "If you don't we can find another place."

We both loved it. McNulty's wife was Japanese, or, as they call it out there, Nisei, born in America of Japanese parents. McNulty was in his middle thirties, his wife perhaps five years younger, a slender, lovely woman, with a kind of charm that was very new to me.

The restaurant was in a part of downtown Los Angeles they call "Little Tokyo," very little, and, I imagine, not too much like Tokyo. The restaurant was small and a bit too warm, but after a while we forgot that and concentrated on stuffing ourselves with tempura, *shabu-shabu,* a kind of delicious Japanese fondue, pork chops teriyaki and cakes and little hot fried rolls, the name of which I cannot remember, and tea and saki. It mellowed us. It made us all lean toward the improbable, a receptive attitude for hearing my story.

I saw no reason to hide anything from McNulty, and I told him everything, the few facts, the many guesses, the coincidences, and, of course, the lack of any sense to the pattern. "Except," I finished, "that a professional gun trailed me from my apartment and fired two bullets into the car—as I told you. That was real, too damn real."

McNulty listened intently, and when I had finished he and the others were silent for a while.

"What do you think?" I asked.

"A damn strange story, Lieutenant."

"That it is."

"But if Courtny let you come here, he must have sniffed something."

"Something. I guess so."

"And now your mission is to find Dr. Herbert Green?"

"Right."

"What do you figure to get from that?"

"I don't know. I feel my way."

"In the darkness and going nowhere," Fran added.

"The thing that gets me," McNulty said, showing that he was no dummy, "is that each time it happened in a restaurant—and with Alan, the Israeli guy, it happened a few weeks later. But if something specific was put in their food, something that would trigger this medicine, then whoever our mass killer is, he must have money, power, influence, and a damn important motive."

"He's motivated," I agreed. "Even if he's totally demented, he's motivated."

"All right, Harry, if there is a shred of truth in this crazy business, then Green committed a crime in Beverly Hills. I'll talk to the captain, and tomorrow you and I will poke around and we'll see what we can find. Meanwhile, let's eat."

His wife, Hanna, was a doll. She said that she'd pick up Fran the following day, and while we were poking around, she'd show her some of the sights of Los Angeles, which were not many at all, but that was nothing to deter Fran. The next morning I left Fran girding and polishing herself for the sights of Los Angeles, while I settled myself next to McNulty in his prowl car, admiring the repeating shotgun clamped to the roof and the quality of upholstery in these nifty little cars that the City of Beverly Hills provided for their finest.

"We'll stop at the station house," McNulty said. "I just wanted to be absolutely sure that there was no Dr. Green, so I left one of our clerks calling every Dr. Green in the phone book. You told me Alan went to an office in Beverly Hills, so Doris will see whether one of them has a Beverly Hills office. It doesn't mean much, but it clears our starting point."

I sat in the car at the back of a great mass of a building, a combination of baroque and Renaissance architecture, that was the Beverly Hills city hall, courtroom, and police station, punctuated all about with palms and other improbable trees.

McNulty came out shaking his head. "Nothing."

"Next stop?"

"They have a lot of these functions around town for Israeli VIPs—fund-raising. Don't forget, this is where the money is. If they want to pick up a quick million for Reagan, here's where they go. New hospital, here. You name it. Anyway, most of the Israeli things are coordinated by the United Jewish Appeal. They're over on Wilshire Boulevard, and there's a Mrs. Levinson who runs things. The big names around it are just big names. She runs things."

He was not exaggerating. Everything that was happening in those offices on Wilshire Boulevard, which was like Sixth Avenue, only a little classier, spun around Mrs. Levinson, a tall, large-bosomed woman with flaming red hair that was not dyed, since her eyebrows and lashes flamed with the hair. She embraced McNulty, kissed him and said to me, "Just took at him. He's beautiful. He could be my son."

McNulty blushed and stammered.

"See? He's a nice boy, and I embarrassed him. But he helps me. When I need help, I call him. Who are you?"

I told her. She nodded, the simple nod stating that my calling was improper for a Jewish boy. She would have preferred Dr. Golding. She then warned off the people in the office who were besieging her, closed the door to her private office, instructed her secretary that there were to be no calls for the next half hour, and asked us what she could do for us. I glanced at McNulty, who nodded.

"There was a party for Asher Alan a few weeks ago."

"Of course. Of course. At the home of Peter Senter, the director. I shouldn't have been involved, because it was not exactly a UJA party. That's United Jewish Appeal," she explained to me, reasoning that a Jew who became a cop instead of a physician would not know that UJA stood for United Jewish Appeal. I felt like begging her to understand that my family had barely enough money to eat, much less send me to medical school, but that my brother was a full professor. I let it pass.

"It was a party to raise money for the Jerusalem Fund. A lot of people confuse the two different funds, even some of them who were there. Myself, I don't push one thing against the other, and just between you and me, at the UJA we're top-heavy with organization. With the Jerusalem Fund, every dollar goes to the rebuilding of the holy city, also, the man who does it there, he's absolutely a saint. That's Teddy Kollek. You know who he is?"

"The mayor of Jerusalem," McNulty said.

"So you know something, good." She loved McNulty, but she could not forgive me for being a cop.

"Asher Alan is also a saint, he should rest in peace. I loved the man. So when the Jerusalem Fund was the object, I didn't turn my back."

"Do you think," McNulty asked, "that if we went to Mr. Senter, he could tell us something about the party?"

"No, because he was in Canada directing a picture when the party took place. He has a very large house. That's important when you give a fund-raising party, and he's not Jewish, which always helps to broaden things, and he once met Asher Alan and fell in love with him, so he let us use his house. What do you want him to tell you about the party?"

"People who were there, some of the guests, who they were . . ." I was cautious. I certainly did not want Mrs. Levinson on the track of anything that concerned us.

"So. You don't want Mr. Senter. Absolutely not. Who you want is Rosie Forer, Dr. Forer's wife. She's an encyclopedic yenta—gossip, Lieutenant Golding. Yiddish." I nodded weakly, and Mrs. Levinson went on, "I am not putting her down. She's a good friend. But you want to know what color dress somebody there wore and how much her diamond bracelet probably cost, ask Rosie. She will tell you. Wait, I'll call her and make an appointment for you."

Afterward, I tried to describe to some friends in the East what that part of Beverly Hills which they call "The Flats" is like. It has nothing to do with the eastern concept of a flat as an apartment. It's simply a flat area of the town, stretching between Santa Monica Boulevard and Sunset Boulevard, and filled with unbelievable houses, some of which you could buy for as little as a million dollars. Dr. Forer's house was a Spanish Colonial, pink-colored, with a swimming pool and a tennis court in the very large backyard. Rosie Forer, a pretty little woman with a small, piping voice, sat us down alongside the pool, under striped umbrellas, and served us iced tea and delicious cucumber sandwiches, followed by a tray of small pastries. Since it was already past eleven, McNulty and I had an excellent substitute for lunch while we talked.

"I could have told you that your Dr. Green was no doctor at all," Rosie Forer began. "Well, I couldn't be sure, and I didn't want to interfere. Out here we don't simply have doctors who go to medical school and get a degree and go on to become interns, etcetera and etcetera, as my husband did. No indeed. That's what they have where sanity prevails and where the sun tires of shining once in a while. Here we have naturopaths and vegopaths and holistic healers and hands healers and aura healers and gurus and yogis and heaven knows what else, not to mention tennis and astrology." She had a sense of humor. "So I couldn't just walk up to Asher Alan, poor soul, whom I revered, and tell him that Dr. Green was a great big phony. Could I?"

"No, I guess not."

"I wanted so much to say a few words to Asher Alan, or at least to hear what he was saying, but there was no way to stop this Dr. Green. Well, I mean there simply is no reputable physician in Beverly Hills or in West Los Angeles I don't know—well, that is a bit of an exaggeration—"

"But you did see him?"

"Asher Alan?"

"No, I mean Dr. Green."

"Of course I saw him. There was a circle of people around them, but I pushed through and listened for a while, and then I went to get my husband and see whether he had ever seen this Dr. Green anywhere. By that time, Green had disappeared."

"You must have seen on TV how a police artist works?"

"Oh, yes indeed."

"Do you think you could guide a police artist to a portrait of Green?"

She nodded eagerly, but McNulty said, "We don't have a police artist as such, Lieutenant. Not enough business in a place like this, but we have an alternative that works pretty well—"

"And," Rosie Forer broke in, "something else."

"What else?"

"I can tell you what street his office is on. Camden."

"You say he actually had an office? You said you were certain he wasn't a doctor."

"And if he wasn't a doctor, he can't have an office? I heard him tell it to Mr. Alan."

"Did you get the number?"

"No."

"A lot of doctors on Camden," McNulty said.

"How long is Camden?"

"The office part? One block."

"Well, let's start."

"We need a picture of him first," McNulty said.

The three of us got into McNulty's Ford, Rosie delighted to be riding in a police prowl car, and we drove over a twisting, narrow road into what McNulty called "the Valley," properly the San Fernando Valley, which is to Los Angeles what Queens and Nassau are to New York. The pass that led into the Valley was called Coldwater Canyon, and at the bottom of the low mountain we had crossed, the road cut through a busy boulevard called Ventura. All of this, curiously enough, took us only a few miles from Beverly Hills, even after we had turned right on Ventura Boulevard and had come to a sprawling old studio, its pink stucco walls cracked and decaying in the hot sun. The sign over the gate said: LAVARA ANIMATION.

Driving there, McNulty explained that while a small police force like the Beverly Hills had no reason to keep a staff artist, they did have the artist of a much larger Los Angeles police force available. That meant red tape. McNulty had discovered that the animation artists at any of the major animation studios were probably more skilled than any police artists in the country. "Not the animators who work on the cells," McNulty said, leaving us to guess what cells were, "but the originating artists, those who create the characters and set the style." In this case, the artist was an American-born Korean, Jack Park by name, who shook McNulty's hand enthusiastically, and ushered us into his studio, a large room with a skylight, the walls covered with watercolors and pastel drawings. The place was furnished with two light tables, an easel, and three tilt-top drawing tables. Everywhere, paints, inks, brushes, pens and pencils.

"It's a busy day," Park said to McNulty. "I can spare a half hour, not much more."

"Let's get to it."

Park drew two folding chairs together and asked Rosie to sit down next to him. "We'll work very quickly, Mrs.—?"

"Forer."

"Mrs. Forer. Best that way. Now just watch me draw. The human head can be placed in three shapes, round"—he drew a near perfect circle—"long, or between the two, a sort of egg shape. Which?"

"The egg shape, but maybe narrower."

Park tore off the top sheet of his pad and his heavy black pencil created another shape.

"This?"

"Yes, I think so."

"Hair?"

"Dark."

"Heavy or balding?"

"Heavy."

"Age?"

"Thirty-eight, forty."

"Nose?"

"Straight."

"Like this?"

"A little heavier."

"Mouth?"

"Funny. Like a woman's."

"Cleft on the upper lip? Like this?"

"Perfect."

They were both marvelous. I had never seen anyone use a

pencil the way Jack Park did. Our New York City police artists use transparencies which they shift about, predesigned parts of the human face printed on plastic. Park used his pencil. Sheet after sheet was ripped off the pad, and each time another version of the face appeared, and Rosie Forer was right with him. I could understand why she had earned her reputation as the queen of yentas. Nothing missed her eye, nothing was forgotten. Park came to a point where he and Rosie were both satisfied with a line drawing, after which he filled it in, shading and highlighting the planes of the face, deepening the drawing, fleshing it out.

"It's him," Rosie said, satisfied at last, "in the flesh," a picture of a very ordinary face with a black mustache, a rather good-looking face of a man who might once have aspired to be an actor, not a distinguished face, but not very ordinary either.

"What does he charge for that?" I asked as we drove back to Beverly Hills.

"One hundred dollars. Thirty-two minutes. Not bad at the price. The city will kick, but they'll pay. For him, it's a public service. The studio pays him two thousand a week—nice work if you can get it."

Rosie Forer protested when we dropped her off at her house. She felt she was entitled to see where the investigation led. After we left her, McNulty said that if Rosie came along, we might as well put it in the press. I felt that we might have to. Park had given us two photocopies of his drawing, and McNulty suggested that we each take one side of the street and give it a quick run. You must remember that we are not talking in New York terms. Running a picture through a street in New York could take a couple of cops a long time, but this was not New York. The single business block of Camden could have been covered by a good worker in a few hours. On our part, we were lucky. McNulty chose a four-story white brick medical building as his starting point and he drew blood. The janitor recognized the picture. McNulty saw me come out of my first building, and he called me across the street to join him. He was standing with the janitor, who led us into the building and up to the second floor. There was a door with a bright brass plate, and the plate read, HERBERT GREEN M.D. The janitor opened the door and led us into the waiting room—old-fashioned but very nice. We prowled through an office and an examining room, the walls of both resplendent with Dr. Green's framed achievements.

The janitor was a Mexican. His name was Pedro Gonzales. I asked him when Dr. Green would be in the office.

"Ah-hah, that's a question, huh? Now look. I got a good job here in Beverly Hills. Family man—me—right, all papers. You want to see my papers?" McNulty shook his head. "All right. My English, pretty good, no? I live thirty years in Los Angeles. I tell you about this office. This is Dr. Goldstein's office. Old man, but damn good doctor. Three week ago, he die. His son live in San Francisco, he tell me, leave my papa's place the way it is. Rent paid. I come down next month clear things up. Okay. Then this guy Dr. Green come along, he tell me I need office one week, just the way it is. I'm doctor from Chicago University, need a place to examine one, two rich patients. Old friend the old man, Goldstein. But you listen, Sergeant, first I telephone Dr. Goldstein's boy in San Francisco. All right I rent office one week, one patient? Sure, he says, go ahead, but keep an eye on papa's stuff. So Green pays me five hundred dollars and I rent him office one week. Only I don't believe he's doctor from Chicago."

"Why not?"

"Because Sally Stisson, nice girl, works for Dr. Konetz, says Dr. Green is living in same condo as her girl friend."

McNulty and I looked at each other, and he whispered to the janitor, "Where?"

"Up the other end of the Valley, just past San Fernando. You wait here, I get address from Miss Stisson."

"Do you believe that?" I asked McNulty.

"It happens, you get lucky, you get unlucky. It happens."

"It also doesn't happen. It's too easy. Why didn't he cover himself?" I didn't like it. It was too quick, too smooth.

"Why should he? He didn't know you'd come highballing out here to bust him for killing some Israeli politician. Without your wife's nose for something, the way you tell it to me, nobody would have picked up any of the pieces. And even if

99

we bust him, what's the charge? Writing a phony prescription? We'd have to prove that he wrote it. Since the prescription had a phony address and phone number, how do you trace it to here? Practicing medicine without a license? But who says he ever practiced it, and if you don't use them to defraud, printing fake diplomas and honors is a gag, not a crime. Every carnival does it. So why should he worry about covering up his tracks? What has he got to cover up? He can say the whole thing's a practical joke. It looks like one."

"I'll think of something."

"Sure, sure, I'm not saying to walk away from it. After looking at that office, I'm ready to go along with you. At least a little way. So we'll find him and push him around a little and talk about a nice, clean premeditated murder rap; and then if he's not a total idiot, we'll walk away no smarter than we came."

It was about twenty miles from where we were in Beverly Hills to San Fernando, most of it through uninspiring flat country, carpeted with tract houses. The condo we were looking for was on the edge of the town of San Fernando. It was typical "Valley" condominium construction, according to McNulty, two stories high, oblong in shape, and enclosing a swimming pool. The pool, unoccupied, was surrounded on three sides by apartments. On the fourth side, a path ran through a lush growth of tropical plants. Since there was no indication of a concierge, we walked into the place and paused where a pretty young woman in a bikini lay on a lounge sunning herself. She was alone on the terrace that surrounded the pool. She smiled at us—while I recalled some of the endless flow of jokes about Valley girls. McNulty shrugged, as if to say, Why not? There are no rules or road signs in Wonderland. He unfolded the picture of Dr. Green and showed it to her.

"Fuzz," she said, with neither approval nor disapproval. "What did poor Smitty do? Rape someone?"

"Smitty?"

"Bert Smith. He's a dodo. Like he's on uppers five times a day. You fellers are cute."

"He lives here?" McNulty asked.

100

"Second door." She pointed. "Apartment D. You going to bust him?"

"Is he there now?"

"Think so. He came in about ten minutes ago."

"What does Smitty do for a living?" I asked her.

"Oh, this and that. I'm in G."

McNulty knocked at the door of apartment D after the chimes produced no effect. The knocking produced no effect either. McNulty tried the door. It was open and we went inside, where there was a small living room, a tiny closet of a kitchen, and a door to a bedroom. We went into the bedroom, and there was a man sprawled on his back on the floor next to the bed. There was no question about his being the man in Park's pencil drawing. The only way in which his face differed radically from the face on the drawing was that the real Dr. Green or Smitty had a hole in the center of his forehead and was quite dead. The hole might have come from the same pistol as was used on Sanchez and Fitzpatrick. I couldn't tell just by looking at it.

A little while later, I walked into my hotel room and slumped into a chair. A voice from the bathroom asked, "Is that you, Harry?"

"In the flesh."

"Just doing my face," Fran said. "Tonight, you and I are going to drift down Wilshire Boulevard to the Beverly Wilshire Hotel, where I peeked into a very classy dining room. We'll charge half to the cops and half to me. That Hanna McNulty is an absolute darling. What a nutty day, but this is a nuthouse, Harry, so what can you expect? First she took me to the local museum of art, because she figured I was very much a culture bug. But on the way, I convinced her otherwise, and we stopped on a street called La Cienega for me to take a picture of the door to a whorehouse where you can get laid with five different credit cards, all of it printed plainly on the door. The museum is sort of nice, and then we looked at some tar pits where the less brainy dinosaurs got trapped millions of years ago. Then we went to a strange tourist trap called the Farmers Market. She apologized for taking me there, but explained that it was de rigueur for anyone visiting Los Angeles. We had a sort of sloppy catch-as-catch-can lunch there, mostly Mexican, after which we visited the MGM film studio, where her brother works in the art department, which is how we got in, and I saw three absolutely valid stars, Paul Newman, Meryl Streep, and another one who's kind of fat and jolly, but his name slips my mind. Harry, a movie lot is a crazy, fascinating place—" She came out of the bathroom and saw my face and cut off the tour guide resume. She stared at me for a long moment, and then asked gently, "What happened? Something terrible?"

"Sort of."

"Did you find Dr. Green?"

"Yes, with a bullet in his head."

"Oh, my God." The joy and excitement disappeared.

"Funny," I said. "We got there maybe ten minutes after he was shot. The killer must have used a silencer, because no one heard anything, and he calmly walked out of the back door of Green's apartment. Yet in those few minutes, he cleaned the place. This is all he missed." I held out a slip of paper. "In Green's watch pocket. Today, most trousers don't have a watch pocket, and I suppose that's why the killer missed it."

"What is it?" Fran asked.

"A carbon proof of a check for ten thousand dollars, made out to Bert Smith, Green's name or one of his names. Issued by the Wabash Protection Company, on West Eighteenth Street in New York. I suppose it was his fee for the doctor job."

The telephone rang. It was McNulty to tell me that the bullet that killed Green had come from a .32-caliber gun. The San Fernando cops would make blowups and send them to New York.

Chapter 7

ON THE PLANE, returning to New York, I leafed through a booklet put out by the Los Angeles Olympic Committee. It told of some of the preparations Los Angeles had made for the coming Olympics, gave facts about housing and transportation, and had illustrations of the various places in and around Los Angeles where the games would be held. One of the photographs showed a new type of arena built specifically for water games and races. It could hold ten thousand people; it was near the beach in a well-landscaped setting; and it was named the Pan American Water Arena. It was by no means the only water arena, but it was the newest and largest. It had cost over sixty million dollars to build and it was the gift of one Alfred Gomez Porfetto, certainly a magnificent gift. Just below the photograph of the arena, there was a photograph of Porfetto and his wife, Birdie May. Porfetto was perhaps fifty, well built but not fat, riding breeches and boots, open polo shirt, tanned, a good head of hair and rugged, strong features. Birdie May was forty or so, tall, slender, blond, and beautiful. The caption informed me that the picture had been taken at their ranch near Santa Barbara. Their home base was on East End Avenue in New York City. They also had an apartment in Monte Carlo and an estate in the Bahamas. Mr. Porfetto bred horses on his ranch, raced a string of horses in Europe as well as in America, and had recently, at the request of his wife, given up motorcar racing. His wife, Birdie May, had been born in South Carolina, and she devoted herself to charitable interests. Both would be honored at a hundred-dollar-a-plate dinner, to be given at the Waldorf, in New York, proceeds to go to the State Olympic Committee.

"Sixty million dollars. I'd love to say, here's sixty mil, build something for posterity. And I never even heard of this guy Porfetto."

Leaning across my arm and reading, Fran said, "Because all you remember is the crime news. I've seen his name before. Keeps a very low profile and wallows in money. One of those Onassis types."

Our attention was diverted, and for the moment we forgot about Mr. Porfetto. Dinner was served, and soon after that we landed in New York. As we walked out of the airport building at Kennedy, Fran said to me, "Do you know, I'm getting used to it."

"To what?"

"To being frightened. It really doesn't trouble me so much any more."

"It troubles me," I said, refraining from adding just how much it would trouble me if it turned out that the same gun had killed Green and Sanchez and Fitzpatrick. Happily, Fran had not made the connection. Los Angeles and New York were far apart, and I had chattered away about how easy it was for a cheap grifter like Green né Smith to get himself killed. But I think we were beginning to leave things unsaid, so far as each other was concerned; it was easier to leave them unsaid than to offer them for discussion.

"At least we're back where it's cold, dirty, and real. When Alice went to Wonderland, she knew afterward that it wasn't there. Los Angeles is very much there, and you might as well know, Harry, that I don't believe our Dr. Green's death was a coincidence. I've stopped believing in coincidence entirely."

Driving into the city from Kennedy, the cabdriver said, "In on the L.A. plane?"

"That's right."

"Missed St. Patrick's Day, didn't you?"

"Oh, God save me!" Fran cried. "Mother of God forgive me, I'm the greatest dumbbell of all! How could I?" It was now half past eight in the evening. "Today. Of course—oh, Harry, I never missed a St. Patrick's Day parade before. We always marched together."

"I'm sorry, darling. There's always next year."

"If we live to see next year."

The next morning, at the station house, I was greeted with this from Sergeant Lasky at the desk: "The captain's burning, Lieutenant. You went off and left your car locked and double-parked in front of the precinct. We had to call in Lassiter from Manhattan South to do a wire job because your wheels were locked into the curb."

"Come on," I snorted. "Toomey has my key."

"Toomey's sick with the flu."

"It's in his desk. Didn't anyone think to look in his desk?"

"They looked in your desk."

When I got upstairs to the detective division, I was almost as angry as Courtny was said to be. He saw me through the glass and yelled for me to come into his office. The detectives weren't grinning. They should have been grinning.

"That was a dumb thing with your car," Captain Courtny said, "but I'm not going to burn your ass over it. I know how much you thought of the kid, and that'll give you enough grief for one day."

"What kid? What are you talking about?"

"Jimmy Oshun, the medic from Bellevue. He was killed by a hit-and-run driver yesterday."

I shook my head dumbly. I guess tears started, at least enough to moisten my eyes.

"I'm sorry, Harry."

"Who did it? Where's the driver?"

"We didn't get the driver, Harry."

"Well, what does the investigation show?" I shouted. "Who killed the kid? What have they found out?"

"There hasn't been any investigation, Harry."

"What are you talking about? What do you mean, there hasn't been any investigation?"

"I told you once, Harry, don't get snotty with me!" His voice hardened. "You liked this kid and the kid was killed. That don't give you the right to come in here and run off at the mouth like some hopped-up jerk. In the first place, the hit-and-run was on Manhattan South turf. In the second place, yesterday was St. Patrick's Day, and aside from the cops who were marching, the department had to put two thousand uniforms on the street. It's the numero uno nuthatch day, and you're asking me why we didn't take over a Manhattan South hit-and-run?"

I didn't wait to hear any more. I stormed out of his office and out of the station house. My car was in front, still double-parked. I drove to my brother Oscar's apartment, found Shelly at home, still in a dressing gown, and told her I needed a telephone and privacy. Whatever I sounded like, I sounded enough like it for her not to question me.

I haven't written of my daughter, Sarah, or my son, Gavin, because they haven't come into this account as yet. Gavin was a junior at Harvard, on scholarship, Sarah on partial scholarship at Wellesley. I called Gavin first. He's a brilliant, wonderful boy, but stubborn.

There was no answer from Gavin's room. The college operator, whom I called next, said he was in class. I said this was New York City police priority, and that I didn't give a damn where Gavin Golding was because I wanted him on the phone immediately. I suppose that being a cop half a lifetime does something for your voice, because ten minutes later I was talking to my son.

"What is it, Pop? Something wrong?"

"Damn wrong. Now you listen to me, Gavin. You resisted things I told you to do in the past. No sweat. It was give-and-take. Good. But now your life is at stake, and unless you do exactly what I'm telling you to do, you will be dead within a week."

"Pop, are you crazy?"

"Now you listen to me!" I said, in a tone I had never used before. "How much money have you?"

"About thirty dollars."

"Your charge card, do you have that?"

"Yes."

106

"Your passport?"

"Yes, but Pop, tell me what's going on. Is Mom all right?"

"Mom is all right and I cannot tell you what's going on. I want you to live and I want your sister to live, and your lives depend upon your doing exactly as I say. Leave college now, right after speaking to me. No luggage, just whatever you put in your pockets. Hat and coat. Drive to the airport and take the next flight to Ireland. Use your charge card. When you get to Shannon, wait there at the airport for your sister. Unless, of course, your sister reaches Boston airport before you. But wait for her. She may be delayed. When you reach Shannon, hire a cab and drive to Dublin, where your Uncle Sean will be expecting you and will put you up." His Uncle Sean Murphy was headmaster at St. Joseph's school in Dublin. "But don't call our apartment from anywhere in Ireland."

"Pop," Gavin pleaded, "I can't do anything that crazy. I'm not built that way. You know that."

"I don't give a damn how you're built. Unless you do exactly as I say, you may have your mother's life as well as mine on your conscience." It was a low blow, but it convinced him. We spoke for a few minutes more, and finally he agreed to everything I said.

Sarah made things less difficult. She was one of those gentle women, innocent without ever being simple and unaware of how lovely she was with her silken red hair and deep green eyes. I could almost feel her terror over the telephone, and I begged her not to panic.

"I won't, Daddy. I'll be all right. You just don't know how strong I can be. But you and Mommy—"

"We'll be fine. Your father is a tough old cop, and believe me, there is no one as tough and careful as a New York City cop. You know that, don't you?"

She laughed and that helped. "I know that, Daddy. But take care of Mommy, please."

She didn't question my instructions, but then she knew me better than Sean did and in a different way. For the first time in my life, I regretted that I didn't share my wife's religion. If I had, I would have gone to the nearest Catholic church and bought out and lit every candle in the place. Instead, I drove back to the station house.

"Now what kind of an asshole have you turned into?" Captain Courtny demanded. "I'd like some explanation of that lunatic performance of yours."

"I had to do something, and I had to do it too quickly to waste any time with explanations."

"I'm glad to know that any time spent with me is wasted. You didn't even stop to review the time you were gone and to put out some assignments."

"I would have to catch up in any case, wouldn't I? The squad is working. Life goes on."

"Sit down, Harry," Courtny said, his voice softening. "Let's talk. It's time we did, and time you stopped chasing shadows. I got some pictures from the West Coast today, pictures of a thirty-two-caliber bullet. I spoke to Finelli over at the Twenty-fourth, and the pictures don't match up. Finelli thinks maybe you been working too hard and worrying too much, and now this business of the medical student downtown. I been talking some more to Manhattan South, and they know about this kid. He's a nut. He's been bugging them with crazy accusations."

"That's what you want to talk to me about? That because this kid is killed by a hit-and-run, he's a nut?"

"No. What I'm saying, you don't walk into this."

"Who says I'm going to?" I demanded.

"I know you. But you don't. You leave it alone. It's Manhattan South. They'll do what has to be done."

"Are you kidding? With a hit-and-run? They'll file it and forget it."

"What in hell do you think you are, supercop for the whole fuckin' city? I don't want to lose my temper again, Harry. We been together a long time, and you're a damn good cop. A smart one, too, and they don't grow on trees. And I like you. I don't kiss ass when I like someone, but we work together pretty good. But now you've gone off the loop with these mirages of yours."

"Mirages hell! Stanley Curtis, Asher Alan, Sanchez, Judge Fitzpatrick, Jimmy Oshun, and Bert Smith, the guy in L.A., six people tied into a murder machine that doesn't stop—"

"You know what ties them in, Harry?" he yelled. "You! No reason, no motive, no connection with anyone to anyone else! You have become a nut! Now you listen to me, Harry. I'm getting a lot of flack. I'm getting it from downtown, where people know people and they put on the pressure. I'm getting it from a Dr. Hyde, who also knows people. I'm getting it from the commissioner who is an old friend of Stanley Curtis and his wife, and the wife let go at you before she went on a sail around the world. And I'm getting it from San Fernando where the local cops want to know what your nose was doing there when a local bum got wasted. So altogether, I am getting a lot of it, and that's the end of it. You forget about Curtis and Alan and you let the Washington cops worry about Fitzpatrick and there is to be no pushing by you into the Oshun hit-and-run. Over. Done. That's the word from downtown and that's the word from Manhattan South."

He slammed his fist down on his desk, and then we sat in silence for a time, and then he said, "Well?"

"There are just a few loose ends—" I began placatingly.

"No! I said it's done. Whatever file you got on this, either tear it up or send it downstairs to be stashed away. There is nothing here that concerns us. Start being a cop again."

I nodded shortly and rose and started to leave.

"Harry!"

I paused.

"Don't turn snake on me. I won't work with a cop who turns snake. This is professional, not personal."

I turned around and we shook hands. At a moment like that, I didn't need enemies. Courtny went out to lunch, and I took the folder with me and drove up to Columbia University. I knew Fran's schedule, and when she came out of her last class, I was at the door, waiting. She was taken aback, but only for a moment, and then she looked at me without speaking. She took my arm, embracing it tightly as we walked to my car, and before we got into the car, she said, "You know, dear Harry, you can't do this every day."

I shrugged, and we got into the car. "Harry," she began; but I cut her off and said, rather sharply, "I don't want to discuss anything just now." She started to speak again, swallowed her words, and nodded. "Okay."

I took the transverse through Central Park at Ninety-sixth Street turned down Fifth Avenue and entered the park again at Seventy-second Street. Fran had hunched around and was staring through the rear window of the car.

"We're not being followed," she said.

"I know."

I drove west on the roadway at Seventy-second Street and parked in the little paved circle to the west of the Bethesda Fountain. I motioned Fran out of the car, took her arm and began to walk. "We'll stroll a little," I said softly. "It's a nice day."

"You think it's bugged—the car?"

"Yes."

"That's pretty scary, Harry. What happened?"

"They killed Jimmy Oshun yesterday."

"The kid at the lecture? Oh, my God," spacing the words out slowly, but with no hysteria. There were things in Fran I had never suspected. We walked on through the gentle, early spring ambience of Central Park, and we had passed the Bethesda Fountain before she spoke again and said, "He kills. That's his tool, isn't it? He has a functioning death squad. Death squad. You know where the words come from —from the place where the method was devised, from Santa Marina. No arguments, no arrests, no threats—just death. You kill whatever troubles you, whatever interferes with you, whatever annoys you, whatever disagrees with you, whatever threatens you—you just kill it. Harry, I think I'm going to start screaming."

"No, you're all right."

"Harry, the kids! The kids are easy! They'll kill our kids!"

"No, not so easy. Right now our kids are on a plane on their way to Ireland—" And then I told her what I had done. She didn't react at first. She stood very still, a handsome, strong woman, her carrot-colored hair, tied in a bun at the back of her neck, streaked with gray, reminding me, always reminding me, of all our good past years together, of the way I teased her about the great mop of flaming hair which I considered the most beautiful thing in the world.

110

She stood very still and tense, facing me, her hands gripping my arms so tightly it hurt, her big purse, always stuffed with books and notes, slung over her shoulder, and finally she said quietly, "You did the right thing, Harry. It will scare the very devil out of them, but they're good kids and they will follow your orders. They'll be safe with Sean; I guess safer than anywhere else, and Sean would give his life for us and the kids. Did you use a clean phone?"

"I called from Oscar's apartment."

"I guess that's safe. But what do we do, Harry? How long? I'm so frightened. Our lives, our family—it's all disintegrating."

"An hour at a time, a day at a time."

We walked back to the car. I told her what Courtny had said.

"Maybe he's right, Harry."

I lay down on the ground and squeezed under the car. The bug was inside the front right fender. "It's only a beeper," I told her. "It spots us."

"Then they know where we are?"

"Roughly. They would have to hone in on the signal to find us."

"Or they might be watching us right now from over there."

About a dozen cars were parked around the circle. They were all unoccupied, nor was there anyone else standing by a car.

"Maybe. The cars look empty. It doesn't really matter."

I threw the bug away, and we got into the car and drove out of the park. It was somewhat odd, my throwing the bug away, like cutting some kind of umbilical cord. The bug was evidence. If you're a cop, you don't throw away evidence, even if you don't know where the evidence points or what it proves. We drove home—which had become a euphemism for a battleground. I intended only to touch base.

We went in together, my gun half drawn, but the apartment was empty. I motioned for Fran not to speak, and then I went over the place and found four bugs. By God, they were thorough. Putting my lips to Fran's ear, I whispered, "Small suitcase, three or four days." I left her to do the packing, while I filled a large briefcase with our checkbooks, our telephone-number books, address books, and anything I could find that might indicate that Fran's brother was the headmaster of what was called in Ireland, as in England, a "public school." I also took the guns. Almost every cop keeps an extra gun, sometimes with him, mostly at home. I kept two extra guns in the apartment, as much as both Fran and I disliked them, both of them .22-caliber automatics. The larger one was a twelve-shot automatic, backed up to fire special longs. The bullet was small, the force large, and the shells were a type of .22-caliber longs no longer manufactured. The gun was experimental, produced briefly during World War Two, and after a few hundred had been made, both gun and cartridge had been discontinued. I bought the gun one summer in New Hope, Pennsylvania, with a single box of eighty cartridges. When they were used up, the gun could be thrown away or kept as a curiosity. The one I bought had never been previously fired. I tried it with about ten rounds and scored high. It fired very true. The other gun was a very small purse automatic pistol, Italian-made and holding eight .22 shorts. I bought it for Fran, but I never had the courage to give it to her and ask her to carry it. I had the feeling that if I had, she would have turned on me angrily and demanded to know why I thought she would touch one of the filthy things. She didn't turn on me now as I handed it to her. She simply made a face and tucked it away in her purse. I put my gun in my jacket pocket with half a dozen extra shells. As I have said, in all my years of police work, I never fired my gun off the range until that night on the highway, and I figured that half a dozen extra cartridges were enough for anything that might come up. Which did not mean that I was a bad shot. As a matter of fact, I was a damn good marksman.

Putting her lips against my ear, Fran whispered, "Will we ever come back here, Harry? I love this place." Her eyes were brimming with tears.

"God damn it, of course!" I said aloud.

Fred Jones, the superintendent of our building, was putting out the garbage cans when we came down with our bags. He was a quiet black man who did his work and minded his own business, and he had been with the building since we moved in. Now he came over and asked whether he could help me.

"Get in the car, please," I told Fran. I gave her the keys. "Lock the doors and stay there and wait for me."

"Where are you going?"

"Just inside for a moment."

After she sat down in the car, I said to Jones, "You son of a bitch, after all these years, after all I've done for your kids and relatives when they got busted. God damn it, your son's in college at Hunter. If I hadn't gone to bat for him, he'd be sitting in jail."

Fred's face tightened with pain. "I was scared, scared. Jesus, you know what it is to be black, Lieutenant. They said they were cops, feds, and that if I didn't cooperate, I go to jail."

"Where are they now?"

"After they went to your apartment, they set up in the supply room."

"With a tap."

He nodded, his eyes wet. "I got shit in my blood," he muttered.

I went into the basement, walked to the supply room, and flung open the door. They had all their equipment in there, hooked up properly, as well as beer and sandwiches and a big wedge of chocolate cake. "All right," I yelled, drawing my gun, "get up! Spread out against the wall! Face the wall —both hands against it." There were plumbing supplies and bags of plaster at the base of the wall, and as they faced the wall and leaned toward it, I kicked back their feet, immobilizing them. One was a large fat man whose pendulous stomach braced him against a toilet throne. The other was small and plump and wearing gold-rimmed spectacles. "This," I said, "is a bust. I am Lieutenant Golding, whose telephone you are tapping. You both fill me with disgust, and if either of you makes any kind of a problem, I won't kill you but I'll take pleasure in shooting out your kneecaps. And I'm good enough to do it, believe me."

"We believe you. Jesus Christ, Lieutenant, we're technicians. We get paid and we do a job. That's all. So don't lay it on us."

"Yeah, I know. You're technicians. Now listen, because I want this formal and clean. I arrest you under the Eavesdropping section of the New York State Criminal Code. Just for your edification, this is a Class E felony, which can be punishable with four years of imprisonment. I am now going to read you your rights. You have the right to remain silent —" and so forth and so on, and when I had finished, Fran's voice came from behind me, "So that's what it sounds like. I always wondered how you used the Miranda."

I glanced behind me. She was standing there, the little pistol in her hand.

"What are you doing here?"

"I don't intend to be a widow. We started this together, we'll finish it together."

I didn't argue with her. I cuffed the two technicians and had them empty their pockets. They had nothing but a few keys and about sixty dollars and change, no identification of any kind. Fran found an old envelope and we put the stuff into it.

"And now. What do we do now?"

"We take them over to the station house and book them."

At the station house, the desk sergeant was O'Kidder, and he looked at me strangely when I told him to book the suspects for Eavesdropping. We don't book too many people for Eavesdropping, and O'Kidder was puzzled. He wanted to know whether it was a city law. Some other cops paused to join in the discussion.

"For Christ's sake, book them!" I snapped. That was unusual. I rarely raised my voice around the uniforms. "It's the state criminal code, Class E felony."

I went upstairs to find Courtny, but he wasn't there, and Toomey said to me, "What is it, Lieutenant? You look terrible."

"I feel terrible."

"Are you sick?"

"Not that kind of terrible. Where's the captain?"

"He went downtown for a meeting with Crown and Roberts." Edward Crown was chief of detectives; Max Roberts was the zone commander; and both of them were very large stuff in the New York City Police Department. "I'm worried," Toomey went on. "There's something coming down that's not like anything we ever had going on before. Do you know what I mean, Lieutenant?"

"No."

"All right." He shrugged. "You don't want to talk about it. I can understand that."

"What in hell don't I want to talk about, Toomey?"

"I don't know—"

"What's happening, Toomey? We been together a long time. If you know something I ought to know, tell me."

He hesitated a long moment before he said, "The thing downtown concerns you."

"How?"

"I swear to God I don't know. It's just that the word's around. You know how the word gets around."

"Yeah, I know how the word gets around. Look, Toomey, I'm not going to explain, but I booked two suspects downstairs. I arrested them myself. I found them operating an elaborate tap on my phone, the kind of thing you put up when you're doing an operation against the mob. I want you to send a couple of guys to my place, the basement, and have them pick up the equipment for evidence, but do it quick. I wanted to talk to Courtny about it, but you can fill him in. I have to go now, but I'll call in and talk to you later."

Downstairs, Fran was sitting primly on the bench, watching the procession of muggers, dopers, hookers, thieves, victims, robbed men, wailing women, battered women, lost children, and other odds and ends of any normal day at the precinct. I guess it was a good many years since she had been to the station house, and she told me that just to sit there and watch was so fascinating that she almost forgot, at least for a moment, the lunacy that had infected our lives. I told her about the conversation with Toomey, and she wanted to know whether I could guess what it was all about. I told her that my guess was no better than hers. We left the car at the station house, double-parked as always—most station houses were built before the prowl car became an institution, at a time long ago when cops walked a beat—and we wandered slowly downtown along Park Avenue. I chose Park Avenue because it was the least populated with pedestrians of all the East Side avenues, and thereby the best place to spot a tail. There was no tail. I'm sure that Fran was thinking what I was thinking, that by now our children were almost certainly airborne and on their way to Ireland. There was no use talking about it. When enough hours had passed, we would call Sean at the school in Dublin. Until then we could only wait and pray.

Once we knew we were clean of any tail, we took a cab down to the Primrose Hotel, a small, decently priced family hotel on 36th Street between Park Avenue and Lexington. The manager of the hotel, Bill Hoffman, had trouble at one time and I helped him out of it. That's one small advantage of being a cop; like a physician, you can do favors that cannot really ever be repaid. Hoffman's sixteen-year-old daughter had fallen in with a pimp, done a couple of tricks for him, and had been picked up. I got her out with no booking, put the fear of God into the pimp, and then arranged, with the help of Fran and her brother, Sean, for Hoffman to ship the kid off to Ireland, where she spent the next three years at a convent school. Hoffman and his wife felt that I had saved the kid's life, so when we checked into the Primrose that day and I asked him to back us up with the register names of Alvin and Clooney Ridge, he was only too happy to do so. I have always felt that anyone who can't trust people is lost, and I explained to Bill Hoffman that this was a matter of life and death, that our lives were in his hands, and that he would simply have to trust me without any further explanations.

"You got it," he said. "One hundred percent." He was a big, fleshy man, a former wrestler. I weigh one hundred and forty-eight pounds stripped. I always felt good having large men on my side.

We had a bedroom and a little sitting room for thirty dollars a day, half of what it would have cost a stranger and one quarter of what it would have cost in any uptown-class hotel in New York City. I told Hoffman that at ten o'clock or so that evening, we would like to put through a call to

Ireland, and that I would happily pay him in cash, if he could keep it out of his records.

"No sweat," Hoffman said. "We still got the old switchboard, and tonight Jenny Dwyer is on it. She's been with us for years—you see, Lieutenant, half our rooms are permanent, old ladies and gentlemen, and they have private lines, and we're a small hotel to begin with. I'll send Jenny to have coffee with my wife, and I'll put the call through myself—no record until we get our bill at the end of the month, and that's almost two weeks away."

Up in our suite, Fran flopped down on the bed, emotionally exhausted. "I won't be human," she said, "or make any sense to either of us until we put that call through to Sean."

"I know how you feel."

"It will be three o'clock in the morning in Ireland. Or is it four? I never could figure it out. But they'll be there by then. They will, won't they, Harry? They'll be there?"

"Take it easy. Things can go wrong, but the kids would still be safe. Sean could be out of town. He could be spending a few days in London. They might not have booked on the first plane out of Boston."

"In March? The planes would be half empty."

"Not right after St. Patrick's Day. Delegations come here for the parade and the festivities, and you know that whenever any of that enormous family your brother married into decide to come to America, they pick St. Patrick's Day. I'm not saying they didn't find seats on the first plane out. I just don't want you to go to pieces if we don't reach Sean first shot or if the kids are not at the school."

"Don't talk like that, please, Harry."

"All right. We switch subjects. You came into that storeroom in the basement like a grim, redheaded Amazon, determined to save her man—"

"Harry, you're terrible when you decide to be literary."

"Not literary. Colorful. But suppose I was in real trouble, at the point of being killed? What would you do?"

"Shoot the bastard. How about that, Harry?"

"It wouldn't work."

"Why not?"

"Take out the gun." She took it out of her purse. "Now shoot something."

"What!"

"Shoot something. Anything. Shoot the lights out on that hideous chandelier."

"Harry, are you crazy?"

"Shoot if you must this old gray head. Anything. Trust me."

"All right. You explain to Mr. Hoffman." She pointed the gun at the chandelier. "It won't. I can't move the trigger."

I took the gun from her and showed her how the safety catch worked. "No gun fires unless you take it off safety. Anyway, do you really think you could shoot at a person?"

"No."

"I don't think so either. Do you still want the gun?"

"Yes."

"Why?"

Humor and horror are not so far apart. "Oh, God," Fran moaned. "Why is anyone in this crazy business? Why are they after us? Why did they try to kill us? Why did they bug our car and our apartment? Why did they tap our telephone? You ask me why I want a gun? Oh, Harry, it's all coming apart."

I lay down on the bed next to her and put my arms around her, and held her to me and kissed her, and she said, "Harry, not sex. I couldn't even think of it now."

"I'm not going that way," I assured her. "I just want to loosen things up. Now listen to me, and I'll spell it out. There's one bit of sense in this whole thing—Santa Marina. Judge Fitzpatrick is linked to Santa Marina twice. First, his decision on the bench. Second, the same gun that killed Sanchez né Bell. Sanchez-Bell is linked to the drugstore and to the prescription that killed Curtis, whatever was on the prescription. Jimmy Oshun—poor kid, he would have made one hell of a doctor—well, he was linked to the prescription and to Mrs. Curtis. And that phony Dr. Green in Los Angeles, well, he connects with Asher Alan."

"And how does Alan connect with anything?"

"I don't know, but—"

"And how do we connect?"

"I started to make waves, the way Jimmy Oshun did. We don't know how long this has been going on and we don't know what's at the core of it. But I have an idea, Franny. You can't go back to Columbia tomorrow. Call and give them some excuse. Then, while I'm working, you get over to the public library, the annex at Fifth and 40th Street. They have *The New York Times* on tape or film, and you can put it on the screen a page at a time. You've worked those machines, haven't you?"

"I have. What am I looking for?"

"Death—accidental death of influential people. Not important people, not celebrities, not stars, but people of influence, movers, politicians, lawyers, judges, writers, important college professors—people who die of unexplained heart attacks, hit-and-run, falling out of windows, slipping on the ice, electrocuted in the bathtub, allergic response, falling in front of a train, killed in a car crash, mugged and killed, robbed and killed. Go back five years if you have the time. Anything you're after will be front page, so you can flip through, day after day almost with a glance."

"Right. I understand. But what am I looking for? Or do I just take all of them."

"No. Only those who connect in some way with Santa Marina."

"Harry, that's a thin thread. Take Asher Alan. How on earth can you connect him with Santa Marina? How can you connect Israel with Santa Marina?"

Without thinking or probing, the way you say something off the top of your head, I said, "Santa Marina was one of the first five countries to recognize the State of Israel."

Fran pulled away and sat up. "Harry," she cried, "Harry, think back to that dinner with Asher Alan. Do you remember what he said about the Uzi guns?"

"You said something about Santa Marina."

"Do you remember what I said, Harry?"

"Yes, you mentioned to him that you weren't Jewish—which I think he might have figured out for himself, and then you said something about loving Israel and being heartsick. I can't remember what you were heartsick about."

"But I do," she said excitedly. "I said I was sick about the

119

news that Israel had sold Uzi guns to the government of Santa Marina, and then he said that if he becomes prime minister, Israel will never again sell arms to a tyrant or a dictatorship. There's your link to Santa Marina—but to kill a man like Asher Alan over that—"

"They don't measure the crime against the punishment. They only kill."

"But at least it's beginning to come together, isn't it, Harry? I mean, perhaps it's no great thing knowing who is going to kill you, but it's better than not knowing who is going to kill you and being killed anyway. Does that make any sense?"

"No."

"But Santa Marina?"

"That only connects, it doesn't explain. If ten people are murdered whose name is Smith, all of them named Smith, well, it still doesn't give a motive for the murder."

"The Uzi guns?"

"It's not enough. Maybe tomorrow we'll put some more of it together."

"Harry!"

"What do you have?"

"Hertzberg, the congressman. Do you remember when he made that wonderful speech in Congress calling upon the United States to turn its back on the gang of murderous dictators we had made our allies? Well, that speech defeated the special Central American military appropriation bill."

"Yes."

"And a week later, he was killed, right here in New York —wasn't it on West Forty-fifth?"

"That's right. A piece of falling masonry. Two other people were killed by masonry from the same building, but this cookie we're after doesn't mind a few extra deaths to make a point."

She was alive again. The enemy had been identified—somewhat. The battle was joined. She rolled over and leapt off the bed. "Harry, I am beginning to feel human for the first time today. I shall powder my freckles and put on lipstick." She opened her purse and rummaged in it, and then her smile faded, her face fell, and she whispered, "Oh, Mother of God."

"What is it?"

Her voice trembling, she said, "Harry, do you remember my little red telephone-and-address book, the one I always keep in my purse?"

"Yes?"

"It isn't here."

"Where is it?"

"I took it out the other day to look for a number and I left it next to the telephone. Did you notice it? Did you put it in your briefcase?"

I shook my head.

Her eyes filled with tears. "Sean's number was in it."

Chapter 8

As I WAS PUTTING on my coat, Fran begged me, "Don't go back there, Harry. Please. They'll be there and they'll kill you."

"Maybe not."

"I feel it."

"If they want to kill me, they'll find me and kill me. Sooner or later. I can't hide here. I have to go to the precinct tomorrow." As I put on my coat, I felt the weight in my pocket. It was the heavy-duty .22 pistol. I left it there.

"Then I'm going with you."

"You're not."

"If you go, I go."

"You'd be no help," I said coldly. "You'd be a damn nuisance."

"Now you're blaming me."

"No, I'm not blaming you."

"My God, Harry, don't you know how much I love you?"

"I know how much I love you," I said flatly, "and you know how much I love you."

I opened the door, and with one arm in the sleeve of her coat, she began to follow me. "I'm going there," she said. "You know that if I make up my mind to do something, I do it. You know you can't talk me out of it. You tried that before."

I did know. "All right," I agreed. "Come with me. But from here on, what I say goes."

"Right."

We took a cab uptown and paid it off two blocks from our apartment. We walked to our building and saw no one we knew. The elevator is self-service. We took it up to the fifth floor and went down a flight of stairs. I told myself that in all probability they were not in the apartment yet, but a few precautions wouldn't hurt. When we got to the door of our apartment, I motioned for Fran to stand to one side of the door frame. I thought that I heard a sound from inside, but I couldn't be sure. I fingered the .22 automatic in my coat pocket, and then I rejected it and drew my service revolver. If I had to shoot anyone, I didn't want forensic recording a .22 long bullet; let that remain pristine pure for the time being. Before I put the key in the lock, I glanced at Fran, and she forced herself to grin back at me. At best, it was a grin; no one could have called it a smile. Then I put the key in, very slowly, turned it carefully, turned the knob quickly, and then flung the door open and catapulted myself through the little foyer into the living room.

He was standing at our one valid antique, an old tilt-top desk, going through the cubbyholes. He wore a raincoat and a hat, and when he heard me, he spun around and I yelled, "Don't! Don't even think about it! Put up your hands, you miserable bastard!" As his hands went up, I snarled at him, "I live here, you lousy creep, and I'm a cop! So it would be a just shooting—square between your motherfuckin' eyes."

"Are you crazy?" he cried. "So I'm breaking and entering! I'm not even armed!"

Still, I felt better, letting out my fear and anger at this skinny little guy in the raincoat. Out of the corner of my eyes, I saw Fran dash to the telephone. The little red datebook was sitting there, next to the telephone. He hadn't gotten to it yet. Fran grabbed it and thrust it into her purse.

"Down on your face," I said to him. "Get down on the floor on your face."

"Come on—"

"I'm itching for you to do something that would give me an excuse. So get down on the floor."

He sprawled on the floor, shouting at me, "You're crazy! Lady, you been watching this. You're a witness to this lunatic. I'm unarmed. What have you got on me—a lousy criminal trespass. That's not even a crime. It's a misdemeanor, and you stand there and curse me out like some kind of nut."

"I got you on a burglary, and that's no misdemeanor. Now shut your mouth and empty your pockets."

"What kind of burglary?" he screeched, twisting from side to side as he emptied his pockets on the floor. "What did I take? Nothing! And you ain't going to plant nothing on me. I'm a Wabash Protection operative. I got my private detective plastic. Go ahead and look at it. You got me on a misdemeanor, and that's all you got." He was such a skinny little wretch; he wore gold-rimmed old-fashioned glasses, and they had slipped off his nose and he was trying his best to keep his head up. He had thin blond hair, and his little blue eyes were watery with frustration and rage. He had about forty-five dollars on him in bills and change, car keys, house keys, his wallet, and a cute little thing that looked like a Boy Scout knife but contained seven little lockpicks instead of blades.

"What are you? Their in-house lock picker?"

"I don't have to say anything to you, and Wabash is one of the biggest outfits in the business, just in case you don't know."

"Good." I opened his wallet and let a string of plastics unfold, the accordion of today's beautiful society and beautiful people. The license was there, Piper Heston, private investigator. Another card informed the world that he was employed by Wabash Protection. I told him to stand up, and I cuffed him. I arrested him formally and read him his rights. Then I asked him what he was looking for.

"I don't have to answer you or talk to you."

I looked at Fran, who had not said a word since we came into the room, but I figured she had been talking to herself and asking, "Who is this madman I'm married to?" But afterward, she told me she hadn't been thinking that at all, only asking herself whether she would consider me a thug if I shot little Piper. They say that hell hath no fury like a woman scorned, but with the three people she loved most threatened with death, Fran's fury topped that.

I handed Fran my gun and told her, "If that little louse moves, shoot him." Her mouth fell open as she took the gun from me; her fury did not reach that far. I was not nervous because the safety was on and she didn't know how to flick it off.

But Piper yelled, "Where am I moving? I'm standing right here. I'm not even moving." He nodded violently at Fran. "Take that gun away from her," he pleaded.

Both Fran and I had developed something neither of us had ever seen in each other, two people so ridden with anger and fear for our children that we were partly out of control, thinking things we had never thought before, saying things we had never said before. Piper was quite right. We were both a bit crazy.

"That gun can go off," Piper whined. "I don't know nothing about you, mister. Maybe you're this Lieutenant Golding, maybe you ain't—but I got nothing against you. They sent me out to shake down this place. It's my job. I'm not a crook. This is my job. You don't have to shoot me."

I called the station house. Toomey was still there. I told him how I had walked into my apartment and found Piper there. I told Toomey that my car was parked in front of the precinct. He had the key. Most days, we shared the car. I wanted him and I wanted a patrol car too.

"You got him disarmed and cuffed?" Toomey asked.

"All done. I read him his rights."

"Then we don't need no prowl car, Lieutenant. I'll pick you up and we'll take him in."

"No, I want the cops to take him in and book him. Don't argue with me, Toomey. And I want him booked for burglary as well as criminal trespass."

"I didn't take nothing!" Piper howled. "You can't book me for burglary."

"I hear him," Toomey said. "He sounds like a squeaky little bastard."

"Name is Piper Heston," I said. "He's a private operator

who works for Wabash Protection," just for the bugs planted around the room, just in case whoever was on the other end of those bugs should decide to descend on us and rescue Piper from the hands of the law. But now that I had put his name and source on record, Wabash would wash their hands of him. They were licensed too. Piper Heston—yes, he worked for us but he had no authority to enter Lieutenant Golding's apartment. Of course it's a criminal trespass, and rest assured that any employee of ours who engages in criminal trespass or any other illegalities is immediately separated from the company. "But you come along, Toomey. We'll go back with you to the house."

When I put down the telephone, Heston motioned with his head, as if to indicate that he would like to move without being shot by Fran. "She won't shoot you," I said, my murderous anger gone. "The safety is on the gun."

"Of all the damn things!" Fran exclaimed. "You would! Harry, you are one large male chauvinist pig!"

Piper shuffled over to me, put his lips close to my ear, and whispered, "Paper."

I thought about it for a moment, warned Fran with a finger across my lips, and then uncuffed Piper and gave him a pad and pencil. *The place is bugged,* he wrote.

I wrote: *Who?*

He wrote: *Don't know. Now Wabash dumps me. No job. I got a wife and two kids. Maybe we deal.*

I wrote: *Go on.*

He wrote: *No burglary. Just criminal trespass.*

I wrote: *What am I buying, Piper? They can only give you a year for criminal trespass, and you can even plea bargain out of it. With burglary, you can sit up in Attica for fifteen years.*

He wrote: *Not likely. Two years maybe. Give me a break. I got something you need.*

I wrote: *Okay. You got it.*

He wrote: *This is what I know. It's all I know. They bugged this place and they got a wire on your phone. Altogether, they got eleven men on you. That is big.*

I wrote: *Why?*

He wrote: *I don't know.*

Fran was standing behind us now, reading each piece of dialogue as it was written.

All I got to do, I wrote, *is to tell these bugs what we wrote. Then they don't fire you. They kill you.*

I know, he wrote.

I wrote: *Why eleven men on me?*

He wrote: *Don't know. Please.*

Fran pulled the pad and pencil away and scribbled: *He's telling the truth. How can you?*

I took the pad back and wrote: *Okay. Criminal trespass.*

The cops came first, and I asked them, "What did Toomey tell you?"

"Criminal trespass and burglary."

"He didn't take anything, so drop the burglary."

Toomey arrived as they were taking Piper away.

Fran said to me, "I almost like you again. It'll take a while more."

Toomey said, "What in hell goes on here?"

I put my finger across my lips and pulled him down, so that he could see the bug under the top frame of the fireplace. I pointed to the door.

Out in the hall, Toomey said to me, "Don't tell me nothing. I'm just a cop. What business do I have asking what's going on?"

"I don't know what's going on."

The presence of Fran prevented Toomey from using more expressive language. Like most cops, he did not use bad language in the company of women, unless they were hookers.

"That sounds a little funny, Lieutenant."

"Sure, the whole world is funny, Toomey. We came home and found a private dick from Wabash Protection going through our apartment. I pushed him a little, and he tells me Wabash has eleven operatives on me. If they had that many on Jack Kennedy, he wouldn't have been murdered. Now the two cops who took Heston downstairs, I told them not to go outside quick, but to stay behind the doors for a while and look around the street very carefully—I wish it wasn't dark—"

"What would they be looking for?" Toomey interrupted with just a touch of sarcasm.

"Maybe two hoodlums in a car with a couple of shotguns —or maybe not."

"Let's go downstairs and see." He pressed the elevator button.

"We'll take the stairs," I said. "I want to see what's coming."

As we went down the stairs, Toomey kept shaking his head. I told him to knock it off. "No comments, Toomey," I said, "not with your head and not with your mouth. If I'm getting the reputation around the house for being a little strange, that's one thing and I can't do much about it. But when you're with me, just cover up on any thoughts about me being a nut."

"Never entered my mind, Lieutenant."

Downstairs, the two cops were still standing in the front hall, with Heston, wearing cuffs, between them. Ours was not one of the new post–World War II East Side high rises; it had been built in 1928, one of those rather small and undistinguished apartment houses in the Seventies and the Eighties, between Park Avenue and Lexington Avenue and between Lexington Avenue and Third Avenue. Nevertheless, it aspired to some upper-middle-class East Side glitz with a nicely decorated, large foyer. Two couples were standing in the foyer, intrigued by the sight of cops with a handcuffed prisoner. But I didn't like that one bit. They were the young upwardly mobile types, mid-thirties, and I said to them, "You know, nothing's going to happen that's interesting. So better move along. It makes it easier for us to do our job."

They went to the elevator. We don't have a doorman, just a buzz system and an automatic elevator. Once they were in the elevator, one of the cops said, "Lieutenant, there's a big, four-door Chrysler across the street, you can see it from here. Four men in it. I don't like that. Four men sitting in a car parked makes me nervous. Window's up now, but before when the window was down, I thought I recognized the face. Benny here"—indicating his partner—"thought so too. Only because he looks like an ape. Crazy Percy Lax, from Chicago. We got his face over at the house, and the feds want him and the Chicago cops want him and God knows who else."

I knew about Percy Lax. He was a very skillful professional, one of the best, not really connected with the mob for whom he worked intermittently, but very much an independent who hired out on contract not only in places like L.A. and Houston and Cleveland and Philadelphia but also on occasion in Europe, which brought much pleading for information from Interpol. Yet it seemed very unlikely that he could be sitting in a car across the street.

"It's me," Piper Heston whimpered. "Your whole goddamn apartment was bugged. While we were up there yakking, they put him there. He cruises when they think there might be a job."

"Who put him there?"

"Someone, I don't know."

"Don't give us that kind of shit!" Toomey snapped, forgetting that Fran was with us.

"Piper," I said, "we can open these doors and kick you out there onto the street. I don't like to be followed. I don't like to have my phone tapped and my home bugged. I'm nervous and angry and edgy, so it would not break my heart to throw you out into the street and see whether that is truly Crazy Percy Lax sitting there in that Chrysler. His M.O. is one of those rapid-fire guns, cut you in half before you knew anything hit you—"

"For Christ's sake, what are you doing to me? I'm a lousy little technician with a P.I. buzzer. I don't know a fuckin' thing, and you want to kill me. I'm a piece of shit but I ain't as low as you lousy cops."

"Piper, Piper," I said softly, "we don't want to kill you. I dropped the burglary charge. You probably won't even go to jail on the misdemeanor rap—if you cooperate. These gentlemen, smart, streetwise cops, tell me that they think a notorious international hit man is sitting in the big car across the street, with three other men who probably carry shotguns. Well, I don't want to shove you out there and have you chopped to pieces. That's a horrible, disgusting fate. I want you to live and tell me who Crazy Percy is working for."

"I don't know! I swear to God I don't know! I swear on

129

my dead mother's soul I don't know! I can tell you Wabash. Sure I can tell you that, and maybe it's true and maybe it ain't. But I don't know and if I tell you that I'd be lying, and if I ever said it under oath, I'd seal my death warrant, because you don't fuck with Wabash, so what in hell do you want from me, Lieutenant?"

Fran, close behind me, whispering, "Don't—it's enough, Harry."

"You know," Toomey said, "they don't care about one empty prowl car, because they know the cops are in here and they can take care of them, but if we call the house and pull over two more, one at each end of the block, it could be that we got Percy, and that would be a nice collar, the way things are now."

I didn't ask him what he meant by the way things are now, because this was not the moment to go into such a discussion. I mentioned that I had thought of the same thing, but that my apartment was bugged. "However," I said to Toomey, "there's no reason why one of the uniforms here can't go upstairs and ring a bell or two and ask to use the phone. How about it?" I said to Benny. "Just nice and polite. If they see the uniform through the peephole, they won't panic. Tell them over at the house to bring in two cars, no sirens, one at the Third Avenue end, one at the Second Avenue end. Tell them who we're looking for, and that a couple of detectives with shotguns should run a backup. Since there are four of us here, they shouldn't need much more. But tell them to hurry." Benny started up the stairs, and I turned to the others.

"It's started. Get away from the door." It was almost eight o'clock. "Fran," I snapped, "get up to the apartment!"

"No."

"Get away from the door!" I yelled. They did as I said, and I pushed Fran down. "On the floor all of us!" The big black car had pulled out into motion. "Benny," I yelled. "Forget it!"

I didn't see anymore of what happened, because we were all on the floor. It had never occurred to me that they might have bugged the hallway of the apartment house. When I yelled to Benny, the two wood and glass doors that led into the foyer of my apartment house exploded. There must have been two large-caliber rapid-fire guns, because they chopped the doors out of existence in a matter of seconds. The moment that was over, the other cop, Toomey, and I leapt through the opening into the street, rolling on our bellies and emptying our guns at the black car, already swinging onto the avenue. It was a futile and useless gesture of frustration. We brushed the dirt off our clothes and went back to our apartment house, where Fran and Heston were the center of an increasing crowd of people, coming from inside and from outside the apartment house. Piper Heston could have walked away, but I had a feeling that it would take a great deal to pry him loose from the protection of cops. Fred Jones was there, his face sick as he studied the two shattered doors, a shattered chandelier, and bullet holes all over the walls.

"Will you please tell me what on earth goes on here, Lieutenant?" he begged me. "You know the way the co-op owners get up so tight if there's a speck of dust around. Just look at this!"

"Take him over to the house and book him," I said to Toomey, nodding at Piper. "Maybe I'll get there later, maybe not."

Joe Hammerstich, chairman of the board of the co-op that owned our building, interrupted at dinner by the machine-gun fire, drew me aside and said unhappily, "What happened, Harry? It sounded like Beirut."

"I'll try to make it short but not clear, because none of this is very clear, Joe, and none of it makes sense. That little guy"—pointing to Piper, who was pushing through the crowd with Toomey—"was rifling my apartment when Fran and I got home tonight. I arrested him, and then he indicated that some people in a large black car across the street would probably kill him. When we decided what to do about it, the gentlemen in the black car were told what we had decided and they swung by and emptied their guns through our lovely old front door."

"What do you mean, they were told what you had decided?"

"There's a bug somewhere in this foyer."

"You're kidding." Joe was a round-faced, overweight, pleasant accountant. He ran the building brilliantly, and instead of gratitude, he got all our complaints. He began to tremble a bit now. "What do you mean, a bug? What's going on, Harry?"

His wife, June, had joined the crowd in the foyer, and she and a dozen others of the co-op family had surrounded Fran as a source of information. Benny came over to me and asked, "What about it, Lieutenant? Should I clear the lobby?"

"Only of those who don't live here. Both of you stick around for a while—at least until Fred"—I pointed to where Fred Jones was sweeping glass together—"until he jerrys up something to close off the lobby." I turned back to Hammerstich. "Joe, I wish I could tell you, but I don't know myself."

"That's crazy."

"Yes. Oh, yes." I began to reload my gun. I always keep a few extra cartridges in my coat pocket. I had fired three times at the car. That was anger and frustration and not very good police procedure, firing into an avenue running right angles to your line of fire, but the target was large and I'm sure we hit the car several times. Toomey would put it on the wire, and we might just be lucky enough to pick up a large black Chrysler with bullet holes in it, except that such luck almost never happens.

"Crazy," I agreed. "I'm sorry, Joe."

"But look at it. Who pays for it? Do the cops pay for it?"

"Come on, Joe. We didn't do any of it."

"You provoked it!" he said shrilly.

"No, no. Come on, Joe. Think about it. The building's insurance will cover it."

"If it's not excluded."

"Joe, did you ever hear of a policy that excludes machine-gun damage?"

Finally, Fran and I were able to slip away, and we walked downtown on Second Avenue. After a few blocks in silence, Fran said, "You're two men, Harry. I suppose all cops are, and I guess what happened tonight is what you call your work."

"You could call it that. This suit is ruined."

132

"No it isn't. I'll brush most of the dirt off tonight. I don't want to watch you working again."

"No, it's not a good thing."

"You begin to get the feeling that I hear crooks have."

"What's that?"

"That one side isn't much different from another."

"They're damn different!" I said angrily.

"Don't turn your anger on me, Harry. I'm all torn up inside. There's that fellow in California, a cop turned writer, and he called his book *The New Centurions,* and do you know who the centurions were, Harry? They were the Roman officers who rolled dice and got themselves drunk under the cross, while our Lord died there in his agony—"

"Your Lord, not mine."

The tears filled her eyes now. "Don't go at me, Harry, please. I'm a failed Catholic who wants only to get down on her knees and beg God's forgiveness."

"For what? For what should you be forgiven?" I stopped and turned her around and put my arms around her. "You're the best person I ever knew. Nothing to forgive you for."

"Harry," she whispered, pulling away from my kiss, "I think we're being followed."

"Two men on foot. A third in the car."

"What shall we do?"

"Nothing. I want to kiss you again, and then we'll walk. It's a beautiful night." I kissed her, and we began to walk again.

"Harry, we are being followed. I can't stand this anymore. What do they want from us? What have we done to anyone?"

"First we get rid of them." I stopped a cab. We got in, and I was relieved that the driver appeared to be under forty. I showed him my badge and plastic and said to him, "I'm being followed. Do you think you can shake them?"

"Goldman—you're Jewish?" the cabby asked.

"What the hell difference—"

"Don't get excited." He had a thick accent. "I'm an Israeli." Half the cabdrivers in New York seemed to be Israeli.

133

"You want to lose a car, we lose a car. No sweat. What kind of car?"

"Dark brown. It looks like a Dodge."

"So we'll lose it."

We picked him up on 78th Street and Second Avenue. He roared down Second, increasing his speed to sixty miles an hour, leaning on his horn, weaving in and out in a manner that reduced our chances of getting through alive—and yet the Dodge hung on our tail. At 65th Street, our driver made a screaming turn. In thirteen blocks, he had overrun the stagger and had gone through four red lights. If Fran had come out of her white terror long enough to ask me, I would have answered that the cops can't be everywhere. There was a red light at First Avenue, and our driver, after squeezing past three double-parked cars at fifty miles an hour, ran the red light, his horn screaming, made a two-wheel turn north, narrowly missing one car, and even more narrowly missing another, and plunged west on 67th Street. There was an enormous garbage truck on 67th Street, and I could have sworn that there was not enough room for a car to pass between the truck and the parked car on the other side of the street. Our driver decided otherwise, and Fran and I both closed our eyes as, once again at at least fifty miles an hour, we shot between the garbage truck and the parked car. I will swear that there was not a quarter of inch of space on either side, and the Dodge following us was simply not as good as the Israeli cabdriver. It hit either the truck or the parked car, I don't know which, and there was the most tremendous crash. A red light had appeared at the Third Avenue end of the street, and our driver stood on his brakes and managed to stop. A police car, its siren going, passed by us into the block as the light changed, the police car going in the wrong direction on a one-way street—something that did not matter, since it would be hours before that street could be used. As we drove west, we heard the siren of an ambulance and the wild hooting of fire engines.

"So I lost him," the driver said.

"You sure as hell lost him," I said. "Go straight ahead through the transverse and drop us at Columbus." There was a Chinese restaurant on 66th, just east of Columbus Avenue, that we both liked.

Fran was lying back on the seat, her eyes closed. "Are you all right?" I asked her.

"No."

"It's over. I mean being tailed. That's over."

"We're alive?"

"I think so."

"The men in the car—were they killed?"

"I don't know. We'll find out on the eleven o'clock news."

"Harry," she whimpered, "I'm tired and frightened, and I want to talk to my kids."

"It's too early. Hang in there, baby."

When I paid off the cabdriver, I said to him, "Remember —we were never in your cab."

"Already forgotten. Even to you, I deny it."

"It helps to have a police lieutenant in this city who owes you one."

"You bet. Only I don't even remember your name."

He drove off, and Fran said, "I don't think I want to go to Israel ever again, Harry. Aren't you going to report this?"

"No. I left the scene of an accident. That's a bad play for a cop. I couldn't explain it. We're so deep in this nightmare, I can't explain anything, not even to myself."

"Amen."

We went into the restaurant. It was past nine now, and Chinese food, like chocolate candy, always helped to elevate Fran's spirits. But she complained that she wasn't hungry and that all she wanted was to call her brother Sean and find out what had happened to her poor children whom I had sent away. I explained that it was too early, that they might have had to wait hours for the plane, and then they had to go from Shannon to Dublin.

"It's already two in the morning in Dublin."

I ordered egg rolls, ribs, spicy noodles, lemon chicken, and Cantonese lobster. Fran nibbled a piece of egg roll, explaining that she wasn't hungry, but she couldn't just sit at the table and watch me eat. She mentioned the connection between the stomach and the mind, suggesting that people who could maintain an appetite under stress were lacking in any real kind of human sensitivity.

"I guess if you knew this side of me you wouldn't have married me."

"Probably not, and it's even worse when those qualities exist in a Jew, who is supposed to be—"

"You still have your illusions about Jews."

"Not so many after tonight. That Israeli cabdriver—are you going to take all of that?"

I had put some lemon chicken on my plate. "It's less than half. You're not hungry."

"I might want to taste it."

"There's enough there to taste. And you know, that crazy cabdriver saved our lives."

"He almost killed us."

I put the rest of the lemon chicken on her plate.

"That's ridiculous," she said. "You know I'm not going to eat that. You're just provoking me. Anyway, we should finish the egg rolls and ribs before we eat the other stuff."

"Why?"

"Why? Oh, you ask the dumbest questions. All right, I'll tell you why. When you grow up in a poverty-line family of numerous Irish kids in New York, you don't leave food on your plate."

"That's reasonable."

"Harry, I can't pretend anymore," she said woefully. "I can't pretend to be charming and bright. It's all too horrible."

"I know. But we'll work our way out of it. Believe me, please."

We finished eating, and then we walked for a few blocks, Fran holding tight to my arm. Then we took a cab downtown to 34th Street and Broadway, from where we walked east to the hotel. The night was cool but not really cold, and Fran wondered whether this was the first day of spring. Myself, I had lost track, but I didn't think so. I counted from St. Patrick's Day.

"Tomorrow," I said.

"But St. Patrick's Day was so long ago."

"Day before yesterday."

"Months." Fran sighed. "What time was it when you called Gavin this morning?"

"Ten o'clock. Give or take a few minutes."

"Almost twelve hours ago. Give it two hours before they got a plane. Six more for the flight—"

"Less. It's west to east, and Shannon's on the edge. With good winds, well, five hours, even less. We made it once in four and a half."

"All right. They should be in Dublin now."

"Just don't count on it. They could have waited hours for seats."

At the Primrose Hotel, Bill Hoffman and his wife, Tillie, were both behind the check-in desk. Tillie was a fat, cheerful lady who was always on the verge of tears, or apparently so, the tears having no connection with sorrow; but when she embraced Fran the tears became real. A threat to us was a threat to the entire world as she saw it.

I gave Bill the number in Ireland. "You know it's about half past three in the morning in Dublin?" he said.

"This is a saintly man. Saintly men don't mind being awakened at three in the morning."

"That wasn't necessary," Fran said. "You don't believe in saintly men."

"I'll put the call through," Bill said. "We could move right through or it could be an hour before we have a connection. But at this time, it should be quick. Then I'll ring your room. I won't listen in."

Upstairs in the room, Fran said, "I don't know how you do it. Wisecracks. One-liners. Doesn't anything touch you?"

"Too much. Do you want someone who possibly can stand up and finish this? Or do you want a wet cloth. I can give you both."

Almost a minute of silence. She sat on the bed, staring at me, and then she said, "I'm sorry, Harry. I have to beat up on someone—otherwise, I'd go mad. You're the only one here."

I nodded. I couldn't go to her or kiss her or take her in my arms. I was in the same condition as she was. "I'll go into the other room," I said, "and I'll sit by the extension. But Fran, baby, whatever we hear when the telephone rings, it's not the end. The kids couldn't call us—that's the thing to remember. A hundred different things could have gone wrong, but they couldn't call us to tell us, could they?"

She shook her head.

We sat in silence, she in the bedroom, myself in the tiny adjoining parlor, and we sat that way for almost twenty minutes waiting for the telephone to ring. It was the longest twenty minutes that either of us had lived through, twenty minutes during which we accepted the fact that our children were lost and gone, rejected it, grappled with it. In that scenario I put together every possibility, that *they*—the unknown *they*—had killed my children as they left their respective universities, kidnapped them, beaten them, had them shot at Shannon, etcetera, etcetera, every dreadful vision that could leap into my mind. Afterward, Fran confessed to the same fears.

And then the telephone rang.

Fran couldn't find her voice. I was shouting hoarsely, "Sean, Sean, is that you? This is Harry."

"Yes, it is myself, Sean, and your kids are here, safe and sound—what's that?"

Fran had let out a squeal followed by tears.

"Your sister, Sean. She's had a hard time. Forgive us for waking you."

"You didn't. Your kids just got here half an hour ago, and now we're all sitting in the school kitchen, where they're eating eggs and good Irish bacon as quick as Mary can fry it up. Do you hear me, Fran? Say something to tell me you're alive and well."

"I'll try, Shanny, I'll try. Right now, I have to weep."

"I'll let the kids talk to you in a moment, but what is this, Harry? Can you tell me something over the phone? The kids know even less than I do!"

"I'm afraid not," I said, "except that no one must know where they are for the next week or so. That doesn't mean that they can't step outside for some sunshine and fresh air."

"There is no sunshine in Ireland in March."

"And have them look a bit Irish, Sean—you know, some old Irish clothes, and if anyone speaks to them, let them put on a heavy brogue so they won't be spotted as Americans."

"For God's sake, will you let me talk to them?" Fran cried.

Sarah was on the telephone first. After a few words, Fran choked up. The day was taking its toll. "Is Mommy all right?" Sarah wanted to know.

"Yes, just full of emotion right now."

"Mommy, Mommy," Sarah said. "You mustn't worry about us. It's just such an adventure, and Gavin taking such good care of me, and really, I feel like someone in a film—" That went on for a while, Fran pulling herself together and managing to talk reasonably well, and then Gavin saying to me, "Look, Pop, I have things under control, and believe me, I won't let Sarah out of my sight, and I can take care of both of us. You know that. And, Mom, you don't worry about either of us. But, Pop, you have to tell me something. What's going on?"

"I can't."

"Just a hint or something."

"No. Nothing. Only, you and Sarah must take new names for the few days you'll be there. I spoke to Sean about other things."

"You're sure? Just a few days? Pop, you have to call both schools, otherwise they'll report us missing."

"I'll do that."

"But we can drift around Dublin, can't we?"

I hesitated. "All right—but always together. And be careful."

"If I didn't know you and Mom, I'd think you were crazy."

"We're not crazy."

"But Pop, you have to admit the whole thing is crazy."

"Oh, no. Now you do as I tell you, Gavin, and when you're out on the street, if anyone comes onto either of you, pushing to know who you are, you get the hell back to St. Joseph's."

I let Fran do most of the talking after that, only cutting in to tell them that we'd call back in a few days.

When I put down the telephone and walked into the bedroom, Fran was standing, breathing deeply. "Oh, I feel wonderful," she said. "They're so beautiful and clever—oh, I do

139

love them. Harry, can he, they—whoever is doing this—can he find them there?"

"In time, I suppose. He would have to find the drivers who took them to the airport and then what airline and then get to the ticket files and then find out who in Ireland has a connection with us, or maybe get it from the cabdriver at Shannon—yes, he could trace them, but it would have to take three to ten days, and only if he felt the necessity to get at them."

"Harry—Why? Why must they find our kids?"

"To close our mouths without killing us. The kids are a trump card. He'd have to be lucky. It wouldn't be easy." She fled into my arms, and I held her tightly. "We just have to get him first," I said, as calmly as I could.

"It would be nice if we knew who he is."

"We'll know. Sooner or later. And we'll stop him."

She shook her head mutely and said, "Turn on the TV."

"Why?"

"Why? Harry, don't you want to know what happened back there?"

"We'll know soon enough."

"Harry," she said firmly, "turn on that damn TV. It's just eleven o'clock, and I want to see the news."

You didn't fuss with Fran when she got that tone in her voice. I switched on the set, and after a rundown on the Hart, Mondale, and Jackson primary campaign, the anchorman turned to local matters, showing us some pictures of a broken water main in midtown. That was followed by pictures of firemen spraying water on what was left of a burning car. Against the film, the anchorman said a few words about the strange chase in midtown Manhattan, then turned it over to the network's man on the scene. He was more explicit, informing us that, "No light has as yet been shed on this strange and somewhat terrible tragedy. As near as we have been able to piece it together, this car had been engaged in a wild chase after a medallion cab. We have a witness here." The witness was a stout middle-aged lady, who, enjoying the position of being observed by millions of viewers, said firmly, "Well, I was just coming out of the store there when I saw these two cars come screeching by. The first car was a cab, and chasing it was this other car which I don't know what it was. Both cars turned the corner so fast I thought they would turn over, but they didn't."

"Apparently," the network man said, taking it back from the fat lady, "the two cars sped down to First Avenue, turned north and then west on the side street. The garbage truck was parked as you see it."

He pointed his mike at the sanitation man standing beside the truck, who shook his head sadly and said, "We always try to park to leave a decent lane, but it ain't always possible. When you get a rotten job of parking, like that car at the curb, we got to block the street until we pick up. No other way. So help me God, I don't know how that cab got through. There couldn't have been more than a tiny fraction of an inch of clearance on either side. The second car hit the truck and then was smashed against the parked car on the other side."

The network man then turned to the fireman in charge. The flames were out and they had turned off their hoses. He said to the fireman, "Both men in the car are dead—right?"

"They're dead, yes. More than dead. They're pretty well burned to a crisp."

"Beyond identification?"

"Oh, yes. I would think so. Even the dental work goes in that kind of heat."

"And the car?"

The fireman shrugged. "Sure, they can look for an engine number or some such thing when it cools down, but it's not likely they'll find anything. Too much heat. It melts the metal. You know"—pointing to two other skeletons of cars —"three fires, not one, and a lot of gasoline. It didn't do much to the garbage truck except to burn the rear tires and some garbage. It's the rubber that makes the smoke and the heat—"

"Let's go to sleep," Fran said.

I switched off the TV. I didn't want to hear any more either.

Chapter 9

SOMETIME DURING THE NIGHT, Fran and I awakened at the same time. That happens to us quite often, as if we were connected some way in our sleep, and Fran felt for my body, as if uncertain that I was there, and then she said, "Harry, how long has this awful business been going on?"

"Not much more than a week."

"No, you're wrong. It's been months."

"No, baby."

"A week?" She was silent, and I lay there with my eyes open. "A week—Harry, do you remember you once told me that if an assassin wants to kill someone and is willing to put his life on the line, he can't be stopped?"

"Did I say that?"

"He's going to kill all of us, isn't he, Harry?"

"Over my dead body," I said, without realizing what I was saying. Then, hearing a strange sound, I asked her whether she was crying.

"I'm giggling, Harry. Over my dead body—did you know what you were saying?"

"Not really, no."

"Why don't we go to the cops?"

"I'm the cops. Try to sleep, Red." I hadn't called her that

142

in years. Only her oldest brother, Charley Murphy, who was a wealthy, important downtown lawyer, called her Red and got away with it.

"Red?"

"I don't know where that came from. Deep inside. The kids on the block called you Red, didn't they? You used to go crazy. But you remember the time old Harry beat up Crazy Louey and saved you?"

"I'm sleeping."

"Good. I always thought that was why you married me. Crazy Louey was twice my size. I was heroic."

And after that, I actually fell asleep for a couple of hours.

I woke up at seven, to the sound of the shower. The woman who came out of the bathroom looked better than she had in days. She had brushed off my suit, and had provided a clean shirt and tie. I was fairly presentable. Fran in a white blouse, blue pleated skirt, and white sweater, looked more than presentable. We went downstairs to the coffee shop, which was the only restaurant the small hotel could boast of, and we ordered a large breakfast. Apparently, speaking to the kids had restored our appetites. Bill Hoffman came by and sat down at our table for a moment and asked us how it went last night.

"Good and smooth."

"Now remember," he said to us, "anything I can help with, including some fat and muscle that's still pretty effective."

I asked him whether he could cash a check, and he said that a couple of hundred dollars would be no problem at all. When he had gone, I said to Fran, "You remember the program?"

"Pretty well."

"I'm absolutely certain they don't know we're here. There's no way they can cover New York, not with a thousand men, and why should they think of the public library?"

"I wish we could stay together, Harry."

"No. The thought of anything happening to you makes me sick, but we have to do it this way, and we have to move very quickly."

143

"And what's our destination, Harry? Will you tell me that. Do you know where we're going?"

"Sort of."

"Sort of? What does that mean?"

"Can't you trust me?"

"No."

"Oh, God," I said. "Please don't start that, Fran. We can't have one of those rotten fights that we fall into. I'm doing the best I can."

"I know," she whispered.

"Walk, if you don't mind—on foot is safer."

"Harry, I love you so. I never mean for these stupid fights to start, and if we ever come out of this, I'll never fight with you again."

"I know. I said to walk, darling, because the more we avoid things like cabs, the better off we are."

She was able to smile. "What things, Harry? There aren't any things like cabs—except cabs."

"I only said it to make you smile."

"Oh, yes. And what's your program for today?"

"To track down the beast."

"That's very colorful, Harry, but a cop doesn't say that. A cop says to arrest the perpetrator."

I stood at the entrance to the hotel, watching her walk down the street. She was a damn fine figure of a woman. She went uptown, I went downtown. At a street-corner phone booth, I stopped to call Oscar. I can now admit that my precautions were paranoid, but at the time I was not in a logical frame of mind, and how did I know that they had not tapped Oscar's phone? I caught him just as he was about to leave the apartment, and he wanted to know what was happening to me, and had I gone off the deep end, and was Fran with me, and why had Sergeant Toomey called him last night, and why had Captain Courtny called him at half past seven this morning to find out whether Oscar knew where I was, and why had my kids walked out of their respective schools and disappeared?

"I'm all right, Fran's all right, the kids are all right."

"Harry, what on God's earth is going on?"

"I can't explain over the telephone. When this is over, I'll give you a blow-by-blow account, but meanwhile I desperately need a favor."

"I'll try." A long moment of silence then. "Harry, are you still there?"

"Where will you be in fifteen minutes?"

"Twenty minutes. In my office at the university."

"I'll call you there," I said.

I walked on downtown. There is no way in the world to trace a call in less than six or seven minutes. At a public telephone on 23rd Street, I called my station house and asked for Captain Courtny.

"Golding? God damn you, Golding, where the hell are you?"

"Outside."

"Well, get your fuckin' ass in here."

"Just hold on!" I snapped back. "What were you doing calling my kids at college?"

"Trying to find you."

"You are a fuckin' liar! I was with Toomey! You knew that!"

"You are stretching it, Harry—you are stretching it. You once were a cop; now you're an asshole. Where are you?"

"Outside. I said that before."

"When can we expect you, Lieutenant Golding?" he asked nastily.

"Three-thirty or so."

He slammed down the telephone. I replaced my phone, walked slowly over to Park Avenue and 18th Street, and called Oscar on a telephone there.

"I thought your phone might be tapped," I explained.

"Harry, are you sure you're all right?"

"You mean have I flipped out? No, I haven't. I am very cool-headed and precise in what I am doing, but I need help."

"What kind of help?"

"I have to talk to someone who knows as much about the financial structure of this country as you know about its social structure, I mean the kind of stuff they keep track of in *Fortune* magazine, stocks, industries, the whole shtick. You must know someone in that line of work."

"I do."

"Good, good. Who is he?"

"His name is Harvey Crimshaw, and he's the head of research and analysis at Denton, Frobish and Kemp."

"And what is Denton, Frobish and Kemp?"

"Only the third largest brokerage house in America, and what Harvey doesn't know about American business is not worth knowing."

"All right. I must talk to him, today. Can you arrange for us to have lunch?"

"Harry, hold on. Just hold on. A man like Harvey has his luncheon meetings scheduled weeks in advance. This is one of the most important financial experts in America. They come to him from Washington when they're looking for a few facts to pad out their illusions."

"Oscar, this is life and death. Not life and death, but the kind of death where you stay dead. It's my life and Fran's life and maybe my kids' lives—and it must be now, today."

"Are you putting me on, Harry."

"No. No, believe me."

"I believe you, and somehow I'll persuade him. I'll be out of my class in an hour and a half. Can you call me then?"

I blessed him and thanked him, left the public phone stand, and walked across 18th Street to the building that housed Wabash Protection. According to the information board, Wabash had three full floors, and the uniformed concierge, sitting at his desk in the lobby, had probably been supplied by Wabash. He stopped me as I started toward the elevator and asked me where I was bound for. I told him, and he pointed to a bank of elevators. "Those for Wabash," he said.

"I want the executive offices."

"Seventeenth floor."

When I left the elevator on the seventeenth floor, on the wall at the opposite side of a large, painfully modern reception room, there was an enormous map of the United States with small lights spotted all over it. The print underneath the map read, THERE ARE OVER TWO HUNDRED WABASH OFFICES IN THE UNITED STATES. A very pretty blond lady, sitting at a desk in front of the map, smiled at me and asked me who I would like to see.

"Whoever runs this place. The top man."

"That would be Mr. Comstock. Do you have an appointment?"

"No."

"Then I'm afraid it's impossible. He sees no one without an appointment."

"Just call in and tell him that Lieutenant Golding of the New York City police wants to talk to him. I think he'll see me." I showed her my badge. "Just to quiet any doubts you may have."

The pretty blonde looked at me, and suddenly she was no longer simply a smiling, pretty blonde, but a tough, sharp-nosed young woman whose cold blue eyes studied me shrewdly. She picked up her phone, punched some buttons, listened after she told them who I was, and then said to me, "Please follow me."

Was I afraid? Afterward, Fran asked me that. Was I afraid? And I told her that I was damned afraid, but then it wasn't the first time. All cops are afraid, except for those few who are genuinely demented. It comes with the job, and here, inside Wabash, I was very much afraid. I'm no hero; I'm just a middle-sized, middle-aged Jewish cop.

The blonde put me into a corridor, where another blonde was waiting. My son, Gavin, who is a science fiction fan, would have called them cloned. I accepted the fact that they used the same hair bleach and wore the same makeup. The second blonde opened the door of an office for me and nodded for me to enter. It was furnished in the tasteless modern style of the reception room, the only interesting piece in it a large free-form marble tabletop. There was no desk as such. The man who occupied the place sat at one end of a big couch, thumbing through a clipboard holding a dozen sheets of paper. Behind him, an enormous painting, meaningless to me, covered with splashes of paint and two large circles, one black and one red. He put aside the clipboard and rose. He was a tall man with a lean face. Quite good-looking. "I'm Comstock," he said, "and you're Golding." He didn't offer to shake hands or ask me to sit down.

"What can I do for you?" he asked, not with annoyance or anger or cordiality—just flat.

"I'd like some information about two of your operatives. One, by name Bert Smith, was murdered in San Fernando. He had been practicing medicine illegally under the name of Green. The other, Piper Heston, was arrested conducting a search of my apartment."

"We don't give out information about our operatives, Lieutenant. You should know that."

"What was one of them doing in my apartment?"

"My dear Lieutenant," Comstock said, "in New York City alone, we have over eight hundred operatives. Do you really expect me to know what one of them was doing in your apartment?"

"Yes, I damn well do."

"Lieutenant, I agreed to see you because I had assumed that you were here on police business. Apparently, you are not, so I am afraid our little chat is over."

It was cold, quick, and humiliating. He opened the door for me and pointed down the corridor. No blonde this time. "The elevators are to your left," he said. Then he closed his door and I was alone in the corridor. Well, what had I expected?

As I started to walk down the corridor to the elevators, the reception room, and the pretty blonde, one of the office doors in the wall opened and a young man stepped into the corridor. He was about six two in height, hair cropped short, his neck the size eighteen of a football player, his muscles filling out his suit very nicely. He had a good-looking boyish face, and he smiled as he informed me that Mr. Comstock would like me to wait around for an hour or two because someone was expected who could answer my questions.

"I appreciate that and it's thoughtful of Mr. Comstock, but I don't have the time."

"It's not your decision," he said. "You must wait."

Then he started toward me, evidently to pick up my somewhat worn one hundred and forty-eight pounds and perhaps put them in a safe place until Mr. Comstock's associate arrived. I moved quickly until my back touched the wall. I like to have a wall against my back in tight places. And then I took my hand out of my coat pocket and with it the automatic pistol that I had put there on the previous day.

He stopped when he saw the gun, and I said, "You know, sonny, whatever you are thinking, don't. Don't even think of how quick you could be, because they only take loaded guns away in the movies. Move one inch and I will shoot you. This gun is semiautomatic. Five shots in your balls and prick. You'd still have your pretty face, but only a squeak could come out. Now drop your jacket on the floor! Quick!"

He did so.

"Loosen your belt. Unbutton the top button in your pants."

He looked at me with his mouth open.

"Hands over your head. Lock your fingers."

He did it, and then, before he could think of what came next, I jammed the gun past his belt into his pants and against his groin. He moved involuntarily, and I yelled, "Hold it, buster, or you'll be a fuckin' eunuch!"

Doors began to open now. People came into the corridor.

"The gun's on automatic," I said to him, "and my finger's got the trigger in. I let go and you'll have a dozen slugs in your young manhood."

"God almighty, don't do it!" he screamed.

The hall had filled with men and women now, Comstock among them, and I shouted, "This kid and I are going out of this building! I've got an automatic pistol against his balls! There is no way you can take me! If you shoot me, I let go and he'll have twelve slugs in his groin. My arm is locked in his belt, so play it smart."

"He's my son!" Comstock yelled. "You son of a bitch Jew bastard, that's my son!"

"You'll never have a grandson if I let go, so why don't you just let us walk out of here quietly, and you'll have your son back, and no one gets hurt."

Comstock was shouting unintelligibly. The men and women in the corridor were beginning to crowd me.

"Comstock!"

Suddenly, it was silent. They stood in a circle around me. "Comstock," I said, "get them back—out of my way. I'm taking him to the elevator. I'm going down the elevator, just him and me. No one else and no one in the lobby downstairs. No tricks! And you, sonny boy, don't even jostle me."

They stood back at Comstock's order, and, pressed against the young muscleman, I got into the elevator, and dropped down to the lobby, where the guard at the desk had his hands up. Evidently, Comstock had gotten word to him. "I'm not making a move, Lieutenant," he squealed. "Not a move."

Two people entered the lobby, pausing to stare at us. The guard waved them away. We went through the doors into the street, and I snapped at the kid, "Drop your pants!"

"Drop your pants!" I repeated when he didn't react. "Now—quick or the gun goes off." His hands trembling, he dropped his pants. The gun was free. I kicked his backside with all my strength, and he tripped over the pants and fell on his face, and then I ran as I hadn't run in years.

His voice, pitched to its utmost power, followed me, "You bastard! You degenerate Jew bastard! You fuckin' bastard!" and so forth and so on until I turned the corner.

I saw a taxi, hailed it, leapt in, and sank panting onto the seat.

"Where to?" the driver asked.

I could barely speak, my heart was pounding so out of a mixture of fear and exhaustion. I had not run with that kind of speed and abandon in years. Uniformed cops run, detectives run, but a lieutenant of detectives doesn't run. He sits on his backside and gives orders and uses his brain, if he has one.

"Thirty-fourth and Madison," I said to the driver.

Then I sat back and reflected that no one in that crowd of smartass private detectives, operatives, or whatever else they called themselves, had enough brains and cool to remember that no automatic pistol—at least none that I had ever heard of—fires an automatic clip when the trigger is released. A hand grenade does that. In a pistol, the trigger is pulled.

Then I told myself that I could thank God that Fran had not witnessed this maniac ploy. But what else could I have done? What other way of getting out of there alive?

Chapter 10

I WALKED OVER to the Primrose Hotel. Fear is a diarrhetic and also an emetic, and while I had been a cop for seventeen years, I had never come up against anything like this. I used the toilet, and while I did not throw up, I came close to it. Then I splashed water on my face, dried my face, and stared for a long moment at the sad, dark-eyed lonely visage that returned my stare from the mirror.

There was a telephone message from Fran, which had been slipped under the door. It said: *Beginning to pick up bits and pieces. See you later.*

I called Oscar.

"I couldn't believe it," he said. "Harvey said he'd rather lunch with you than Shultz, with whom he's lunching tomorrow. 'The one who pulled that incredible Vermeer ploy? And he's your brother?' Well, he pushed Shultz up a day, and he'll meet you at twelve-thirty at the Harvard Club."

Suddenly, Oscar was scoring points on the basis of being a cop's brother. He took it gracefully, except that when I asked him where the Harvard Club was, he replied, with a note of incredulity, "You've never been there?"

"No, Oscar."

"Forty-fourth Street, just west of Fifth. I believe the number is twenty-seven."

I walked there from the hotel. The more I avoided cabs, the safer I was. They say that New York City is the best place in the world to drop out of sight, but as a cop I can refute that. It may be true of the other boroughs, but you can walk down a street in middle Manhattan and meet two or three people you know; and since I was convinced that Wabash Protection had several hundred operatives out looking for me, I had no reason to relax.

As for the Harvard Club, that was a part of New York life I had never studied intensely, and since the place was in another precinct, I had never even been invited to look at a robbery or a member who had keeled over from a heart attack. I was not entirely ignorant of New York City club life, that very important part of the city that keeps so low a profile that it casts almost no shadow at all. Oscar was a member of the Century Club, which, as he explained to me, has as its membership the bright nucleus of the literary and publishing establishment. If I had gone there alone, I would have concluded that the main qualifications for membership were to be age sixty or above and to wear creaseless trousers. At the Harvard Club, the ceilings were higher and the food was better and the mean age lower.

Harvey Crimshaw was about my age, a bit taller, slender, graying hair, and a set of humorous blue eyes. I had never thought of eyes as humorous until I faced the problem of describing Harvey. He had a look in his eyes that was just short of laughter, and of course he was a man who laughed readily. He greeted me with pleasure, shook hands warmly, informed me that he was an avid reader of detective fiction, and that my own caper—his word—was better than anything he had read lately. He seemed to be genuinely delighted to lunch with me.

"Of course, it's a first for me. Never lunched with a lieutenant of detectives before."

"And I've never been in the Harvard Club before."

"Well, it's comfortable and the food's good. Will you have a drink?" I shook my head. "No, of course. You're on duty. Well, suppose we order."

After we had ordered, Crimshaw said that Oscar had put this to him as a matter of life and death. There was a note of apology in his voice. "I mean," he said, "that Oscar might well have felt the need to exaggerate. He needn't have felt that way. I made him understand that I was delighted to meet you, and the previous date, which I canceled, was of no great importance. But just for my own benefit, is it actually a matter of life and death?"

"The question I'll ask you won't sound that way, but your answer can save several lives."

"One question?" he wondered.

"Just one—yes."

The food came. "Please," Crimshaw said, "let's not stand on ceremony. I want to hear that question. And call me Harvey."

"All right. Here's the question. Who owns Wabash Protection?"

"Wow." Quietly. He sipped at his drink and stared at me with what appeared to be new interest. "Wabash Protection," he said. "You wouldn't want me to ask you why you want this information?"

"Later, perhaps." I picked at the beef stew on my plate. I had no appetite. I was still sick inside over what had happened this morning.

"Well," Crimshaw said, "how do we go at this, Lieutenant? I have only another hour."

"You're kidding."

"Well, perhaps I could stretch it. On the other hand, since this is so desperately important to you—and since it's Wabash, I can understand why it might be—I had better begin at the very beginning and spell it all out. Do you want to take notes?"

I shook my head. "I'll remember. I've had a lot of practice at that."

"All right, from the beginning. Private protection agencies, or detective agencies, are an old fixture on the American scene. Pinkerton is the best known, and they began during the Civil War as a private secret service for the Union Army; but until fairly recently, the private detective agencies were small potatoes and the protection agencies were not much larger. You have the image created by Dashiell Hammett and by television of the shabby little office and the private eye who barely keeps body and soul together. Well, I suppose there's some of that still around, but by and large, it belongs to another era. The tremendous increase in crime has produced something else. But of course you know that."

I nodded. He took a few bites of his food and then lost interest in it. "I find this terribly exciting, but then I live a fairly dull life. Where were we? Oh, yes, do you work on the East Side—that is the Upper East Side?"

"Yes."

"Then you know how many streets in that area have their own uniformed private guards. Now let me just inject a bit of stock market data. Three of the most active growth industries were hardly listed on the pre–World War Two exchanges. The first, of course, is computers. Second, hospitals and all the associated industries, and thirdly, and much less known, the protection industry. This last has truly mushroomed, not only here but all over the country. Now let's get down to Wabash. It came into being eight years ago, created by a man by the name of Ellis Wabash. I think he was a private detective in Cleveland. He had six operatives, and as I understand it, they operated out of a cheap office on West Forty-seventh Street. I'm well up on this part of Wabash history, because I had lunch last week with the analyst who covers it for our firm."

"Analyst?"

"I can see you don't dabble in the stock market."

"On a cop's wages—oh, no. My wife would kill me if I did. Whatever savings we have are in money market accounts."

"That's good, very good indeed. You get a well-protected nine percent or better and absolutely no risk, covered by federal insurance. I wish more people had your good sense. Anyway, the stock market is for those who can take it, and I'm afraid the country could not survive without it. Brokerage houses must know about the stock they buy and sell for their customers, and that's where the analyst comes in. In a large brokerage house, such as ours, each analyst will have two or three or four or ten companies, or perhaps a whole industry that he must study. A really good analyst will sometimes know more about a company than the president of the company or the board of directors, and my thankless job is to whip the analysts and get to know at least a part of what each of them knows.

"Back to Wabash. As I said, Ellis Wabash opened up some eight years ago, had reasonably good luck and good management, and in one year he was working with six operatives. He had created a good, solid reputation, and according to his wife, he was prepared to double his work force. Then he died, and his wife had to sell the company."

"You mean he was killed."

"How did you know that?"

"He was killed?"

"Well, not killed, no. It was an accident. He lived out in Queens, small house. Came home late one night. The garage door closed, and he fell asleep with the motor going."

"How simple. How very simple. All problems solved in one simple manner."

"Lieutenant?"

"Just thinking. I'm sorry. Please go on."

"His wife got a good price for it, considering that it's a service business. She tried to make something out of his death, because she told her that he had been asked to take on work that would have paid well, but he was afraid and refused. That's all she knew. I suppose it was an accident, don't you?"

"I don't know—"

"As I said, she got a good price for it. A man called Henson ran it for the next sixteen months. He had money, evidently a good deal of money, but we know nothing about him, not even his first name—I guess we could find out more, if we had to. Henson increased the business enormously. He took a whole floor in one of the older office buildings, increased his operative force to better than a hundred, and opened branch offices in Boston and Philadelphia. Profits soared, and after sixteen months, Henson decided that the Wabash Company would go public. That means, as I'm sure you know, they were going to sell the company to whoever bought the stock."

"That much I'm familiar with," I said.

"It was all perfectly legal, but odd. Usually, when a person or a group develop a company, they sell off a portion of the stock and keep a bundle for themselves, at least fifty-one percent if they wish to continue in control, or less if they wish to continue as investors. Of course, with a large company with say ten or fifteen million shares of stock, a small part of that might be enough to maintain control. But Henson sold every share and then took the money and ran."

"How much money?"

"They issued two hundred thousand shares at five dollars a share, one million dollars, less about ten percent for expenses. A very fair price for a labor-intensive service company of that size. On the other hand, with a bit of pushing and glitz, they could have gotten twice that."

"Would you explain?"

"Yes. Small companies," Crimshaw went on, "that decide to go public and retrieve their investment—and very often a substantial profit on top of their investment—frequently sell their stock at a much higher price than the real net worth of their companies warrants. Their position is that they are selling future possibilities, managerial skill, a continuing pattern of growth. Now when you consider the growth in both size and profits of Wabash in the sixteen months of Henson's management, you see a pattern that could extend into the future. In terms of that possibility, the price of one million dollars was low—even in preinflation money. However, the two hundred thousand shares of stock were presold, that is they were spoken for immediately. A bit of improper shading there, but it happens."

"And Henson was never heard from again?"

"Oh, no. Disappeared. But there's no law against that, is there?"

"No, I guess not. Who bought the Wabash stock?"

"Not easy to know that entirely at this point. But Listerman-Reed bought about forty percent of the stock, and subsequently acquired enough to give them a fifty-one percent hold."

"And what is Listerman-Reed?"

"Sporting boats, fishing boats, surfboards, tennis equipment, a hockey team which they own, vitamins, some over-the-counter drugs—a nice, healthy company, sells health and very good at the job."

"All right, if this company makes healthy profits, which you seem to say, why didn't they grab all of Wabash if they wanted it? A million is not that much in your world, is it?"

"No, indeed, it is peanuts. But a stock like Wabash is two things. It is a protection agency and it is also a money machine. Now I am sorry, Lieutenant, to have to lead you down all these twisting garden paths, but there is no easy answer to the question you asked me—and I am sure you want the complete answer?"

"I do, absolutely."

"And I still have most of my hour. Now I may be telling you a good many things you already know, and I'm not trying to be insufferable. It's just a shorter road if I lay out everything. If you had asked me about General Motors, I could have answered in two minutes. Wabash is different. Now what do I mean by a money machine? That much-maligned old gentleman Karl Marx was once asked a seemingly unanswerable question: What determines value? His answer was very clear and simple: The value of anything, in economic terms, is its price. If Listerman-Reed had owned all of the stock, there would have been no market price because there was no stock on the market. So, very shrewdly, they established a market, first over the counter, then at the American Stock Exchange, and three years ago at the New York Stock Exchange, the big board, as we call it. Now starting with a price of five dollars about six years ago, the stock went up to fifty-two dollars and then it split. Subsequently, the stock split four more times and its market price today is somewhere around sixty-one dollars a share. That's what I mean by a money machine. That market stock, sold originally for about half a million is today worth more millions than you can count."

"But how did that money machine benefit them? They couldn't sell any stock without losing control."

"But they could. When a company becomes the size that Wabash is today, you don't need fifty-one percent for control. But the fact is that they did not sell a share of their own stock. Instead, they bought. They bought and bought their stock back into their treasury until they had established what we call a very thin float, that is, a limited number of shares on the market. According to the specialist on the floor, that is the man at the Exchange who makes the market on Wabash, over eighty percent of the stock is now owned by the company."

"Then the answer to my question is Listerman-Reed?"

"I'm afraid not, Lieutenant. We have only begun our journey through the jungles of high finance. We should note that when Listerman-Reed bought Wabash, they were buying a fairly small outfit. Today Wabash is enormous, the largest agency of its kind in America, and while the stock sells for sixty-one dollars, the company earns only two dollars a share. Which means that Wabash is selling for a fraction more than thirty times earnings. That is," he continued, seeing the blank look on my face, "two dollars of earning per share, and they have never paid a dividend. It's the very narrow float and this ups the price as well as the pattern of earnings. They have millions of shares, most of them owned by Listerman-Reed, and vast profits which Listerman-Reed uses to expand Wabash, not only in branches and personnel, but with every scientific advance that might be useful. Nevertheless, Listerman-Reed does not own Wabash—"

"Hold on. You said they did."

He had the waiter take our plates away, most of the food uneaten. Harvey Crimshaw was delighted and excited—because, as I sensed, he was opening a problem that had bugged him as well as me.

"Yes. They do and they don't. Listerman-Reed is privately held, not a public corporation. Yet it's not privately held. It's a laundry machine. You know how money is laundered?"

"That, I do know. The mob instructs us on that."

"Well, the purpose of Listerman-Reed is to launder power, that is to be an innocent-appearing instrument in the laundering of power. Who owns Listerman-Reed also owns Wabash, with its huge private army of thugs—I say that advisedly, although their guards are used by businesses all over the country."

"That," I said, "is interesting. I'm going to call you Harvey now. That, Harvey, is goddamned interesting. And it's legal?"

"Just as legal as can be."

"You can create an industrial army of armed men, no limitations on size, and it's perfectly legal?"

"Perfectly legal. And profitable too."

"Harvey," I said, "how long have you been brooding over this?"

"Brooding?"

"A moment ago, you specified a huge private army of thugs. That, if I'm not mistaken, is somewhat libelous. I just don't see a respected part of the financial establishment dropping a line like that. Also, how come you sit there like the city's number one expert on Wabash? When Oscar asked you to have lunch with me, he had no notion of my interest in Wabash."

"Or you of my interest in Wabash—by golly, you are one suspicious gentleman."

"My trade."

"Name's Harry?"

"Harry."

"Now look, Harry. We have customers who trust us more than they trust their wives or their mothers. They give us money and tell us, Put me into a stock. They don't tell us what stock—usually. But sometimes they do. Or they say, Why don't you put me into Wabash? Wabash splits and doubles every few months, they say. And we tell them, Hold on now. Wabash is selling thirty times earnings. We think that is imprudent for serious investment. We can buy some of the finest companies in America, or in the world for that matter, for six or seven times earnings, and they pay dividends. Wabash doesn't. Well, when sufficient customers complained that we had denied them the privilege of becoming rich by refusing to put their money into Wabash, we decided the time had come for some special research and analysis. We did not like what we found, but neither could we put our finger on anything illegal or anything that we could bring to the Securities Exchange Commission. But I found sufficient evidence to justify my use of the word *thug.*"

"This becomes, as Alice would say, curiouser and curiouser."

"Even to the point of a lieutenant of detectives who quotes Lewis Carroll."

"My wife teaches English at Columbia. It rubs off. You still haven't told me who owns Wabash."

"We passed that. Listerman-Reed owns Wabash. The question now," Harvey Crimshaw said, "is who owns Listerman-Reed." He was enjoying himself. He paused to ask my desire and then told the waiter that we'd both have brandy, specifying Napoleon and mentioning that the Harvard Club dispensed the real thing, not one of the endless imitations. I decided that one brandy would not incapacitate me for duty, but I must admit that I felt a wave of guilt at the thought of Fran eating a frankfurter from a wagon outside the public library while I, with any number of people pledged to kill me, drank valid Napoleon brandy at the Harvard Club. Harvey Crimshaw, on the other hand, appeared to have no guilts or qualms at all. I was sure that he was picturing himself relating this adventure—for research can't be very exciting—to a group of friends around a dinner table. I decided to puncture that immediately.

"Harvey," I said, "before we go any further, I must say that this discussion can't go to anyone else. I have to be very firm on that point. No mention to your associates, your friends, or your wife. We're talking about a deadly disease. It's too easy to become dead."

He considered that for a long moment, and then he said, "You're very serious, aren't you?"

"Damn serious."

Harvey was no fool. "You used the word *killed* about Ellis Wabash." He paused. "What do you suppose happened to Henson?"

"Heaven only knows."

"He didn't do anything illegal. He made a large killing in the market. When people do that, they don't drop out of sight. Henson must have had a lot of offers."

"I'm sure he knew things he shouldn't have known. Maybe he tried to use some of those things."

"Hold on—that sounds crazy. Harry, I've spent all of my

adult life in the financial community, and that kind of thing is the stuff of Hollywood. We are a sober and law-abiding bunch. Oh, we may bend the law a bit and now and then we throw enough weight around Washington to change it to our advantage, but we don't—"

He did not finish his sentence. Perhaps the thought was too unsettling to be spoken aloud. He sipped his brandy and stared at me.

"Who owns Listerman-Reed?" I persisted.

"Home base. You see, Harry, as I mentioned earlier, Listerman-Reed, a privately held company, owns Wabash—that is, a controlling portion of Wabash stock. But the question of who owns Listerman-Reed is something else, quite. The owner has no other connection with the company than the one hundred shares of stock that the company issued when it was incorporated by Stephan Listerman and Betty Reed in 1922. They were young people, just married. Stephan Listerman owned a small family boatyard at Woods Hole in Massachusetts. Betty Reed's family made skis in New London, Connecticut. A few years after they married, the fathers of both died, and the youngsters decided to combine the business. For the next fifteen years, the business barely managed to stay alive. Then World War Two came and Listerman-Reed began to get orders for lifeboats. As our merchant marine fleet expanded from virtually nothing to the largest cargo fleet in the world, Stephan Listerman, now running the company while his wife raised children, controlled his share of the expansion, both prudently and intelligently. They built good lifeboats and they amassed a good deal of wealth, and after the war they played a major role in the field of sport and pleasure equipment. But boats remained their major source of income, pleasure boats, special boats for the America's Cup races, sport boats and yachts— good boats, as good as any built in America."

I nodded, leaned back in my chair and closed my eyes. Harvey's hour had passed but he made no move to wind up our lunch or leave the table. Patiently, he waited a minute or two before he asked me whether I was asleep.

"Hardly."

"Thinking? I have to close my eyes to put something together."

"Yes. Oh, yes. Tell me, Harvey, did you ever do jigsaw puzzles? Fran and I love them, especially when we're on vacation. Not the kid puzzles, but puzzles where you have no complete picture to go by. You drive yourself crazy—and then, suddenly, you recognize the picture. It's always one small piece."

"And you found the piece?"

"The *L.R. Sweetheart.*"

"What on earth is the *L.R. Sweetheart?*"

"They call it that. Nobody thinks of Listerman-Reed, any more than they think Columbia Broadcasting System when they say CBS. The *L.R. Sweetheart* is a boat, a perfect beauty of a boat, thirty-seven-feet long, sleeps four, and can outrun a Coast Guard cutter. Manufactured by Listerman-Reed."

"Are you going to tell me how and why?" Harvey asked, his tongue hanging out, at least in a manner of speaking.

"You read it all in the papers—even in *The Wall Street Journal.* Friend of mine, Finelli by name, he calls the station house and tells me something has come up that he has to move on immediately. He needs at least four more detectives, plainclothes. I ask him why doesn't he find some uniforms and undress them, but he has some explanation about no time for that, and since one hand washes another I agree. Fortunately, my boss, Captain Courtny, wasn't there. Finelli is over on the West Side, not far. Four of us pile into a car, unmarked, and ten minutes later we meet Finelli and his boys at Seventy-eighth Street and Riverside Drive. The West Side marina is at Seventy-ninth, right down under the highway at the river edge. Finelli tells me that he was tipped on a boat tied up at the marina, a big boat called the *L.R. Sweetheart.* Finelli spaces us out on the various paths leading into the marina, paths that go under the express highway, and to make a long story short, we close in on the boat and pick up two guys and their bimbos, and one billion, two hundred million dollars' worth of cocaine. Twelve hundred million dollars, street value, one of the biggest drug collars in history."

"Wow!"

"You can say that again. Of course, it was Finelli's collar, so all we got was an assist and a small reflection of the glory; and myself, a good dressing down from Courtny, my captain."

"Why?"

"Because he's a miserable bastard, and couldn't see himself left out. Claimed I should have found him and consulted him. But that's beside the point. The point is that this was a Listerman-Reed boat, carrying cocaine that came from—oh, God forgive me, I will go to whatever hell is reserved for stupidity."

"You'll find a lot of friends there," Harvey said, "myself included. Of course, I read the story and never made a connection between *L.R.* and Listerman-Reed. You know about the cocaine."

"Yes, it came from Santa Marina."

"And apparently you should have remembered that yesterday or a week ago. A very strange man you've turned out to be, Lieutenant, an unusual cop or maybe not. I don't have much to do with the police. But I still haven't told you who owns Listerman-Reed."

"Listerman sold it?"

"That's right. Ten years ago, Stephan Listerman was seventy-four years old, in fairly good health, and still very much in love with his wife. At least, so people said. He had built a very special forty-foot boat, and he and his wife were going to cruise around in it and enjoy their twilight years. A nice thought. Two good, solid New Englanders, having lived a useful life, putting out to sea. So they made a deal and sold their company for forty-one million dollars. Not a bad price."

"And who bought it?"

"Ah," Harvey said, "don't you want to hear what happened to the Listermans?"

"I can guess. Not that I want to. How did it happen?"

"You can guess, can't you? Do you know, Lieutenant, I am sitting here in the Harvard Club in the heart of what I have always considered the most civilized city in the world,

163

and I'm beginning to be very much afraid. I don't like the feeling."

"Welcome to the club."

"My youngest child, little boy of six, had a puppy. It developed meningitis and we had to put it away. He was brokenhearted, and he said to me very accusingly, that it was easier to kill it than to fix it."

"Yes," I agreed. "It's a way to solve problems. What happened to the Listermans?"

"Their boat blew up—down in Florida. Their lawyer, a close friend, and their daughter were with them. No survivors."

"And it just happened," I said slowly, "that only the lawyer knew who the purchaser was."

"Yes, it just happened."

"And the money? The forty-one million dollars? It had to be drawn on something. It had to be paid—otherwise, the company would go to his heirs. Did he have heirs?"

"Two sons."

"When your outfit does research, they do it."

"That's how I earn my bread. No, there doesn't have to be a check or money. Whoever bought the company bought it with forty-one million dollars' worth of bearer bonds. United States government bonds. No way to trace them, and the bonds were on deposit in the vault of Listerman's bank."

"Back to square one. Is that what you are telling me? I don't believe it. Do you mean that a large company, a transaction of forty-one million dollars can take place and not be recorded?"

"Absolutely. The law doesn't require it."

"A whole different set of laws down there in Wall Street. A pharmacist must keep a record of every prescription he writes. We keep a record of every stolen article we repossess. But you lads can sell giant companies and keep no record at all."

"Really? Then how about the billion dollars' worth of cocaine? As I seem to remember, it disappeared. Quite a scandal."

"Something else entirely. Anyway, that was not the city cops. It was the feds who mislaid it. Come on, Harvey, we haven't been sitting here for two hours for you to tell me that you don't know who owns Listerman-Reed."

"Who owned the boat at the marina at Seventy-ninth Street?"

"No papers, nothing. The two bums who were running it claimed they picked it up secondhand in Santa Marina. No way to trace that, not in Santa Marina. But, Harvey, that wasn't my turf. I like to think that if it had fallen in our lap, we would have made more out of it. Maybe Finelli could have too, but his captain, a cretin by the name of Hallihan, just took his hide off for not calling in the feds and involving our precinct, and then Hallihan handed it over to the feds. This happened two years ago. A lot happens. You forget."

"I can understand that."

"What about tax returns. They have to file returns. They have to be signed."

"Not by the owner. The president of the company or the manager can sign—the owner doesn't have to appear."

"So that's it. You sat here for two hours in this goddamn Harvard Club, and from the beginning you knew damn well that you could answer my question."

He had the upper hand now. He grinned at me. I began not to like him as much as I had before.

"I answered your question. I told you who owns Wabash, which is what you asked me. And I never said I didn't know who owns Listerman-Reed. I don't lead people down the garden path. You never asked directly."

"What's the difference, Harvey? You're involved now. I'm sorry I had to drag you into it, but you're in it. All right—straight on: Who owns Listerman-Reed?"

"The funny thing is that the isolation and concealment of that ownership was nearly perfect. I got the answer from the son. When Listerman went off on that boat trip, he told his oldest son, Ernest, to go to his house and pick up a small suitcase he had forgotten. Now understand, no word of the buyer had passed Listerman's lips. His son had pressed him on that point, but Listerman said that he was not certain, and until he was certain, he did not want to discuss it. Evidently, the purchaser was certain that Listerman did not know who he was. The purchaser acted through his lawyer, as an agent with power of attorney. Now in some manner—the son doesn't know how—Listerman discovered who the purchaser was. Most likely, he knew someone who knew the lawyer who acted as agent, and possibly this is why Listerman was killed."

"No. This man clears his trail, always."

"Yes, perhaps. But when the son went for the suitcase, he saw a small notebook, leather-bound, in which his father made notations. He thought that his father might want it with him, and he dropped it into his pocket. Then when he delivered the suitcase, he got to talking with people who had come to the party on the yacht and forgot all about the notebook. When I spoke to the son in the course of our investigation of Wabash, he mentioned the notebook. I suggested that we go through it, which we did. I guess with all the grief and problems surrounding the death of his parents and his sister, he forgot all about the notebook. In any case, he considered it of no importance. The name of the purchaser was not vital to him."

"But you found it in the notebook," I said.

"That's right. No proof, Lieutenant, but a name that fits everything. Listerman dealt with the principal's lawyer, a rather shadowy fellow called Sienta—Marco Sienta. I say shadowy because as far as I could determine, Sienta has only one client. Evidently, Listerman came to the same conclusion, and the notation in his little reminder book, as near as I can remember, read like this: *Forty-one million—very decent price. Prefer to deal with the principal. It must be Porfetto.*"

"Give me that again, please, Harvey—slowly."

"Prefer to deal with the principal. It must be Porfetto."

"Porfetto. I know the name—damn it, where?" I slapped my hand against my head, and evidently that shuffled some tired brain cells. It came back to me. "Gave a swimming arena to Los Angeles for the Olympics."

"That's the boy. He wallows in good works. As a matter of fact, he's guest of honor at a big fund-raiser in support of the Olympic team. Our firm bought a table, one thousand dollars, seats ten. One of our partners won a bronze medal in the ancient days."

Pulling it out of my memory, "Alfred Gomez Porfetto. Has a wife with a silly name."

"Birdie May. Not a silly woman, no indeed."

"Who the hell is he, this Porfetto?"

"A most unusual man, does good works everywhere, friend of widows, orphans, and various organizations for cancer research and such. He has even set up a Porfetto foundation which seeks out worthy young folks who need college support. Horse breeder, sportsman. This, Harry, is extracurricular, not a part of my Wabash investigation except where it links up. I've heard a good deal about Alfred through the years. He's primarily a West Coast figure, very low profile. Avoids publicity when he can. We came across him years ago when we participated in a stock offering of a company that grew fruit, oranges, avocados, and peaches. Southern California. There was no substance, and the stockholders who had put up four million dollars found themselves with peeled fruit, so to speak. It wouldn't happen today, but at that time every Jack and Joseph was going public. We don't like to be involved in such things and we rooted around and discovered that Porfetto had sold the land to the fruit company for two million and that he picked up another million out of the stock deal. As I said, he's practically unknown here, but he has enormous land holdings in California. Sunland City with it's thirty thousand population is his. He owns the land, the stores, shopping centers, hotels, even the fire company. Only a drop in the bucket. He claims to have been born here in America. He owns one of the largest steel companies in Brazil. His English is faultless, but people who know Spanish told me he is not a Brazilian, not by any means, and that his Portuguese leaves a lot to be desired."

"Where do these friends of yours think he comes from?"

"Santa Marina."

"Bingo. We're well past the hour you offered me, Harvey."

"The hell with that. This is the first exciting thing that's happened to me in years."

I nodded and said, "All right, let's scratch away at it. Myself, I'm just a city cop, but my wife spends a good bit of her life denouncing injustice, and she even feels that the women of today can prevent the world from going down the sewer. One of the things that really sets her going is our intervention in Santa Marina, which she claims is ruled by as vicious a set of killers as ever existed. The word around, she tells me, is that the cocaine and banana business in Santa Marina is controlled by a single family, the same family that operates the death squads, and that a very important branch of that family operates here in the United States, very quietly, very effectively."

"We've talked about that at our research meetings. Porfetto's wealth runs into billions, and by the way, it's a common name in many places down there. But there's no way to track wealth today. You have numbered accounts in Switzerland, substitutes, washing machines, and of course a whole web of masked foreign interests. We heard that Porfetto sold eight hundred thousand acres of mahogany stand in Brazil. I can't imagine what the price was—bought by the government with money lent by New York banks—nor have I any notion of where the money went. Why did he want his own boat manufacturer? Obvious enough—if indeed he's connected with the drug trade."

"Why would he be? He has more money than God."

"That's true," Harvey agreed. "But the dozen or so families who own Santa Marina and run the death squads there base themselves on cocaine. Family loyalty is strong down there. We pour millions into Santa Marina and we've been pouring millions into the place, all based on the threat of a communist takeover. Well, part of it is tanks and guns, but untold millions have been poured into the place for food and medicine. Ask anyone who's been there whether they've ever seen a food or medical program backed by us."

"What are you telling me, Harvey? That this money has gone to Porfetto?"

"And the others. Where do you think his capital came from?"

"That could be, I suppose. Tell me, Harvey, you're a conservative, a Republican—right?" He nodded. "And you voted for Reagan?" He nodded again. "And you talk about our policies in Santa Marina exactly the way my wife does."

168

"Harry," he said slowly, "we're in the money business, and in the money business, you have to be purer than Caesar's wife. Every day, we buy and sell in the millions, not for ourselves but for others. A customer telephones and tells us to sell ten million dollars of whatnots at a dollar each. Then we owe him ten million dollars. No paper, no written order, not even the whatnots—nothing on either end but trust. We're not good guys, we're not bad guys, we're not for or against justice. We're in the business of making money, pure and simple. You can do it two ways—with integrity or as a bandit. We don't like the bandits. Porfetto took us, and we don't like that. And when you say that he's running a Santa Marina death squad in the United States—"

"I didn't say that."

"It's there, Harry. You've been pulling teeth for it these past two hours."

"Maybe yes, maybe no. For the moment, between ourselves. Yes?"

"Yes," he agreed.

Chapter 11

I USED THE TELEPHONE at the Harvard Club. Public telephones can be a damn nuisance. They're usually broken or occupied and they mostly share a lack of privacy. The telephones at the Harvard Club were both comfortable and private, and when Harvey had steered me to them, and had shaken my hand and pledged himself to ride by my side, if the need arose, I called Finelli and reminded him about the big cocaine bust.

"Don't remind me, Harry. I got medals up my ass. Would you believe it, not even a commendation?"

"Why?"

"Because Hallihan, that asshole captain of mine, said that I had broken the proper pattern of procedure. You ever hear of anything like that? He was stuffing his mouth in Foo Ling, that Chinese restaurant over on Broadway, and he claims I should have called him. How the hell did I know where he was, but he was burned up because the media didn't give him the play."

"Joe," I said, "is this wire naked or do you have extensions on it?"

"One line. Pure."

"Got a few minutes?"

"All you want," Finelli said. "Nothing but hookers and

170

transvestites. All of a sudden, we got transvestites, and this big six-foot boy tries to run and he breaks his ankle on the high heels. It's no lead-pipe cinch, walking around in a skirt and bra."

"Hallihan—is he there?"

"In his office, out of earshot."

"Now about that cocaine—"

"Harry, what in hell's your interest in the coke? That was two years ago."

"It's come out of the grave, believe me, Joe—"

"Hold on!" Finelli snapped. "You calling from the station house?"

"No. Outside."

"Your apartment?"

"No. Outside and as clean as the driven snow." Now it was my turn to ask what he was driving at.

"They put a tap on your phone—at the station house."

"Come on, Joe, that's crazy. Why in hell would they tap my desk at the house?"

"Damned if I know. But I saw Kenelly at a bar last night, and when I asked him what was new over there, he told me that this was going around. Who knows? Why?"

"The hell with that. Just go along with me and maybe we got a little personal noise to make. Now where'd you take that coke when you removed it from the boat?"

"Harry, I been through that a hundred times. You saw how it was packed—pound bags, plastic, fifty pounds in a wooden box. We made a checklist in triplicate right there on the boat and then we put it into our own panel truck. You saw it, I saw it, five other guys saw it and swore to it."

"Yeah. I left you there and went across town. You took the coke to the station house, right?"

"Right. I wanted to drive the stuff right down to the property clerk's room at Police Plaza, but the others said no, don't do it because Hallihan is such an asshole about procedure; he'll kick ass because we didn't check every bag at the station house and then call downtown and see if our cops wanted custody or whether the feds should have it. So we took it to our house and we stored it in the property room until the narcs could test it. They ran their tests, and by the time it was finished and we called downtown, the guys at Police Plaza said that it was late and the driver of the property truck had gone home and it wouldn't make any difference if we shipped the stuff down there tomorrow, but actually what they wanted was time to call the media and see themselves on TV. So we left the stuff overnight in our property room."

"Where is your property room? Downstairs behind the desk?"

"No, we ain't got your class. We use a big old closet that opens off the captain's office."

"And what happened next day, when the truck came from downtown?"

"The media came with them," Finelli said. "These days, everyone is in competition for the media. So we gave them the coke and they took it downtown."

"How? I mean what happened when you knew they were there for the coke?"

"Nothing. Hallihan opened one box, handed me a bag, and said try it. He said he wanted to know that none of those clowns downstairs had been tampering. I ain't got no equipment, I tell him, but he says take a little and that I'm no stranger to coke. It was coke. No doubt about that. So we tied up the bag, put it back, nailed down the box, and I yelled downstairs for the guys from downtown to come and pick them up. Now what the hell are you making of this, Harry?"

"I'll tell you, Joe. Put a few guys out in the neighborhood, very quiet, good guys you can trust, and see whether they can find a big buy on powdered sugar two years ago. It always comes in small boxes, so someone might just remember a real big buy."

"You got to be kidding."

"Maybe."

"Jesus God, do you know what you're putting to me?"

"You're an old, hard-nosed cop," I told Finelli. "If it's bullshit, put it in the bullshit basket and forget about it."

"What in hell's going on? They tap your phone, they try to kill you on the highway—what in hell is going on, Harry, and how does it connect up with the coke?"

172

"I don't know—yet."

"It's two years."

"So it's cold and you forget about it. It's just a thought."

I put down the telephone and left the Harvard Club. Nice lunch, I said to myself. It would be nice to be able to drop into a place like this every time the mood took you. It would be even nicer to come out of there and not have to say to yourself that maybe it's the last time. I walked uptown. I mentioned before that a police lieutenant doesn't walk. He rides; wherever he's going, he has to get there quickly. I'd walked more these few days than in three months past. At 59th Street, I swung west, and at Central Park West and 72nd Street, I went into the old Dakota and rang the bell at Dr. Jacob Miller's apartment.

Dr. Jake, as my kids called him, had lived in the Dakota forever or anyway before all the movies were made about the apartment house and before the apartments cost a million dollars each. We found him when Fran became pregnant with Gavin, and he has been the family doctor ever since. He is the only physician left in the city of New York who still makes house calls and who doesn't take Wednesday off to play golf. There were only two patients in his waiting room, and when the nurse told him I was there, he managed to see me only thirty minutes later.

Jake was a small man, very small, white-haired and equipped with the last pair of rimless spectacles extant. He studied me carefully, motioned to a chair, and said, *"Nu,* Herschel, how is the crime business?"

"To paraphrase Abraham Lincoln, God must love criminals, he made so many of them."

"Possibly. All our notions of God are open to revision, like everything else. What hurts?"

"Nothing, thank God. This is no time for me to be sick. I come to you for enlightenment. Can you give me ten minutes?"

"Sarah, Gavin, and your wonderful redheaded wife?"

"All good. Fine. I don't want to waste your time, Jake." And then, I went on to tell him, as concisely as I could, the circumstances of the deaths of Stanley Curtis and Asher Alan.

When I finished, he said, "So what are you asking me, Herschel?"

"I think they were murdered."

"Oh?"

"Could it be?"

"Herschel," he said gently, the only one aside from my mother who called me Herschel, "sure it could be. We live in a time of great killing. Perhaps it has always been that way, but communications were not very good. We only knew what happened close to us. Ah, enough of my drugstore philosophy. Instead we'll go to the drugstore and talk about pargyline. Pargyline—" He spread his hands. "Why pargyline? There are a dozen prescription drugs where a double or triple dosage taken for a week will kill. I don't think it was anything they ate in the restaurant. Maybe just salt, and that was the straw that did it. Restaurants load their food with salt. Maybe a double dose of pargyline. But there are so many miraculous, important prescription drugs that given a double dose can cause stroke. Nobody questions the doctor. Thank God most doctors are decent people. Could you ever convict a doctor who said it was a mistake?"

"But both in restaurants?"

"A coincidence. You know, a lot of people die in restaurants, too much rich food, too much salt, too much drinking —and then all of a sudden, a heart attack. Once I went on a cruise with Elsie. We were going to have a quiet beautiful vacation. Never again. Every other night, after a huge dinner, at eleven o'clock, they served a buffet, corn beef, ham, smoked salmon, caviar, smoked turkey, pilaf, herring, all these delicious salty things. Every night the passengers stuffed themselves and washed it down with beer or wine, and every other night or so, I was awakened at least once to help the young ship's doctor with one or two heart attacks. So you see, guns like that nasty one in your belt are not the only lethal things."

Nevertheless, guns are lethal. I was on foot and alone and untracked in the belly of a great city, and I felt good because there was no way they could know where Fran was or where I was. I was so relaxed that my brain stopped working and it never occurred to me that they knew sooner or later I'd

174

come back to the station house, and that if they put a few men on the cross streets and on the avenues leading there, they'd have me. Also, for the first time, I began to realize that I was not the kingpin of what was going on, but had simply stepped into the middle of work in progress. As far as they were concerned, Fran and I were simply nuisances that had to be eliminated. But that idea was only beginning to dawn on me. What happened three blocks from the precinct house was the first edge of the dawning.

It was not the kind of hit-and-run that the mob engages in; it was paced, cool and deliberate. I was walking east, three blocks from the station house, when at the other end of the street a man stepped out of the doorway of a fairly posh apartment house, spun toward me and raised what looked like a very heavy automatic, a Mauser or some such gun. I didn't have time to observe the gun. A number of things were happening simultaneously, and as they say, I went with the action. When the man appeared, the first moment of his appearance, something triggered my warning system. He was a good shot, an incredible shot, and in spite of the fact that I leapt aside, that first shot took a tiny bit of skin from my earlobe. I was down on my knees as he got off his second shot, and it went over my head. At the same moment, a private school, located on my side of the street and between the shooter and myself, erupted, pouring nine- and ten-year-old boys and girls into the street, who saw the man with the gun and who began to scream. The last thing in the world that I desired at that moment was to pull out my own gun and shoot back. On target, I'm the best shot at the precinct, but still I might hit one of the kids. A long shot, and kids running every way. It was just no good. I crouched and ran for the corner. No more shots. I swung around the corner, pulled up against the avenue side of the corner building, drew my gun and gripped it with both hands. I was about four feet from the corner of the building. He would come on this side or across the street: either way, I'd have no more than a fraction of a second lead before he saw me, either my first shot or his.

The next hundred seconds or so were interesting, but I would not want to live through them again. He didn't come.

Instead, after two minutes or so, I heard the sound of our patrol cars. It was an absolutely beautiful response. We can do it when we have to.

Toomey got out the first-aid box and patched up my ear-lobe. "It's bleeding, but it's just a nick. You don't want to go to the hospital, do you?"

"Good God, no."

"Well, it ruined your jacket, Lieutenant. Scars of the wars, but what makes me feel good is the fact that the bad guy missed you. Who was trying to ice you?"

I shook my head hopelessly.

"He's going to ask you," nodding at the captain's office, and at that moment Courtny opened his door and yelled, "Golding, get your ass in here!"

"Sweets for the sweet," Toomey muttered.

I marched into Courtny's office. He didn't ask me to sit down. Instead, with a note of utter disgust, he said, "What happened to your ear?"

"A guy with one of those big old automatic pistols, the kind that can stop a tank, took two shots at me. One nipped my ear."

"I know that much. What am I, a spectator here? God damn it, Golding, it's time you learned that I run this place."

"So they tell me."

"Now what the hell does that mean?"

"A stupid remark. It doesn't mean a damn thing. If I am talking strange, it's because for the past week people have been trying to kill me."

"What was this creep who took a shot at you? A mugger, a mob guy, or what?"

"A hired pro. Maybe Percy Lax."

"Come on, how do you know that?"

"Because I been in this business seventeen years. Who else carries cannons? And I hear Lax is our local tourist."

"What did you get off?"

I studied him for a while before I answered this one. Something had happened to Courtny, and it was part of the growing realization that had begun with the hit man's attempt to kill me. It started very slowly, with just a little

176

blossom of comprehension that was much more doubt than understanding. Until that moment, it made very little sense that they should go to such efforts to kill me. I didn't have anything like that kind of exalted opinion of myself. I was pretty much the run-of-the-mill cop who distinguishes himself by pushing for promotion because his family can't get by on what he makes. Not worth great effort to eliminate me. But now I began to realize that they had their own large reason, which I had only begun to smell, and with the smell came this difference in Courtny.

I was not crazy about Courtny, but no one was. He was crude, nasty, and reeked with the smell of the cigars he smoked, maybe twenty a day. He was never without one. Nevertheless, we had worked together pretty well for the six years he had been captain at the precinct. He had a reputation for being a very good, hard-nosed street cop who in his time had worked in Manhattan South, Fort Apache in the Bronx, and out in the Bedford-Stuyvesant area as well as other Brooklyn spots where with small effort one could get mugged or killed, yet it had been hard for him to make promotion. There was a rumor around for a while that he was being talked about for chief of detectives, but after Koch and the commissioner spent a couple of hours with him, they sent him back to the precinct post haste; but of course that was only a rumor.

Right now, he had changed. He hated my guts. And when he asked me what did I get off, it meant how many shots had I fired at this gunman, as a brave cop should. I was number one marksman in the precinct—as a matter of fact in the whole zone. Why didn't you shoot him, Harry?

"Not a shot, Captain. You see, at the moment he lined up his first shot, the one that got my ear, about two-dozen kids bolted out of a private school on that block and into the street. I don't toss bullets into a street where there are people or kids."

"But he did. I hear he took a second shot."

"He shot high, thank God. That cannon of his is an instrument of slaughter."

He picked a fat folder up off his desk and said to me, "You see this, Golding? This is your record. Seventeen years on

177

the force and you never fired your gun, never took out one of those bums out there on the street—always with an excuse not to use your gun. What is it with you and a gun? You got shit in your blood?"

"Yeah," I said in disgust. "Maybe we share a syndrome, Captain. I'll tell you something else for that folder—when those kids piled into the street, I ran. If the Olympic Committee could have clocked my speed from there to the corner, I'd be on my way to Los Angeles, in spite of my age. I don't know whether I would have run if the street had remained clean, but maybe I would have. I'm not Marshal Dillon out there in Dodge City, shooting it out with some lunatic who decided to make killing his profession and who took out a contract on Harry Golding. To hell with that! That's not what I'm paid for."

"Then what are you paid for—being an egghead, taking your wife to Los Angeles? Let's talk about taking your wife to Los Angeles on police work, after the song and dance you gave me."

"Is that what you're sore at?" I asked, incredulous. "Because I took my wife to Los Angeles? It didn't cost the department one damn bloody cent, and you damn well know that!" I had raised my voice. Thin partitions and glass panels separated Courtny's office from the detective room, and every one of the men in there was listening. "I went on police work! Don't ever forget that! And it might just end with the biggest bust you ever dreamed of."

"Get the hell out of here," Courtny said. "And change your jacket. You look like shit."

"All right. I'll go home and change, but I want Toomey and two other men with me."

"Why? Are you picking up a suit of armor? Nothing doing."

I turned from leaving to face him and said coldly, "I'm the chief of the squad, Courtny, and I'm carrying out police work according to my best judgment. There's witness outside"—pointing to the detectives—"to that effect. If my going there alone should result in my death"—I dropped my voice—"you might just whisper good-bye to your pension, maybe to the department too," I added.

He faced me out for a moment; then he muttered, "Go ahead. I don't give a fuck what you do because you won't be doing it very long. You want to be an asshole, be an asshole."

I left his office and asked Toomey who would be available for a half hour, and he grabbed two detectives to go with us. I asked Toomey whether my car was still outside.

"Double-parked. You been cussed out by everyone in the place, including me."

"Why you?"

"I got to move it four times a day."

"Why don't you curb-park it?"

"There ain't been curb-parking around this precinct for years. You know that." He handed me my keys. "You drive."

"I'm going to my apartment to pick up a fresh suit, but I don't think it would make any sense to any of you that I need four men to pick up a clean suit."

"That's all right, Lieutenant," Bolansky said, sitting next to Keene in the backseat. "You don't have to explain. It's a beautiful day. I'm happy to get out of the pisspot station."

"The point is, I don't want you to think I'm crazy. This is goddamn serious."

"Oh, Christ," Toomey said. "Don't go on like that, Harry. We don't think you're crazy. You been acting mighty peculiar, but nobody thinks you're crazy, not after all that wiretapping stuff in the basement. Of course, why they tap you—that's another matter."

"Shut up," I told Toomey.

"Sure."

"I said I'm dead serious, and I am. Two things: First, my apartment is bugged, every inch of it."

"So why don't you send Tony Cabreni over there?" Cabreni was the best man we had on bugs, in or out.

"They'd only bug it again. I'd rather leave it alone and use the bugs. Bolansky," I said remembering, "get out before we take off and check under the car for trail bugs." And then, when Bolansky came back to report that there were no trail bugs under the car, I told them, "The second thing is that over at my apartment there will be two or maybe three men

179

waiting to kill me, and one of them uses something like a World War Two Luger, one of those big things that can stop a tank."

"You're kidding."

"Like hell I am!" I snapped.

There was silence for a long moment as they stared at me, and then Toomey said, "I'm going inside to get a couple of shotguns. You say there're armed men in there—I don't go busting in with a pistol in my hand, like some dumb hot-dog kid who's watched too much TV and wants to be a hero."

The reference was to Keene, who was sitting in the backseat with Bolansky. He had done it once, with two armed men in the room, kicking down the door and all the rest. He took it nicely. "I'll take one of the shotguns," he said.

"You know, it's my apartment," I said, "full of things Fran and I cherish. So if we take shotguns—ah, the hell with it," I finished. "Get three, Toomey. I don't want one. What do I say to Fran if I bust up her whatnot chest?"

"What's a whatnot chest, Lieutenant?" Bolansky asked.

Toomey came back with the guns, and he said that he wouldn't be surprised if Courtny had a stroke, the way he was letting go of everything around him.

"Ah, well, poor man," I said, "he carries a heavy burden."

"We carry the burden," Toomey said.

We double-parked, and then we moved into the house quickly, our guns out and ready, and a couple of people who noticed us almost fainted. "Police," I said. "Please move on." A silly thing to say, but on the other hand, I felt very silly.

In the elevator, I told them shortly that I would turn the bolt with my key. I could do that almost silently. I would fling open the door and dive in, flat on the floor, and Toomey and Keene would cover me, one each side, and Bolansky in the doorway. The elevator stopped and we stepped into the hall.

"You let me take that dive," Toomey whispered. "I'm younger than you, and I used to play football."

"You can't take a dive with a shotgun." I felt that I was spelling out a pattern of lunacy, and I was still amazed that these nice old friends didn't flip me into a straightjacket and run me right down to Bellevue. It was indeed a tribute to their trust in Harry Golding who had given them this incredible song and dance about men in his bugged apartment waiting to shoot him. Also, ever since television took over the human race cops have become increasingly self-conscious, hooked on the cop shows on TV and always wondering whether there isn't a camera right over their shoulders.

Anyway, we went through all the motions. I flung the door open, dove in from a crouch to flat on my belly and lost my grip on my gun, which sailed across the room. Toomey and Keene charged after me, just like in the movies, and Bolansky crouched in the doorway, his shotgun at ready, and of course the place was empty. The only plus for the good guys was that we had not kicked down the door. We advanced from room to room, a careful and brave selection of New York's finest, and they were all empty. Then we returned to the living room and they all looked at me, and perhaps because cops do have compassion, no one said anything.

I was saved from being hustled to the nearest shrink by a cigarette. It had been crumpled into an ashtray, but it was still smoldering, a thin line of smoke rising from it, and I pointed to it before they had a chance to say anything, and then I pointed to other things, a brown bag on the coffee table with half of a corned beef sandwich sitting next to it, a container of coffee that was still warm when I poked my finger into it. Toomey picked up the cigarette, put it back, and then went to the coffee table and put his finger into the container of coffee.

"They could have been on the stairs when we were in the elevator," Keene said.

"Maybe not quite that close." Toomey started to speak again when I put my finger across my lips. He understood and nodded.

"You want any of this stuff for evidence?" he asked.

"Evidence of what? The hell with it! I'll go into the bedroom and pick up a few things. I won't be more than five minutes. You fellers make yourselves comfortable." I touched my lips to remind them of the bugs. "Talk about literature. It's enlightening."

In my bedroom, I stripped down, got rid of the dried blood on my neck and shoulder, substituted a small flesh-colored Band-Aid for the large one that Toomey had applied, and put on fresh clothes. I packed a small suitcase with some extra shirts and a robe and slippers, simply to make life in a hotel suite a bit more comfortable and then paused at the open closet to stare at my uniform, something that I wore only for parades and funerals. I can't define the run of thought that impelled me to pack the uniform. It's possible that, as I folded it carefully into the suitcase, I had some vague notion of what I intended for it—but the notion, if there, was very vague indeed.

I finished packing, joined the others in the living room and led them silently out of the apartment. Even in the car, I couldn't get over the feeling of someone listening, and I turned on the radio, finding some music to blur our speech. I parked on Third Avenue.

"We can talk here," I said.

"Oh, Lord," Keene said. He was a good-looking black man, and it was only after being shaken that he lapsed into broad southern. "I sure enough don't want to break into any junkie or some other bum's apartment ever again. I do hate that. It just gives me a bad stomach for days."

I said to Toomey, "When I was having my ass burned by Courtny for telling him that I wanted three more men to come to my apartment, who was in the detective room?"

"Us."

"You and Keene and Bolansky?"

"That's right."

"I thought I saw Hennesy there."

"He was there. But then he went downstairs to bum a butt. We don't smoke."

"That's right," Keene said.

"Could you hear what we were saying in Courtny's office?"

"Come on," Toomey said. "You know you can."

"You know what I'm driving at?"

"What am I?" Toomey demanded. "Some kind of moron?

Of course I know." And pointing toward the backseat, "And they know too. It might be a hell of a lot better if we had some idea of what's going down here."

"What else is new?" I said. "Look, you heard Courtny make that smartass crack about a suit of armor. Was Hennesy in the room then?"

"How about it?" Toomey asked Keene.

"No."

"Bolansky?" I asked. "Do you recall?"

"No, because, you know, Lieutenant, he made some crack about being sick of hearing Courtny's crap, and then he got up and said he was going downstairs to bum a butt off someone."

"I'm pushing because it's important," I said. "We got to know whether Hennesy was there or not, because if he wasn't . . ." I let it go.

"He wasn't," Toomey said, "but it still could have been some kind of coincidence, Lieutenant."

"No! I am sick to death of trying to explain this thing with coincidence. Coincidence doesn't follow you around trying to kill you. They had a shot at it this afternoon, and they were waiting there in the apartment. You know that. You saw the cigarette, the food, and when we left the station house, our own sweet Captain Courtny picked up the telephone and called my apartment and told them that four cops with a lot of nasty firepower were on their way over and they were to get the hell out of there before we arrived. Now if any of you see it any other way, tell me!"

"Trouble is," Keene said, "that none of us seems to know what's going on here, maybe not even you, Lieutenant. How about that?"

"If what you say is true, Lieutenant, then Courtny's in this neck-deep. So what do we do?"

"I'll be damned if I know."

"What do you want us to do?" Keene asked.

It was getting dark now. Fran would be back at the hotel. A sudden wave of fear shook me. What if something had happened to her?

"Nothing. Play it cool. Let's see what happens tomorrow."

"You shouldn't be alone," Toomey said.

"I'm not. Fran is with me."

"You won't go back to the apartment?"

"No."

"The station house?"

"I'll be there in the morning."

"How can we get in touch?"

"You can't. I'll call in first thing in the morning."

I picked up a cab there on Third Avenue. I was fairly sure that we weren't being followed, and I had him drop me at Lexington and 34th Street. All my years in the police department, I had been at the other end of the stick. I had tailed people, instructed others to tail people, and had on two occasions led seminars in my squad on the art of tailing. And it is an art, believe me. But now, for the first time, I was being tailed. That had never happened to me before, and it called for a whole new set of reflexes and observations that would lead to a decision as to whether I was being followed or not. This time, no tail.

I walked to the hotel, nighttime now, about seven o'clock in the evening, and when I entered our suite, I was almost certain that Fran would be there.

She wasn't. I felt a rush of fear, a sense of something clenching my heart and with it a feeling of total despair.

Then the door opened and Fran walked in. I didn't say anything; I simply held her in my arms.

Chapter 12

WE HAD DINNER that night in the small dining room of the Primrose Hotel. It was a great relief not to have to go out into the street, but to be able to hole up here where at least for the moment we were safe. I asked the waiter to put us in a corner, where we could talk softly and not be overheard. It was very pleasant indeed, almost like a dinner date of long, long ago, and at least for the moment, with the children secure in Dublin, we could relax and even smile a bit. I had asked Fran what her day was like, but she only said that she had spent ten hours in the New York Public Library and had returned with a bundle.

"You first," she said. "Your day and then my day. Anyway, I have notes. You don't have notes."

"No notes, but one hell of a day. I look back and I can't believe it. It's eight-thirty now, so that was less than twelve hours ago—when we said good-bye this morning."

"Poor dear," Fran said. "Let's order first."

A good woman is always practical. We ordered our food, and then I told Fran what had happened since we parted in the morning. She listened intensely, her lips parted. The food came, quite good, yet I had to remind her, "You're not eating, Fran."

"Heavens to betsy, you want me to eat and listen to this?"

"Yes."

"All right, I'll eat," she said meekly.

I went through the day, blow by blow. When we came to the coffee, she had it all. "Harry," she said hopelessly, "I don't understand."

"Join the club. But does it match up with your day, even around the edges?"

"I think so, around the edges perhaps. But where does Courtny fit in?"

"I've been working with that. First I thought Courtny was just a miserable old bastard getting more miserable as he aged. No. I am convinced that he's in this, neck-deep. I told you how I kept after the guys to establish that Hennesy was not there, and then walking over to the hotel tonight, I was able to get it into focus, and I remembered seeing Hennesy leave. So it was Courtny who called the apartment and got them out."

"You look nice. I always felt that a man can't dress better than to wear a blue blazer over gray trousers. But you took another suit?"

"The brown one."

"Yes. That's nice. But didn't I see your uniform?"

"Yes, you did."

"Why? Having a parade?"

"Clever. No." I hesitated. "I had a notion—"

"Tell me."

"Later."

"Get back to Courtny. How does it connect? The cocaine?"

"I think so. That's just a wild guess, but he's an old pal of Jake Hallihan over at the West Side, and Finelli thinks it's not too crazy to figure that Hallihan made the switch with the coke. You know, we live in a peculiar society. The people who run this country have a notion that you can stop something people want by making it illegal. That's what they did with the Volstead Act, and it was Prohibition that turned petty larceny and bank heisting into organized crime. If you're going to run whiskey, that requires organization. If you're going to brew beer and distribute it, that also requires organization. The feds try to cover themselves by saying that it's the Mafia and that the mob came here from Italy. Baloney. We created the mob, right here, with that crazy Prohibition. There never was anything like it before Prohibition. Then when Prohibition was repealed, the mob was organized and they turned to prostitution and heroin. The dope required international connections, so the mob became a little more organized. But heroin is limited. You can make junkies out of thousands of poor kids who don't know any better, but they can only feed a habit by stealing, and that makes an uncertain and limited market. The mob needed something else, a drug that could base itself on the middle class and the upper class, a drug that didn't frighten them and a drug that didn't leave hen tracks all over the doper's arm."

"Cocaine," Fran said.

"Absolutely. The caviar on the mob's table. A drug whose horrors revealed themselves slowly, an in-drug, fashionable, smart, sniffed at parties by the best people, a real fancy upper-class drug, the dope dealer's dream. And it's big. Fran, it is the biggest illegal that ever hit this earth, billions and billions of dollars."

"That makes sense. Hallihan switched the coke, and you think Courtny was in it with him?"

"Why not? Two of the most important precincts in the city, if not in the country. I think we have the best and most honest police force in the world, but cops are human and they can be bought. And if you're buying a cop, why not a precinct captain? Buy the best."

She nodded. "I'm even more scared now."

"But it has to be connected. Can you connect it after today? Did you find it?"

"I think so." She stared at me thoughtfully. "You know, Harry, after what happened today, I don't think they're going to try to kill us anymore."

"Baby, I wish I felt that way. Why not?"

"Because too many people know. Toomey and the other two, and their wives and certain other relatives too, and cop pals of Toomey and Keene and Bolansky—"

"They promised not to talk."

"Harry."

"Fran, I'm not arguing. I am sick to death of being a target. I hope you're right. But if they don't kill me, what then?"

She shook her head, her eyes filling with tears. "I don't know, but they'll find a way to crucify you. We're making too many waves."

I signed the check and we went up to our rooms. There was fresh ice in the tiny sitting room, and Fran poured two glasses of Lillet, and I fell into a chair and sipped my drink while Fran assembled her notes in the table.

"I picked 1974 as a beginning point. I felt that farther back than that, I couldn't handle. Also, 1974 was the year Eric Bellamy was killed. First, manner of death: Speeding car, hit-and-run. It rings a bell, doesn't it. Now to connect: Eric Bellamy was CIA. He left, fed up and disgusted, and wrote a book. Did I mention that he lived in Cleveland? The book was titled: *Kill Me, I Love It.* Now listen, no card on file for the book in the library, no copy. But I found a review, small one, in *The New York Review of Books.* Bellamy's thesis was that the money we were pouring into Santa Marina, ostensibly to help the crazy generals down there fight a 'Marxist rebellion' and to feed the hungry, actually went in two directions. One to buttress and develop their cocaine industry, and two to enrich the family that practically owned Santa Marina. Bellamy claimed he had proof that this family collected at least thirty million a year out of the funds Congress voted Santa Marina. The main residence of the family was here in the United States, and their home country of Santa Marina was used as a source of wealth, since in addition to the money I mentioned, they did a thriving business amounting to millions a year, selling the military supplies we shipped down there to the Middle East, the PLO and Iraq being their main customers. On the basis of this capitalization, the family had become the most powerful privately owned business entity in this country and had also imported the death-squad method of dealing with their enemies."

"Well, the name?"

"Ah. Sit back, Harry. Mrs. Murphy's daughter is no fool,

188

and I decided, when the name did not appear in the review, that the editor had decided that the book was absolutely actionable, and that his paper was not rich enough to print the name and stand the libel suit."

"So you called *The New York Review?*"

"Right from the library, Harry. Any chance they still had the book? No way. Did they have the original copy of the review? No way. Would anyone there remember? Ten years —no way."

"No other reviews?"

"They must have stopped every one—except this. Overlooked it, I suppose."

"And you asked a librarian why no book?"

"I did."

"And?"

"She suggested that I call the Library of Congress, that they must have it. So I got a purse full of quarters and I called the Library of Congress. No book."

"I kind of admire that. That is control."

"Footnote. About a week after he was killed, Bellamy's house burned down, wife and daughter dead in the burning house. Firemen thought it might have been torched but they weren't sure. But—no man is an island unto himself."

"I'm listening."

"In 1976, Stanley Curtis charged, in a speech he made at Berkeley, that three members of Congress were in the pay of Alfred Porfetto. He didn't repeat the charge and nothing was made of it—which is curiouser and curiouser, and even curiouser when a year later Stanley Curtis came up with the racing yacht, *John Paul Jones,* in which he began to train a crew for the America's Cup trials. He was very mysterious about his backers, except to say they were old-money Newport. He eschewed publicity about the million-dollar yacht, yet it was known that it had been built by Listerman-Reed. Of course, that didn't connect until you told me about your lunch at the Harvard Club. Now it connects."

"Good girl."

"Don't thank me. I spent the day in a tunnel of death. The world will never be the same to me after this. He had a secretary, name of Thelma Goode, thirty or so, good-looking, maybe they had something going between them. She drove her car into a tree up in Connecticut. What were they doing, Harry, teaching her a lesson?"

I said nothing. She blinked, shook her head, and said, "Let's go on. We have a United States senator, Peter Lomast by name, and after he was elected, it came out that Porfetto had put up most of the money for his campaign. Laws broken, scandal, some unsavory hints about Porfetto. All of it blown away, and ever since, Mr. Lomast has been the lead Republican hound dog denouncing the Santa Marina rebels.

"A story in the *Times* referred to an article in *The Nation*. They had some young fellow with more guts than caution who went down to Santa Marina to cover the recent election. He found out that if you don't vote, you are listed and become a prime candidate for the death squads. During election time, the death squads were run by a degraded creature, name of Primo Porfetto. He asked whether Primo was related to Porfetto. Denied it."

"Did you read the *Nation* article?"

"I did. Porfetto here denied it as well."

"What happened to the kid on *The Nation?*"

"Nothing. But then, he was publicly connected, as a reporter, and well squelched. He became a correspondent in France, sends an occasional story to *The Nation*, and is paid almost nothing. But he seems to get along. At least, that's what they tell me there. Then I looked up Porfetto in *Current Biography*. He was born in the U.S.A. We both took it for granted that he was born in Santa Marina. Well, Santa Marina has a consulate here, a little office, I would imagine, in an office building practically across the street from the library. I telephoned there and asked about the Porfetto family. They said nastily that they didn't give out such information. Then I switched to Spanish, told them my name was Betty Lou Jamison, that I was one of the president's very important secretaries, that he had decided to give the Medal of Freedom to Mr. Porfetto and had instructed me to call for background information. I said that if there was any concern on their part, they could call the White House and confirm me."

"You're kidding," I gasped, beginning to laugh for the

first time in a long while. "You're wonderful. Medal of Freedom. Oh, God, it's so absolutely appropriate."

"That's what they thought. Call back to the White House? That would be an insult to the great President of a great country. Oh, Harry, stupidity and wickedness seem to go together. I said that the President wondered, since Porfetto was born in the United States, whether he actually maintained any family connections in Santa Marina. He would like to link your brave and steadfast country to the Medal Of Freedom. It doesn't sound so hokey in Spanish, Harry. But of course, of course, a Porfetto's heart is always in Santa Marina, wherever his body is. Also, not so schmaltzy in Spanish. Long ago, in the 1920s, when the rather unbelievable Warren G. Harding was President of the United States, Porfetto's father came to this country at the invitation of President Harding himself, after President Harding had sent a brigade of marines to Santa Marina to fight off the Bolshevik menace. That was before it became a communist menace and then a Marxist menace. President Harding felt that the presence of one of the leading families of Santa Marina in the U.S. would assure the children of America a constant supply of healthful fruit, mostly bananas. So does joy and gladness enter our hearth and home."

"Medal of Freedom—and it feels perfectly natural. Why not? Every stinking dictator, capo, mass murderer on earth is on our payroll. Why not drape them all in medals of freedom? You know, what it amounts to is that we're handing Porfetto enough money to eventually buy this whole country. And how many has he murdered that we know? Curtis, Thelma Goode, Asher Alan, Sanchez, Fitzpatrick, Oshun, Bert Smith, Ellis Wabash, his wife, Listerman, his wife, his daughter, his lawyer—"

"Listerman?"

"I told you about them downstairs—and those only begin the list. This, Fran, is a death squad. This is what it means to live in Santa Marina and make one little bleat of protest. We're a big country, but it's only begun, and Wabash is their damned legal private army of killers. And nobody says one word. Everything is either an accident, a coincidence, a mob

191

rubout—and did I leave out that congressman hit by a piece of stone from a building here?"

"Harry, take it easy," she begged me. "Cool down. Let's talk about this quietly and sanely."

"You know they'll find us," I said. "Another day, another two days—"

"No," she said, quietly and coldly, "they will not find us and they will not kill us. You men have made a monster out of this world, and always it's the same. You take the children we have given life, and you murder them, with your wars and your death squads and your dirty little fascist-pig dictators. That has to stop, Harry. I am no candidate for sacrifice and neither are you."

"Yes," I agreed. "It has to stop." There was no way to argue with her, but what would stop it was beyond my imagining.

"Shall we get back to Porfetto?"

I nodded.

"The good man's a benefactor. Throws money everywhere. He has just given a new wing to the museum. It is to be called the Mayan Wing, as the *Times* put it, to be directed toward better understanding of the people south of the border. There was an art critic who wrote for *Leonardo,* a small and very esoteric art magazine. I went through half a dozen copies in the library, and this art critic, whose name was Felix Sandly, was outraged that the museum would accept a gift from what he called 'the butchers Porfetto.' I suppose he knew something, and I imagine that if we were to investigate it, we would find that Sandly had been to Santa Marina, or something of that sort."

"Of course, the poor bastard's dead," I said bitterly.

"Died of a stroke. The magazine in which he defied the powers that be was bought and folded. It was losing money anyway."

"Is that it?"

"More or less. Harry, I had to call Oscar with a question today. Don't worry," she said, seeing the look on my face. "I didn't tell him where I was calling from. But do you know what he told me? Deborah is back in New York, Deborah Alan. Oh, Harry, I want so much to see her."

192

"No. That's out. Why is she here?"

"Some mission for the Foreign Office in Israel."

"Fran, you can't even think of seeing her. You can't. It's too dangerous. They must have Oscar's house staked out and watched constantly, and they probably have his phone tapped as well. I'm so tired," I said. "It's been a grim, awful day. Let's go to bed."

Suddenly, she began to cry. "I've been so busy," she said through the tears, "showing how clever I've been all day, and I never stopped to give some thought to what happened to you."

"Nothing happened to me."

In bed, she clutched me and whispered, "Please, please be careful, Harry. What would I do if something happened to you?"

"You know, Fran, danger increases the sex drive."

"Harry."

"It's a well-known fact."

"It is not. The reverse is true. Danger dries up the sex drive and makes people impotent."

"Look at the James Bond movies," I reminded her.

"You're not a bit like James Bond, Harry. You're shorter. You're getting bald. You have a nice little belly and you never shoot anyone. But, you know, you do make love better."

That was nice. It made up for other things.

Chapter 13

IT WAS RAINING in the morning, a bleak, cloudy March day, the kind of a day where the brief promise of spring slips back under the edge of winter. You want security on such a day. You want to be inside where there are lights and warmth and people.

"Not the worst day in the world to curl up and read."

"Harry, I have nothing to read," Fran said.

"You could watch television."

"Daytime television. Have you ever tried to watch daytime television?"

"Sure. Last year, when I had the flu. It's like taking a sleeping pill. You doze off and time passes. The point is, Fran, that I want you to spend the day here. I don't want you to leave these rooms. It's only one day, and that's not too terrible."

"It is too terrible. The way I feel, I'll simply go out of my mind. I don't mind the rain, Harry. If I could just take a walk—"

"Please."

"All right. I won't argue. I love you and trust you, Harry. Don't let anything terrible happen."

We had slept late and I was already late for the station house. I called and asked for Toomey. Tracing a call in New

York is much harder than the movies make it out to be, and there was no reason for me to imagine that anyone at the station would try to trace a call from me. When Toomey answered, the first sound of his voice told me that if it had been bad before, it was worse now.

"Lieutenant, where are you? I've been trying to find you."

"What happened?"

"I know you and Finelli are old friends—"

"The hell with that! What happened to him?"

"He was shot."

"All right, tell me."

"About an hour ago. I guess he was coming here to talk to you. He parks across the street, and as he gets out of his car, a car rolls up and puts three slugs into him, heavy stuff, forty-fives, and then takes off and we don't even have the license plate."

"Sure. That's great, right in front of the goddamn police station. Is he alive?"

"He's alive, but he's hurt bad," Toomey said. "He's over here at Lenox Hill. We're lucky the hospital's so close."

"Toomey, you put a uniform over there outside his room, and do it right now."

"Courtny—"

"To hell with Courtny! Go downstairs and let them arrange it. Courtny doesn't have to know. I'll go straight to the hospital. Suppose you meet me there, say fifteen minutes."

I put down the phone, and turned to Fran. "Joe Finelli," I said. "They shot him."

"But he's not dead. I heard you mention the hospital."

"He's badly hurt. The way Toomey talked, it doesn't seem that he has much chance. Frannie, darling, please stay here."

"Okay, I'm here."

She hugged me again, and then I left.

Toomey and the uniformed officer were already at Lenox Hill Hospital when I got there, and there were two of Finelli's squad and Paula and Finelli's daughter, a sweet-looking kid of fourteen or so, and Finelli's mother, a little old woman in black who sat on a bench in the hallway, hunched over and weeping quietly. When Paula saw me, she threw her arms around me, crying and begging me to tell them not to let Finelli die.

"It's going to be all right," I lied. "You don't kill Joe Finelli with a couple of bullets."

She pulled me over to Finelli's mother and said, "Mama, this is Joey's friend, Lieutenant Golding. He says Joey ain't going to die. That's what he says, Mama."

"You love Joey," the old lady said to me. "He's a good boy." Her words came faintly through her sobs. "Nobody has such a good boy."

"He takes care of her," Paula said. "He always takes care of her."

A doctor in a green operating gown came through the double doors at the end of the corridor, and he stood there waiting and looking around. I went over to him and told him who I was and that I was Joe Finelli's friend.

"He's gone," he said softly. "We tried. Those big slugs ripped him to pieces."

I suppose his face was enough and they must have caught some of his words. Finelli's mother let out a shriek, and Paula began to sob uncontrollably. One of Finelli's squad went to her and put his arm around her. The doctor drew me aside. "Is your first name Harry?"

"That's right."

"Then he must have meant you. We were beginning the anesthesia and at the moment he was feeling no pain. The nerves were shattered. He said, 'Hey, Doc, tell Harry I found the sugar.' " The doctor paused. "Does that make any sense to you?"

"It makes sense, yes."

"He's a Catholic, of course?"

"That's right."

"Who'll take care of things? Our priest was with him. She'll want to know that."

Pointing. "That's his wife. The old lady's his mother. Those two men are from his squad. They'll take care of everything, and they'll notify his precinct and the people downtown." I went over to the uniformed cop from our precinct, and I told him that there was nothing for him to do there and that he could go back to the station house.

"Let's go," I said to Toomey.

"It stinks," Toomey said. "The whole goddamn thing stinks. Being a cop stinks."

"You can say that." I went over to Paula, who was kneeling on the floor, her face in the old lady's lap. Mrs. Finelli, the mother, was keening a soft wail of pain as old as time. I raised Paula to her feet as gently as I could.

"I'm Joey's friend," I said.

"I know, Harry."

"I'm still his friend. You know that. His soul knows that. And when you think of him, he's there."

"I know, Harry."

"So if you need me, I'm here. And the department will take care of things—everything, Paula. You'll always have enough to live on, you and the kids."

"Thank you, Harry." She embraced me. "God bless you."

It's not as hard with Catholics. They still believe in something. I wished to God that I believed in something as I walked out of the hospital with Toomey.

On the street, careful, nervous as a deer in the woods, my hand on my gun, I got into my car, which Toomey was still driving, and I said to him, "Toomey, ask me who killed Joe Finelli."

"I'm asking."

"And I'm going to tell you, and do you know why? Because I'm walking a tightrope between the Trade Centers, and any moment it can break. So if I'm dead, you stay alive and run this down, or Finelli and I will haunt you for the rest of your life."

"We'll both of us stay alive, Lieutenant."

"Maybe. Now listen. Jake Hallihan is responsible for the death of Joe Finelli."

"The captain over—"

"Just listen. You remember that big cocaine bust at the Seventy-ninth Street marina?"

"Yeah, the one where the coke got lost."

"It didn't get lost. Hallihan had it stored overnight in his office and he switched it for powdered sugar. I suggested to Joe that he ask around the neighborhood for a store that might remember selling out maybe its whole stock of powdered sugar. Not so hard, because over there on the West Side, only a couple of supermarkets stay open to midnight and maybe half a dozen delis. Before Finelli died, he told the doctor to tell me that he found the sugar. The doctor asked me did it make sense?"

"Hallihan. My God, that's hard to believe."

"Believe it. I think Courtny's in it too, but I have no proof. It ties into a guy named Porfetto, who runs a killing machine that makes the old Murder Incorporated look like kids' play."

"Porfetto?"

We were at the station house now, double-parking as always.

"That's right."

"Lieutenant, is he the guy who's getting an award tomorrow at the Waldorf?"

"Same one, yes.'"

Toomey shook his head and said, "It beats me. I used to try to figure it out. No more. It makes no goddamn sense at all. Courtny tells me to take Keene and Bolansky and Henderson and stake out the motor entrance to the Waldorf, where Porfetto is the big man tomorrow. It's a lot of plain-clothes cops in a situation where they got uniforms outside as usual, and I tell him I can't put it together until the lieutenant gets here. Fuck the lieutenant, he says. This is from Washington, and I'm still captain here. That's what he tells me."

"What's from Washington?" I asked him. At this point, far from thinking straight, I was hardly thinking at all.

"The extra protection for Porfetto."

"Well, they ask for it when they think a diplomat's in danger."

"He's not a diplomat. You going to take this from Courtny?"

"Toomey, what the hell do I do? Go up there and tell him to keep his lousy fingers off my squad? The hell with it!"

The reporters and the media had just been coming into the hospital as we left, but here at the station house they were all set up, the trucks from CBS and the other networks and the newspaper people, too. When they grabbed Toomey and me,

I explained that nothing was coming down here and that the people from Lieutenant Finelli's precinct were over at Lenox Hill Hospital. Some of them exchanged looks, and the lights went on, the cameras focused on Toomey and me. One of them asked Toomey to stand aside, so that they could get me alone. Toomey led the way into the house, and I followed him. The regulars at the precinct from the *Daily News* and the *Post* tried to get to me, but Keene, evidently waiting for us, interposed his huge bulk, pulled us into the men's room, and put his weight against the door behind him.

"Whatever your reason is, thank you," I said to Keene.

"Lieutenant," Keene said, "I just couldn't let you and Toomey go up there without some warning. They got two of them pissbellies from Internal Affairs waiting for you."

"Internal Affairs—you got to be kidding."

"I am not kidding. Some asshole leaked it, and since the video kids were here for poor Joe Finelli being shot, they figured they'd get a few frames of you. How is the lieutenant?"

"He's dead."

"No. Poor guy, poor guy. I used to work with Finelli about seven years ago. He was tough and hard, but you come to him with bad trouble, he'd give you his last dollar. I seen it."

"What are they here for?" Toomey asked. "For the lieutenant or me?"

"I guess it's mostly the lieutenant, Sergeant. But they said they want you there."

"All right. We'll go upstairs now."

We moved quickly, out of the men's room and up the staircase at the back of the station, which led to the detective squad room. The TV people were inside now and they tried to get to us with their mikes, but Keene spread his arms, pushing them back and explaining that police work required all the floor space in the station and they'd just have to go outside. It worked. It always worked with Keene because of his deep, rumbling voice and the spread of his arms.

I never met a cop who had anything good to say about Internal Affairs, and yet it makes sense that a police force like ours, with over thirty thousand men and women in its various parts, needs a disciplinary force. It doesn't matter that we have the best police force in the country, and as I have said, maybe in the world. We have Christians and Jews and a sprinkling of Muslims, blacks and whites, and men and women, and Irish, Italians, Hungarians, Russians, Poles, Chinese, Hispanics, and any other ethnic group you can think of. And we work together with more human decency and compassion than any other cops I ever heard of, and we have higher IQs and a damn sight more common sense than those fancy but not so bright clean-cut characters who make up the FBI and the CIA—but we're people; and in a group of people that size, you're bound to have a reasonable selection of crooks, con artists, bunco players, and plain bums who are on the pad. It couldn't be otherwise, and you couldn't run our force without an inside force to police it. That's Internal Affairs. That doesn't mean anyone likes them.

I didn't like them, but I had been able to avoid them in terms of direct involvement. Now they were waiting for me, one of them pudgy, natty, wearing a three-piece suit, a pale mustache, and glasses, the other a middle-aged athlete with the neck of a line tackle. They introduced themselves as Flecker and Smithson. They told Toomey to wait and they took me into the interrogation room. As we passed Courtny's office, he grinned with pleasure and nodded.

They weren't unfriendly. We sat down around the table, and they said I could smoke if I wanted to. I said that I didn't smoke, and they said that they didn't smoke either. Flecker, the neat one, took a folder out of his briefcase.

"It's your record," he explained, opening it and glancing at it. "We been through it already. It's a good record, a damn good record."

"Actually, what we did," said Smithson, the line tackle, "was to compare some dates. Did you know that Inspector Max Roberts, the zone commander, was due to retire first week in April?"

Before I could answer, Flecker cut in, "You know, Lieutenant, you're not obliged to answer any of our questions, and you're not under arrest or duress or even suspicion. This is just an inquiry for the good of the force."

And I was born yesterday, I thought, but said, "Yes, I understand that."

"And about the zone commander?"

"I had heard some rumors. I didn't pay much attention."

"Just indifferent to it?"

"No, not exactly indifferent," I said, wondering what on earth the impending resignation of Max Roberts had to do with anything. "Officers resign. They get old, they get sick, sometimes they get sick and tired."

"So the passing of Inspector Roberts wouldn't mean a thing?"

"That isn't what I said, and I damn well don't want words put into my mouth. I said inspectors retire. Of course, I'm interested in who becomes the zone commander. Inspector Roberts is a very nice and intelligent man. I work well with him. I have a squad of detectives that I'm responsible for, and a zone commander could make my life miserable."

"Would you mind if we record this?" Flecker asked, reaching into his briefcase.

"I would! I sure as hell would! I don't know why you're here, and I don't know of any reason why you should be here. I'll answer your questions and I'll talk to you, but I won't be recorded without an attorney."

"Okay, okay," Flecker said. "Don't get excited."

"Excited? I'm not excited. I am sore as hell. I am pissed off that you characters can come here and interrogate me with stupid prosecutor talk. I want to know why. And I want to see that tape recorder in your briefcase. I want it here on the table, where I can see it's not running."

"You're too suspicious, Lieutenant." He took out the tape recorder, a small one, and placed it on the table.

"Not running. Try to trust us."

"That'll be the day. Now what's all this about Inspector Roberts? Suppose you give me a straight answer and stop trying to be cute."

"You're not Mr. Nice Guy." Smithson sighed.

"None of us are."

"All right, Lieutenant. Did you know that last month your name was put up to fill the post of zone commander after Inspector Roberts resigned?"

"Come on. What kind of crap is that?"

"It's the truth."

"It's bullshit. They don't pick up lieutenants and make them zone commander. They don't go over the heads of the captains and the uniforms. Well, maybe it could happen in Manhattan South or at Fort Apache. Not here. We don't have that kind of war here."

Flecker shrugged.

"Why should we lie?" Smithson asked.

"God knows."

"All we asked is did you know that your name was put up?"

"No, I didn't. And who put me up?"

"Captain Courtny."

"Oh, Jesus God, that's to laugh."

"Why?"

"Courtny. I'm poison ivy to Courtny."

"Maybe he wanted to get rid of you. Maybe he wanted to get you out of here, if you're such a pain in the ass to him. He wasn't out of line. You got a brilliant record, Golding, but I can see just sitting here that you could be a pain in the ass to work with."

"Thank you. But tell me this—what in hell difference does it make whether or not I knew that my name had been put up?"

"It's a question of motivation," Flecker said. "If you knew about your nomination and if you wanted it badly enough, you might just have done what you're accused of. It could give you a real running head start for the job."

"I won't ask you what I'm accused of," I said tiredly. "I'm in a mood to tell you both to fuck off and walk out of here."

"Look, sir," Smithson said, "maybe we came on too strong. How would you like our lousy job?"

I stood up and said, "I'd starve first or clean toilets."

"Sure. Come on, Lieutenant, sit down and let's talk civilized about this. We have a charge against you that we have to talk about. It may satisfy your ego to walk out of here, but in the long run, it can only hurt you."

"Okay." I sat down. "Talk. I'm listening. But don't try to be cute."

"You ever hear of Paul Grogan?"

"No. Should I?"

"He's one of the millionaire types on the board of directors of the museum."

"Go on."

"You never heard of him. We thought maybe you had and that he was working some kind of personal vendetta because maybe you gave him a fat ticket."

"I'm a lieutenant of detectives," I said icily. "I don't give out tickets."

"Joke. All right, this here Paul Grogan swears out a complaint and hands it in downtown where he knows Ed Crown, the chief of detectives. It charges you with stealing that Vermeer the media made such a fuss about and taping it under the bench, so you could discover it later and become a big media hero and maybe walk into the zone commander job."

"What?"

"Yeah—that's it."

"Why don't you say joke again? You two are full of jokes, but this does it."

"We didn't write the complaint, Lieutenant. Why don't you talk to us instead of putting us down? What the hell are we, lepers?"

I nodded. He was right, and I told him so.

"Let's begin with first things first. Is there any substance to this complaint?"

"None. I didn't know one damn thing about the zone commander job, and if I had I'd have enough brains to know how the department works. I could kiss the commissioner's ass in Macy's window for forty-eight hours and it wouldn't buy me that job, and I would have to be a low-grade moron to think up such a crazy caper as that Vermeer thing to buy points."

Flecker nodded. "I see it that way. But we got to go through the motions. Point two—do you have any connection whatsoever with this Grogan?"

"Never met him, never heard of him."

"When was the last time you or your wife visited the museum? I mean before the robbery."

"We haven't been there for months."

"Grogan asserts he spoke to a guard who says otherwise."

"That's to be expected," I said. "If this bastard Grogan wants to frame me, he might as well buy a guard for the package. What else have you got?"

He reached into his briefcase and came out with a brown envelope, from which he extracted a handful of paper scraps and paper ribbons.

I told him, "They learn from TV. The killers are the idiots of the world and they suck on a glass tit."

"I take it that means something, Lieutenant. Meanwhile —" He held up the tangle of paper scraps.

"The magazine pages from which the ransom note was cut. You found it in my apartment, which has now become a corridor. I carefully saved those incriminating pieces because if I put them in the garbage someone might find them and discover my heinous crime. So I put it all in an envelope and shoved it into my desk or the fridge or some such place. That's because I was born brain-damaged and didn't have enough sense to put them in an ashtray and burn them or flush them down the toilet."

"That's what it looks like," Smithson said. "What can we do, Lieutenant? Tear up the complaint and say it's too stupid to float? We couldn't do that. You know that, and there's been so much talk about how you reached under the bench and found the painting that as crazy as this complaint is, it makes some kind of point."

"What kind of point?"

"Beats me. Anyway, we talked to you."

"What are you charging me with?"

"We're not charging you, but for the time being, we got to recommend your suspension. So you better hand over your badge and gun to Captain Courtny."

"That's it. That puts me out of the running, doesn't it?" I thought of what Fran had said this morning about crucifixion taking the place of execution. It wasn't exactly crucifixion, but it hurt.

Flecker said, "Lieutenant, why don't you go downtown

today and have a talk with Frank Opperman. He's the D.A. who takes most of the bunco stuff, and he'll be dealing with this. He's a good man."

"Bring your lawyer," Smithson said. "That's the best advice I can give you. You don't want to talk to Opperman without a lawyer."

Flecker said, "Ask Sergeant Toomey to step in here."

"What do you want Toomey for? He had no part of this. He wasn't involved in the museum thing."

"He's your number one man, right? All we want is to check out some dates and places."

"Are you going to suspend him?"

"No. We got no complaint about Toomey. We just want to talk to him."

I told Toomey that they wanted to talk to him. Hennesy and Keene were working at their desks with a couple of pushers or muggers or robbers, and they looked at me but didn't say anything. I went into Courtny's office. He wasn't grinning. He simply watched me in silence as I put my gun and badge on his desk. As I turned to leave, he said, "Golding, you're a good cop. I don't believe any of this shit."

"Yeah. Thanks."

I walked through the detective room and downstairs and out of the police station, and I left behind me seventeen years of my life, and if I were given to crying, I would have cried like a baby. I was a New York street kid. The kid fought day in and day out, first with his fists to cover his brother, Oscar, who never knew how to use his fists, to beat up every bastard who called him a damn Jew, and then with his head to make something of himself when there was no money to make anything of him, and who for some freakish reason always wanted to be a cop. Now I wasn't a cop anymore. If they had the power to do this to me, then they had the power to keep me off the force—one way or another.

I left the car at the station, and walked away from there. I was quite certain that I was not being tailed, but I went through the motions of evading a tail. My original conclusion was correct. I was not being tailed. They didn't even have to kill me. Whatever fangs I had were drawn.

The rain had finished, and the wind was tearing the remnants of the dark, angry storm clouds to shreds. In New York City, the March air is electric. Breathe in and you have life and energy. The shock and trauma began to recede, and by the time I had reached 57th Street, a notion that had been nibbling at my mind for days now began to grow and take shape. It pushed my misery aside. There is nothing more elevating to the spirit than a proper decision, but while it elevated my spirit, it did not decrease the rage I felt against these bastards who had killed Finelli and who could kill me or frame me or remove any human being whom they felt was in their way.

Fran was reading a copy of *The New Yorker,* which she'd bought at the hotel newsstand. She put it aside and looked at me. Afterward, she said she had never seen me appear so woeful before. Fifteen minutes ago, my spirits had been elevated; now they were back at rock bottom. I still knew what I had to do, but it gave me neither excitement nor hope. I told her that Finelli was dead and how it happened.

"Poor man," Fran said. "I must ask God to forgive me for all the rotten things I said about him and his wife."

"He was an angry bull. I never let him get close to me. I wish I had so that I could remember him better. But however you cut it, he was a good cop."

"Yes. What else happened to make our morning bright?"

I had stopped on my way down to buy sandwiches and beer. The sandwiches were corned beef, favorite for both of us, and with the sandwiches, a container of coleslaw. I suggested that we eat first. The sandwiches were excellent, thin rye piled high with lean corned beef. The beer was imported Pilsen.

"I'm glad you're here," Fran said. "I didn't think I'd see you all day, and I didn't know whether it would be here or in the morgue. It's no way to live, Harry."

"Amen."

"So you might as well break down and tell me why you're here and not back at the station."

I told her. She listened, and then I asked her what she thought of it.

"Well, it makes a kind of dumb sense."

"What's that supposed to mean?"

"I mean the Edgar Wallace story you told me about. If you hadn't read that story by Edgar Wallace, Harry, would you have thought of reaching under the bench?"

"I don't know."

"Harry, about ten or twelve years ago, another small painting was stolen from the museum, and it was never recovered, and no one ever thought of looking under the bench."

"What are you trying to tell me, Fran? You mean to say you think this garbage could add up to a viable case?"

"Yes," she said unhappily. "If we don't stop it—and if we couldn't, Harry, what would it mean?"

"I don't know. It's grand larceny theft, but nothing was taken off the premises. It was only moved from one place to another. But the ransom note makes it bunco, fraud, attempted fraud, and if they could make a jury case out of that —Fran, I just don't know, except that I could go to jail. But who would believe a crazy story like that?"

"A lot of people who hate anyone who's a little bit smarter than they are. I found myself wondering for a moment—"

"Oh, Jesus Christ, Fran, not you."

"No, no, Harry. I threw the thought away. But it had to leap into my mind."

"You know, I was at my desk in the squad room when the call came in. That was about noontime. You know, it was one of those mornings. If I remember right, there was a sort of big bust over on Lexington Avenue near the hospital, two men selling dope to kids, and the same morning there was a flare-up at Hunter College where two black students jumped a dope dealer and beat him half to death, and while that was going on, a professor had her purse snatched. On top of the usual parade, so it added up to one of those mornings, and in the middle of everything, the museum called in that the Vermeer had been stolen. You know I don't have any kind of regular office, just the two tin and glass panels to make the corner, so everyone in the squad room saw me sitting there and the detectives were in and out of my office—so how on God's earth could I have lifted the Vermeer?"

"Harry, did you tell this to Internal Affairs?"

"No. They can't do a damn thing to help me, so why tell them?"

"And you didn't tell them about the Edgar Wallace story?"

"Oh, no, you can be sure of that."

"All right," Fran said, "they told you to get a lawyer and see the D.A. with him. We're going to get us a lawyer right now."

"Who? We don't have a lawyer."

"My brother Charles Murphy. Charley's with one of the most prestigious legal firms in the city, and that's what we need—a prestigious legal firm."

"Honey," I said, "you're sweet and loyal. But we haven't spoken to Charles for over a year, and we can't just descend on him and tell him that he's hired with all of twenty cents as a retainer."

"Harry, Italian families see each other every day, Jewish families, once a week at the Friday night dinner table, but with an Irish family, it can be five years and there's still love or if not love, dues to be paid. Now, see whether I'm not right." She took her address book and dialed a number. "Mr. Murphy, please." Pause. "His sister—yes, love, his sister; he has one sister, Francesca O'Brian Murphy."

Then I heard Charley's deep voice booming over the phone, "Francesca O'Brian Murphy, is it? And what in hell made you remember that you had a brother on this side of purgatory? Is it that miserable cop you married that stole you away from a brother who cherished you?"

"Charley, we're in terrible trouble. When will you be back from lunch? We must see you."

"Sister, I'm having a sandwich at my desk. I'm neck-deep in work and meetings all afternoon. Maybe tomorrow."

"Charley, today. Don't you understand me? Today. We could be dead by tomorrow, all of us, Harry, myself, and the two kids. I'm not kidding, Charley, if my life is worth it, cancel the appointments and give us the afternoon."

"What have you gotten into? I thought Harry was riding high on that Vermeer caper."

"Please. When can we come?"

"Now. You haven't forgotten the address—Twenty-five Broadway. Should I order a sandwich for you?"

"We've eaten. Oh, thank you, Charley."

I threw on my coat and got hers from the closet, but she drew back and said, "Just a minute or two, Harry. You didn't ask me what I did today."

"No, but you were here."

"I called Sean in Dublin."

"Good. That's all right. Did you have Bill Hoffman put the call through?"

"Yes."

"Did you talk to the kids?"

"No." She hesitated. "Harry, the kids aren't in Dublin."

"What! What do you mean, they're not in Dublin? Where are they? What happened to them?"

"Harry," she said, gripping my arms, "I'm all right. So the kids are all right. Now cool it and listen. The father of one of Sean's students has the cab concession at Shannon. He had heard about the two American kids who were with Sean, and when he found an American asking his drivers whether he had driven two kids fitting the description, which he had down pat, he got in touch with Sean. First he threw the man out of his garage. He thought it was a CIA man, and they don't love the breed in Ireland. The next day, Sean noticed someone watching the school, a man he had never seen before. Mary, Sean's wife, has an uncle who's second-in-command of the Dublin police, and Sean gave him some story that got him to pick up the man, and he had a gun on him, so they were able to hold him for at least a few days. Meanwhile, Mary called her sister, who runs a little seaside hotel in the south of England. You remember her sister. She came over to visit when we were in Dublin, a tall, skinny lady, very sweet, but she never married. Anyway, she said, of course, bring the kids over. And I think Sean is wonderful to handle this himself."

"He is wonderful," I agreed. "He's a great human being."

"You can say that again, and when I told him that the kids were running from the same gang who murdered those poor nuns in Santa Marina, he said that he was given a deed of grace, and that's just like Sean."

"Where are the kids?"

"In England, with Molly Flannigan, Mary's sister."

"Did Sean cover his track?"

"Oh, yes. They flew to England, and then by cab to London. In London, they made sure to lose anyone who might have been following them, and then they went down south by bus. Sean knows how to do that and it was a great treat for the kids."

"He didn't give you any address or telephone?"

"No. He was very careful."

"All right. The kids are safe for the time being, and we'll end this thing tomorrow."

"Tomorrow? You want to talk about it?"

"No. Let's get down to Charley's office."

Chapter 14

IT WAS LIKE a long double take, or perhaps the words hadn't registered, or perhaps her mind was in the south of England, but it wasn't until we were in the subway on our way south to 25 Broadway that Fran seemed to realize what I had said and demanded, "What is going to end tomorrow? What thing?"

"I told you. We talk about it later."

"About what?"

"I told you, later."

She didn't like that. She kept glancing at me, as you might with someone on the way off the deep end. She knew me too well, and I'm sure that following the steps she suspected my mind would take, she could guess at something close to what I intended. I hoped not—at least not until I could sit down and persuade her.

By now, it must be fairly clear that Fran and I come from a pair of interesting families. We share an origin in one of the city's more tolerable slums on upper Amsterdam Avenue, and we've come a long way since then, myself able to point to Oscar, and Fran connected to two remarkable men, Sean and Charles Murphy. Charles put himself through Columbia and Harvard law, and then broke his mother's heart by marrying Constance Webber, a very stylish daughter of the Webbers, who have all the money that the Rockefellers and the Morgans don't have, but happen to be Episcopalians. Fran always claimed that Charley was in love with Constance, and that his alliance was no more unusual than hers with a cop.

Howsoever that may be, Charles Murphy was one of six partners in a very important law firm. They occupied three full floors at 25 Broadway, and underneath the names of the partners, graven in a bronze plaque that faced you when you stepped off the elevator, were several dozen names of juniors. It always impressed me.

I must admit that I was very fond of Charley, even though we traveled in two different worlds. Unlike Sean, who was dark and slender, Charley was an oversize, overweight bull of a man, with a barrel chest, a lot of stomach and Fran's coloring, red hair going white here and there and the red beard of a buccaneer. He embraced Fran in a bear hug and his handshake with me was as bone-crushing as ever. Then he poured three shots of Irish whiskey, and would listen to nothing until we put it down.

"It'll do your heart good," he said to me, "even if you're on duty. And thank God there's one cop left in this family of ambitious shanty Irish."

I said, "I appreciate the sentiment, Charley, but I'm not even sure I'm a cop at this point. I've been suspended and I've handed in my badge and gun."

"Jesus God, no! What are the bastards up to?" That was the wonderful thing about Charley. He always knew what side he was on.

"I don't think we can start there, Harry," Fran said. "We told Charley that this is life and death. It is. I think you must start from the very beginning—from the lecture at NYU—and then tell the whole story, every bit of it. It has to be that way. He has to hear all of it. We can't leave anything out."

"That's at least an hour."

"I have nothing to do but listen," Charles said soberly, picking up his phone and saying, "No calls, Sally, not for two hours. I don't care who it is, no calls."

Fran said, "Thanks, Charley."

"Did I tell you you're prettier than ever?"

Fran began to cry. "It's a reaction," I told Charley. "We've been through a lot. Even without that, she cries when you tell her how beautiful she is. But she's right. I have to tell you the whole story, Charley, and don't think I'm crazy, because she's sitting there to back up whatever I say."

"Go on," Charles said.

"It began just—my God, only a couple of weeks ago. Oscar asked me to talk to his class at NYU on the question of homicide, from a policeman's point of view. That's how it began. . . ."

And from there, I went on, leaving nothing out. Charles hardly moved all through the story. We sat on two chairs facing his desk. He was seated in a big swivel chair, facing us, his eyes half closed, turning a pencil between the thumbs and forefingers of his hands. It took over an hour to spell it all out. "And that's it," I said finally. "The kids are in the south of England with Molly Flannigan, I'm suspended, and a lot of good people are dead."

"You're sure the kids are all right?"

"You know Sean," Fran said.

"Yes, I do."

"Do you believe us?" I wanted to know. "That's the main thing—do you believe us."

"Well, you can't put it quite that baldly. Do I believe that you're telling the truth? Of course I do. Why should you lie to me? And since my sister is the best of the lot of us, I believe her. Are your lives and the lives of your kids in danger—no doubt about that. Your apartment was bugged, your phone was tapped, and attempts were made on your lives. But, on the other hand, am I ready to say that this enormous spiderweb you feel exists, this plot to become the power center of the United States through a combination of cocaine trade, industry, and stolen millions appropriated for Santa Marina—that this exists and is factual? Well, I don't know. A death squad, Santa Marina style, operating here for years, killing what may amount to hundreds of people if your theory holds—" He shook his head. "And with Wabash Protection as the private army and executioner of Al

213

Porfetto, who sits on top of this pyramid—Franny, I know Al Porfetto. Not too well. He isn't too social and he doesn't mingle much, but I know the man. You just can't do in America what you describe. The Arabs can't do it, and they could buy and sell Porfetto five times over. I'm a lawyer, and the evidence just isn't there."

The evidence was there. Charley was a lawyer, but I was a cop and I looked at evidence somewhat differently. But I didn't argue with him. Actually, that was only peripheral to my problem—which was what does a cop do when he's being framed and dumped. It's true that Fran and I had both expected more of Charley. He knew the people with power, and we thought he might reach out to some of them and that way help us. We were tired. Tired of running, tired of always being afraid. Finally, four decades after Nazi Germany, I was learning what it meant to be hunted, to fear death from hour to hour, and to have no one to turn to.

I knew anger or petulance wouldn't help, but Fran was his sister and now she let go with, "Damn you, Charley Murphy, you've become like all the rest of these lousy Establishment fat cats. If some swine has twenty cents and a charitable handout, he becomes a member of your club. Well, your club stinks. Harry and I are fighting for our lives and for the lives of our kids, and you tell us the evidence isn't in."

Charley sighed, and I said, "Stop it, Fran. He's helping. We asked for help. He's giving it to us. To hell with that. I want to know what I do now."

"Good, good," Charley said softly. "Just take it easy, Fran, let's see what we can do with the pickle Harry's in. That's what you came here for."

"Yes, I suppose it is," Fran admitted. "I'm sorry, Charley."

"Ah, you're right. We had a great uncle of my name, Charley Murphy, who died fighting in the Sinn Fein Easter, and look at me here now. Oh, the hell with that. We each keep body and soul in our own fashion. Now let's touch it point by point, and mind you, I'll never call you a liar, but I must question you."

"Of course."

"So first, the Edgar Wallace business. We have the spiffiest

214

literary establishment in the country, and the most book-stores and the *Times* book section and *The New York Review of Books,* to mention the snottiest of the lot, and apparently several million people reading like the very devil, and you're telling me not one of them recognized that Edgar Wallace story?"

"I can't say, Charley. Maybe the thief's a reader."

"Hey, you didn't tell the shooflies about Edgar Wallace?"

"No."

"It dies here. No one is to be told. Ever."

I nodded.

"Now, about Grogan. I know him. One of those rich, eager creeps who pushes onto public service where he need not be elected or appointed. Give a million to Lincoln Center, and get on the board of this or that, theater, opera, Philharmonic. They'd put a monkey on those boards if he'd ante up a million. Committee to plan the revitalization of TriBeCa. They have the experts; now they need funding and up steps someone like Grogan—Paul Grogan—oh, wait one red hot minute!" He sat with his eyes closed, hands pressed to the desk. "Ha! Oh, what a memory your brother Charley has!" He picked up his desk phone and almost in a shout, "Sally, find the last annual report of Wabash Protection." Then he turned to me and said, "The two others, the men actually engaged in running the museum, they never brought up the possibility of you being engaged in shenani-gans?"

"No, not at all."

"Now about the ransom note, did you see it?"

"Only the content."

"But since you set up the system for catching the museum thief if he tried to collect the ransom, you must have felt it was genuine. Is that so?"

"Yes. I thought so."

"But evidently, the thief knew the painting had been re-covered. Have you any idea who the thief was?"

"Not really. If I were to run a real investigation, I suppose I would concentrate on the guards. To begin, anyway."

"But you didn't run a real investigation?"

"I brought it up, but Courtny vetoed it. He was right. The property had been recovered."

"You could have pushed for it."

I shook my head. "No. I thought about that. We just have too much work for my squad to handle as is."

"That's a point against us. But we have a few for us."

At that moment, a small, bright-eyed lady, who was evidently Sally, came into the office and dropped an annual report on Charley's desk. "And you're Fran," she said. "I recognize the hair, of course."

She sailed out of the room, and Charley slammed his fist down onto his desk and yelled, "Bingo! I am goddamn brilliant! See this? See this? This is the annual report of Wabash Protection. These annual reports always list the directors, who are very often window dressing and no more. Oh, they may pick up a few hundred dollars for each board meeting and they're supposed to render know-how and experience, but as often as not it's a place for the president's friends to nod their heads. And right here, on the list of Wabash directors, Paul D. Grogan, president of Grogan Industries."

He had been carried away. It was his manner, and it made him a splendid trial lawyer, but I can guess that often enough he's halfway down the road before he knows clearly why he's running. This was a triumphant exercise of memory, to remember that he had seen Grogan's name in the Wabash report, but at the same time it tended to demolish all the staid and serious doubt he had cast at the suggestion that there could be a conspiracy of the size I proposed. His ebullience subsided, and he stared at us rather glumly.

"Hoist by my own petard," he said.

"And what does that mean, Charley?"

"A petard was a sixteenth-century cannon, used to break the walls of a city under siege, and when the cannon broke its anchor ropes, it could spring back and kill the gunners, or something like that."

"I didn't ask you what a petard was. I asked you what you meant."

"Anyway, it isn't that," Fran said. "It was a kind of primitive bomb."

"It means I'm scared," Charley said. "It means that you

two could be right. No, it doesn't!" he snapped emphatically. "What does it matter that Grogan is a director of Wabash? Who told you that Wabash is controlled by Porfetto?"

"Harvey Crimshaw, if you know who he is?"

"Of course I know who he is. How do you happen to know Harvey Crimshaw?"

"Oscar put me on to him, and I had lunch with him at the Harvard Club yesterday. Don't look at me like that."

"Just for your information," Fran said, "Harry doesn't make that a way of life. He's a cop, a poor, battered, lonely cop."

"Oh, for God's sake, Sis, I'm trying to help." And to me, he said, "How much does Crimshaw know?"

"A good deal, not everything. I had to talk to him. Charley, this is a world I don't know."

"Look, Harry," Charley said gently, "the reason I keep coming back to that Edgar Wallace story all the time is because it's the one piece that could hang you. We're dealing with two things: One is the possibility of Porfetto being connected to a gigantic murder ring; the other is the matter of the charges brought against you. You feel that these charges are part of a device to destroy you, and I can understand why you feel that way. But whether or not it's the fact, we have to make a case against the charges, and this Edgar Wallace thing could bring you down if they get hold of it. It would indicate that you used the story not to solve the crime, but to commit the crime. That's why I am so desperately anxious that the story should not get out of this room. Do you understand?"

I didn't reply. I was staring at his desk, a beautiful old Queen Anne piece.

"Harry?"

I slid off my chair and down on my hands and knees.

"Harry, for heaven's sake—" Fran began.

"Harry, what the hell are you up to?"

I crawled under the desk, and then I wriggled back out, holding a small round object in my hand. "It's already out. Every word we said here this afternoon is out. This thing in my hand is the latest beauty in a transmitting bug. It's my fault, Charley, not yours. I should have known that they would think of Fran's brother, and we came running here, just as they knew we would." I dropped the thing to the floor and ground it under my heel. "They're working us, using us, directing us, and we do their will."

"Mother of God," Fran cried, "we told them where the kids are!"

"Did we?"

"We did, we did."

Charley picked up his phone and told Sally to get him the overseas operator. "Use our priority," he said, and then to me, "Do you want to talk to Sean? Harry, I don't know whether you'll ever forgive me, but I'd give my life before I'd see harm come to any of you."

"I know."

Fran was huddled over, sobbing. For the comfort it might give her, I whispered, "They still don't know where we live."

"I think we've gotten through," Charley said, handing me the telephone. It was Sean's wife, Mary, talking to the operator.

"I'll talk to her," I said quickly. "Mary, don't hang up. This is Harry. Where's Sean?"

"He does a seminar at the university. He'll be home about ten."

"Can you get to him?" I begged her.

"Well, I don't know. For what?"

"They know where the kids are. He has to put them somewhere else."

"Harry, it's nighttime here. Sean can't go over to England tonight. And where can he put the children? What is this, Harry? What is happening?"

Charley reached for the phone. "Give it to me, Harry." And into the phone, "Mary, this is Charley Murphy, Sean's brother—yes, of course you know me. Now listen, Mary, we have a corresponding firm of solicitors in Dublin, and one of the partners is Darby O'Sweeney. He's a big, tall, capable man." Pause, and then, "Oh, you know him. Good. Good. I will call him and he'll meet Sean at your place tonight, and they'll both fly over to London. And don't worry about the money. If there are no flights, Darby will hire a plane. Now lock your door, and don't be letting anyone in but Sean or

218

Darby. If they have to, let them call me collect at my office here in New York. Sean has the number. And Mary, you have some kin with the police. Have them put a lookout on the school." He put down the telephone and managed a smile of sorts, explaining that whenever he spoke to anyone in Ireland he put a brogue into his voice. "Got into it as a kid, imitating Pop and his friends. I'm going to call Darby now. He's a fine man, and he'll have a pistol in his pocket for a thing like this. It's a kind of Dublin reaction."

Fran was still sobbing.

"Come on, Sis," he wheedled. "We're going to climb out of this one, believe me."

"Why are they after my children?"

"Same reason they bumped Harry here from the cops. They want a good hold on both of you. But they won't get your kids. Convince her of that, Harry. I have to call Darby."

I put my arms around Fran while he called his solicitor friend in Dublin, and I whispered to her, "As God is my witness, baby, this will be over tomorrow."

I felt foolish as I spoke. We had departed from reality, and I had a sense of speaking lines that someone else had written. The background was Charley speaking to Darby in Dublin, and all of it took on that color of lunacy that one finds in the Irish theater, and I remembered Sean in Dublin pointing with such pride to the bullet marks on the old post office where the Sinn Fein had fought its last fight—Sean so gentle that he could not crush a flea.

"Well, it's in Darby's hands now," Charley said as he put down the telephone. "He's a fine lad."

I felt like telling him that his phony brogue added nothing to the occasion, and that he should stop acting like a team-playing defensive tackle in the game of kill all the Goldings.

Fran had pulled out of her bout of tears. "I can't stand much more of this, my children at the mercy of demented killers three thousand miles away—"

"Fran, no one's going to kill our kids. Stop that."

Charley said, "We still haven't managed anything with the matter of your suspension. We have to put together a defense."

Suddenly, I didn't care anymore. I told him that.

"You'd damn well care about going to jail. I'm going to call the district attorney. We've dealt with him, and he occasionally takes some booze with me at the Harvard Club. I want to set up a meeting. The whole thing is so damned outrageous. The Murphys don't breed thieves."

I didn't remind him that I was not a Murphy. He meant well, and he was certainly rallying around, and I couldn't fault him. He did call the district attorney. There's a good deal of confusion in the public mind about the role of district attorney in a place like New York City. There are five boroughs that constitute Greater New York, each of these a county and entitled to its own district attorney; but the notion fostered by TV and film that there is one D.A. prosecuting like crazy is far from the fact. The Manhattan district attorney, like the others, is not appointed to his office. He's an elected official, but he has working under him over three hundred assistant district attorneys, and he himself, more often than not, is almost impossible to reach. He doesn't prosecute cases; he runs the machine, and since the people who desire to get to him are legion, he is somewhat more unapproachable than the President of the United States.

I was astonished that Charley was able to reach him on his first try, and my estimation of Charles and the weight he carried went up a good many notches. The conversation, as Charley told me later, went like this: Charles began by specifying me as his brother-in-law, which seemed to cut no ice at all with the D.A. It just happened that the D.A. knew all about me. Would he meet with Charles and myself? No way, nor did he desire to discuss the case any further with Charles. Evidently, I was being discussed more than I had imagined, and dispensed with more than I imagined. The D.A. advised Charles to instruct me to proceed along proper channels, and there were men, capable men, on his staff who handled bunco and fraud. Also, as he told Charles, I would be best advised to keep my nose out of things that did not concern me, and that I would know damn well what he was talking about.

"So that's it," Charles said to me. "There's an assistant D.A. named Opperman who runs the bunco department. I'll get to him tomorrow. Leave this with me, Harry. You have enough to worry about. I give you my word—we'll clear this up. You tell me you're not at the apartment now. Where can I reach you?"

I took no chances. I wrote the name and address on his desk pad, telling him to hold on to it. I had a strong feeling that our only chance for getting through this was to keep our address a secret. I told Charley, "If you talk to them again overseas, begin by telling them no names, no places. I'm totally paranoid at this point."

He hugged Fran as we prepared to leave, telling her that he had been a lousy snob of a brother, but that he would make up for it. I thanked him. "For what?" he wondered. "I gave it away. But how in God's name did they get in here to plant that bug?"

"You can get in anywhere if you want to, Charley."

Downstairs, we walked north. Eventually, we'd have to go through the business of shaking a tail, providing there was one, but here in the crowd that thronged lower Broadway, there was no way to go about it.

Fran had tightened her face and closed off the tears. I knew her well enough to suggest that she should stop blaming Charley. "Hell, he makes maybe four, five hundred thousand a year. He's pretty decent for anyone in that income bracket."

"Oh, I don't give a damn about his money. It's just that he's the kind of Irish I like least, clever as hell with no substance, pushing that phony brogue, trying to assure you that even death can be pleasant. Harry, I'm going to Ireland."

"That's what they'd like you to do."

"Don't be so damn smug. I want to be with my kids."

"So do I. But in order to achieve that, we have to stay alive. I don't believe in that heaven your guys preach, and even if I did, I'd want to postpone it."

"Oh, don't be such a horse's ass!"

"Then don't get mad when I talk a little common sense."

"Oh, yes. Common sense."

"Common sense. I should underline that. And whatever you think of Charley when you get mad at him, he does things. He has two good men looking after the kids, but you feel that the situation will improve if they also have to look after you."

"They won't have to look after me."

"Fran, you're not going to Ireland."

"You're telling me!" She turned there in the street, her eyes narrow and angry. "Since when do you tell me where to go and what to do? Since when? Since when have you taken ownership?"

People were turning to look at us. I took her arm, but she pulled away. "Please, Fran, not here. Please."

She strode away, myself after her. I kept pace with her and begged her to wait until we were back at the Primrose Hotel, and then she could tear me to pieces.

"Yes," she replied, "because the quality of men is just beginning to dawn on me. You do nothing, you change nothing, you think of nothing. Like the great maned lion who lies around all day while the lioness hunts, brings back the food, raises the cubs, teaches them—and her lord and master fucks. That's all he's good for." She took a deep breath and added, "And now, you cretins have found an atomic bomb, to blow up the whole world with—oh, what a lot of turds you all are!"

I agreed with her. I assured her that she was right, even though I couldn't immediately connect the atomic bomb with the rest of it. "Frannie, we'll talk this over. If Ireland's the answer, we'll find some way to get you there," adding to myself, at least she'd be out of this. "But now," I said, "take it easy. We're in this together and I'm doing the best I can. That's all I can do—the best that I can. But I told you that this will be over tomorrow."

"How?"

"Let's get something to eat."

"I'm not hungry. Are we being followed?"

"We'll do the routine," I told her, and for the next six blocks we made all the motions that were habitual to us by now, stepping into the proper store, popping out at the right moment, into an uncrowded side street and crossing it, memorizing faces, splitting up to go around opposite blocks —well, we were not followed.

There was a chill in the air. We went into a small restaurant for coffee and Danish, and when we found a table, Fran said, "Take your coat off, Harry, or you'll be cold when we go outside."

"No, I've got a gun in my raincoat pocket."

"I thought you turned in your gun."

"That was the company piece. This is my twenty-two."

"You know, I'm glad you have a gun. I was never glad before. I hated guns. I still hate them, but I'm glad you have it."

"You have your purse gun?"

She hesitated, then nodded. The waiter came and we ordered. Then Fran said, "What happens? I mean, Charley never got anywhere with the D.A. What happens now?"

"If they feel they have a case against me, they'll give it to the grand jury."

"And if they hand down an indictment, you go on trial— is that what we can expect?"

"I hope not."

"Harry, I've heard that if a cop goes to prison, he hasn't much chance of coming out alive."

"That's vastly exaggerated."

"And I'm supposed to take comfort from that?"

"Let's go back to the hotel," I said abruptly. "There's one thing I have to do."

Back at the Primrose Hotel, seated in our little living room in our safe house, safe haven, Fran watching me, I telephoned the district attorney's office. I persuaded the lady who answered the phone to pass me through to someone important enough to tell something very important to. I identified myself, and after a few minutes, I found myself talking to Assistant District Attorney Abel Johnson. Again, I identified myself and said that I would like to put something on the record, but I wanted it taped. I would not speak unless he assured me that what I said was being taped. He asked me whether I could hold on for about five minutes. I said that I could.

"All right, Lieutenant Golding. You're being taped now."

"Okay. This is Lieutenant Harry Golding, making a statement on Thursday, the twenty-second of March, 1984. If I should be found dead any time during the coming week, I wish this to be a deathbed statement and so considered. Two years ago, in April of 1982, a large cocaine bust was made at the marina at Seventy-ninth Street and Riverside Drive. The plans for the arrest were drawn up and led by Lieutenant Joseph Finelli. The cocaine was stored overnight in the property room at the Twenty-fourth Precinct, Lieutenant Finelli's precinct. During the night, Captain John Hallihan, same precinct, switched the cocaine for powdered sugar. Day before yesterday, I suggested to Lieutenant Finelli that Captain Hallihan had made the switch, and yesterday, or perhaps late the night before, Lieutenant Finelli discovered the shop where the large amount of sugar had been purchased. This morning, Lieutenant Finelli was murdered. This is the latest of an endless series of murders, most of them disguised as accidents, committed by a death squad which has its roots in Santa Marina and which is operated here in the United States as part of an industrial-dope complex that has become very powerful and tightly interconnected with the executive branch in Washington—"

I went on, steadily, explicitly, spelling out everything I had discovered, laying out what proof we had, the material that Fran had dug up in the public library and all the rest of it. When I had finished, Johnson said, "Hold on, now. Don't hang up. Tell me where you are right now and I'll get a couple of our men over to guard you. Your life is in danger, if one quarter of what you say is fact."

"What else is new?" I said. "I don't want your men."

"They're good men."

"No, sir. Absolutely not."

"Will you hang in until I put my boss on?"

"I spoke to your boss before."

"Lieutenant, for God's sake, we must speak to you before this goes any further. Believe me. Now hang on."

"No. If you're setting up a trace, well, you should have thought of that when we began."

I put down the telephone and stared at Fran. She said nothing, and then for a minute or so we sat and watched each other.

"Well?" I had to break the silence.

"Why didn't you let them send a couple of men over?"

"At this point, I wouldn't trust my own mother."

"Oh, bullshit, Harry Golding. Bullshit compounded. That's not why you wouldn't let them send a couple of men to stand guard."

"You think he believed me?"

"Harry, you're a lieutenant with a great record and you accuse a precinct commander of grand larceny and murder —they'd have to be nitwits not to believe you. Anyway, I know why you rejected the protection. You have decided to kill Porfetto when he goes to the Waldorf tomorrow to be honored, just as we honor other pigs of his ilk, which is your nutty reasoning to justify what you intend to do."

That really threw me. She lifted it out of the air with such certainty that it took a while before I was able to assure her that she was way off base.

"Harry! God damn you, Harry Golding, I'm your wife. Every time three or four Irish kids on our block decided to beat you up, who came to your aid? Who waded in with a baseball bat? You remember when Mickey Sullivan had you down on the street on your back and he was trying to put out your eyes with his ugly fingers? Who was it shoved my pencil sharpener into his back and told him it was a gun and that I'd fill him full of holes if he didn't get up and hold up his hands, and then when he did, you let him have it right in the solar plexus, and there he was rolled up on the sidewalk, unable to speak or move, and we pulled his pants off and threw them into the garbage truck—"

I was laughing now, doubled over and laughing so hard I couldn't stop, and she caught the laughter from me, and then both of us were doubled over, and I managed to say, "And he wasn't wearing underwear. The schmuck was not wearing underwear."

"Harry, don't ever ask me how I know what you're thinking. It's too easy. It's twenty-seven years since you robbed me of my good Catholic virtue, and when I confessed it to Father Brady, he said that I had condemned myself to a long, long stay in purgatory, by which I'm sure he meant our marriage—"

"You never told him it was a Jew?"

225

"Never! He was by the book. He would have had me burned alive. Oh, Jesus, Harry, danger brings it all out, doesn't it. But you have to give up this crazy notion that you can kill Porfetto."

"You're sure that's what I decided?"

"Yes, I'm sure." We had stopped laughing now. "Well, you can't. I'll tell you something. I don't read thoughts. When you came back here with your cop uniform, I figured it out. You started to plan it then, and now you figure you've got it all worked out, and you're going to shoot Porfetto and then they'll shoot you, and you'll be a dead terrorist and we'll all be safe. If that isn't the nuttiest thing I ever heard of, I don't know what is."

"All right. You have to know sooner or later. I'm going to kill Porfetto. There's no other way to stop this. He's beyond the law, he has the White House snowed, God knows how many government officials he has in his pocket, and he has his own private army. His home base, Santa Marina, taught the world a new form of government—government by death squad—and it's really taking on here. There's only one way—"

"Become a one-man death squad?"

"I don't see it that way."

"Well, my darling Harry, let me put it to you another way. The truth of the matter is that you couldn't kill a fly. Oh, I admit that you're a tough cop, but only because you are able to convince everyone that you're so tough by never raising your voice and by taking stupid chances that a really brave cop wouldn't take in a hundred years, but you do it because you're so scared that you figure that unless you do something really stupid, your job is down the drain. That's a god-awful sentence for a lecturer on English lit, but it makes the point."

"Thank you."

"You going to get mad at me and have another fight, Harry?"

"Not tonight. We can't afford it tonight. But if we ever come out of this alive, I'm going to set aside three days to be so damn pissed off at you I won't even speak to you."

"That's nice."

"Now listen to me. I've worked this out, and it's not complicated. When the uniform's on, a cop is a cop. Then—"

"Wait just one minute," Fran interrupted. "Didn't I hear you say that Toomey is in charge of a four-man uniformed detail that will escort Porfetto into the hotel?"

"Yes. That's right."

"Okay. Go on—tell me."

"I have dark hair. We strip it with peroxide and make me a blond. Blond mustache to go with it. Cars go into the Waldorf on Fiftieth Street. There's about thirty feet between where Porfetto leaves his car and the VIP elevators. Several steps up. Somewhere in that space, I'll get a shot or two in. I'm the best shot at the house."

"Harry, in seventeen years as a cop, until the past few days, you never fired a gun on the street, you never killed anyone, you never even wounded anyone. And now you tell me that you're going to go up against that little army around Porfetto and get him. And Toomey won't know you because your hair is blond. Harry, that's crazy."

"Sounds crazy, but it can be done."

"No."

"It has to be done."

"No. No, no, no!"

"I'd think that after all these years, you'd have some faith in what I can and can't do."

"That's just it. You can't kill a man in cold blood, Harry, no more than I could. That's for animals. We're not animals."

"No. Animals don't murder their own kind. We're something God spun off in a moment of great disgust."

"Harry, that's a terrible thing to say."

"Is it? We get crazy over these death squads, but it's all peanuts compared to the fifty million people who died in World War Two. Who taught these penny-ante, shithead dictators south of the border their trade? We send advisers down there to train them. We pour money into them. And then we tell everyone that they're becoming more democratic day by day."

"Harry, if you go on like that, you'll make yourself sick. We're both suffering from a kind of cabin fever, and if this keeps up we'll be at each other's throats. Now, listen to me. I wasn't joking before. I made a decision, and it's best for both of us. I'm going to Ireland. Either I'll be with my children or near them, or I might as well be dead. I don't care anymore. Someone has to tell Sean the whole story, and if this bastard Porfetto owns half of this country, he doesn't own Ireland yet. And in Dublin, we can still have the upper hand. We have friends and family there and we have good connections with the police. Sean and the others are running about like chickens with their heads cut off, when they should be on the attack. And as for you—Harry, don't you think I know what a weight I am? I'm the albatross around your neck—and even if what I said about your compassion is true, you're still one of the most brilliant cops on the force. You don't have to kill Porfetto. There are other ways."

"Fran, I can't let you take off by yourself."

"We're a team of two, only two. What else can we do? Suppose the kids were in Israel. Wouldn't you feel that they'd be safe if you were with them?"

What Fran didn't realize, with all of her perception, was that from the moment I raised the question again, I was in agreement with her. I wanted her out of the way and out of the country, because whatever her arguments were against my trying to kill Porfetto, I rejected them. I intended to kill Porfetto the following night, and nothing would stop me.

I let Bill Hoffman know about Fran's trip. He cashed another check for me, and our credit card would buy the ticket. I still put up a small measure of resistance, but finally gave in. I asked Bill to trust me, as difficult as it was becoming, and he simply said, "Some debts can be paid. Ours can't."

We packed a small suitcase for Fran, and then I drove her to the airport. I had the feeling that my life was at an end, that all we had built and planned and dreamed of was gone, collapsed and left in ashes. Perhaps Fran felt the same way, but as I held her in my arms there at Kennedy, she said, "I trust you, Harry. Make them believe you downtown. It's the only way."

The hotel room was cold and empty. I had never felt so much alone in all my life. I turned on the eleven o'clock news, and there was the station house, Toomey just entering and Lieutenant Harry Golding a few feet behind him, and the video reporter, who of course knew all about everything, saying that the good lieutenant had been suspended.

"This is the same Lieutenant Golding who, you will remember, made that life-is-stranger-than-fiction discovery of the stolen painting by Jan Vermeer." The video reporter did not mean to suggest that the ghost of Vermeer had returned to steal the painting; it was merely his struggle for clarity that led him into a word morass. But he straightened things out and indicated that the suspension was not unconnected to the mystery of the stolen Vermeer. He tried then to get some words out of Keene, who came out of the station house, but Keene looked at him so coldly and disdainfully that the TV man backed off.

To hell with it, I thought. I turned off the TV and undressed for bed. It was about five o'clock in the morning in Dublin. I said a small prayer asking forgiveness from whoever it is that can give forgiveness for what I intended to do tomorrow.

Chapter 15

THAT NIGHT I slept little and poorly, perhaps two hours out of the whole night, but I dozed now and then, and out of many dreams, there was one I remembered. It was a latter-day reference to an incident that took place years before, when both kids were quite small. We had driven out west to do my three weeks of vacation time fitted into Fran's open summer. College teachers have it better than cops, three months off. During the trip, we saw a good many wonderful sights in such places as Utah and Colorado and Arizona, and then we made a quick dash home. We were in Indianapolis, and I had to go to work the following morning, so I drove until the sun set and then I drove all through the night. Fran and the children slept, and I was trapped in that strange unreal world of nighttime highways. After midnight, the traffic fell off sharply, and by two in the morning, except for a very occasional car, I had the roads to myself. The whole world was bracketed in my headlights, an endless empty road that unfolded before me, mile after mile after mile. There was no other sound than the rush of the car and the breathing of my family. Even the towns we passed through were dark and unpopulated, but for the most part the great highway circled the towns. The world had gone away. The world had ceased to be, and all that was left was the tunnel of light my headlights drove into the darkness.

So in the dream, I had made up my mind to do a thing, and thereby, I had plunged into the darkness, without headlights, without a car around me, but naked into the eternal night.

At five o'clock in the morning, I awakened from this dream, trembling. We had stopped being excessively careful about our calls to Dublin. They knew about Dublin. They knew where the kids had been. So I put the call through the night operator at the Primrose Hotel, but it was almost two hours before the overseas operator could get through to the Dublin number, and during that time, I sat with the bedclothes drawn around me, cold and shivering with fear, and stoking the fear with all the grotesque images my mind could muster. When we got through, Sean's wife, Mary, answered, and when I asked desperately whether Fran had gotten there safely, Mary said, "Ah, yes, poor dear."

"Let me talk to her, please, Mary."

"Would you want to awaken her, Harry? It's never a wink of sleep the poor dear had on that airplane."

"But she's all right."

"Oh, of course. But why did you let her come here? This is a place of danger for her. The school has closed up to let the lads get home for Easter, and the men are gone, and don't ask me where."

"Just the two of you—in that great place?"

"And a few kids who have no place to go, with their parents off to the four corners of the earth. But our doors are stout and we have a policeman or two lurking about. We'll make out. Never you fear, Harry. We're all safe. Only, this must stop."

"Today, it will stop," I told her. "And for Fran, I'm fine and I'll do nothing foolish. Tell her that."

I shaved and then I took a cold shower. Then I put on my police uniform, and I felt ridiculous. It was no good. I was not a policeman anymore, and the only thing on that uniform that maintained its validity was my medal for marksmanship. Out of a match that involved all of the midtown precincts as well as Manhattan South, I had finished first.

Long ago, when Fran and I had just married, we had borrowed an old Ford and had driven up old Route 9W, and then inland on the barely paved roads of Greene County. On a dirt road there, we came across a group of state troopers who had set up targets and were practicing with their pistols. It was a lovely day, and we stopped there for a while and got out of the car to watch. I suppose no healthy young man could have been around Francesca with her flaming head of red hair and her skin like a butterfly's wing without making a pass of some kind. In this case, the troopers gave us a drink of soft cider, and then one of them suggested that Fran try her hand at the target. She refused so winsomely that they had to include me in the invitation and one of them thrust his huge, heavy .45-caliber revolver into my hand. At that point in my life, I had never fired a revolver or any other kind of gun before. He showed me how to cock it, and I raised the heavy gun with no thought of holding it in two hands or trying to really aim it, and I pulled the trigger and hit the bull's-eye on the target, which was sixty feet away. The hole in the black bull's-eye was alone. No one else had hit the bull's-eye, although there were a good many shots in the second and third ring. The troopers were certain it was a mistake, and they urged me to do it again, and I was kind of nettled and put off by their doubts, when they could have just clapped their hands and said, "Good shot, kid," or something of the sort. I didn't care whether I hit the target, or maybe I knew that if I tried, I'd hit nothing, probably not even the target; so I didn't try, just looked at the target and then raised the gun and fired. Bull's-eye again, twice in a row, and if you ever tried to hit anything, even the side of a barn, with a large-caliber revolver, you know what I mean. They wanted me to keep it up, but Fran pulled me out of it, whispering, "Harry, let's get out of here. I don't like it."

She sensed that they were hostile, angry because a kid did something none of them could do, and she was afraid it would grow into something worse than these state cops saying that I was a vaudeville performer or some other kind of phony stage shooter. But that didn't explain to me how or why I was able to do what I did, and this was a gift that had stayed with me. At pistol practice and in competition, I went

232

through the forms and motions, the formal stance, the slight crouch, the two-hand hold—but all of that was to keep the others from regarding me as some kind of freak. I have since read of others who had that particular nasty gift, certain characters in the old West and some others too, and as I said, it was the only part of my uniform that I felt was valid.

The uniform was not. I was no worshiper of uniforms, but the men who wore that cumbersome blue uniform had stood on the edge of civilization for a long time now, and if some of them were not very nice people, I had often wondered what this city would be without them. The cops don't fashion the system and the cops don't make criminals. The system makes the criminal, and then the cop is called in to put his life on the line, and if some of them are on the pad, it's just amazing how few they are.

So after I had studied myself in the uniform and taken appropriate satisfaction in the fact that it had never been let out and still fit, even though a bit tight around the belly, I took it off and hung it back in the closet. My gray suit would do, and if I came out of it alive and not busted as a murderer, I would prefer that the job be laid on a civilian, not a cop—the job being the assassination of Alfred Gomez Porfetto. I knew all of the arguments against this kind of thing, because I had lived a long time with those arguments. I hate terrorism and I despise assassins. I once wrote a letter to the *Times* about the possibility of a New York police force without guns, but I didn't have enough courage to sign the letter with my own name because I was afraid the men I work with would have eaten me alive. I guess that's why the *Times* didn't print it. And now I was working out in my mind the assassination of Porfetto.

Well, circumstances change, as I would tell my wife. It was no longer a question of why with me. It was something I had to do, and even the working out of the coming event was not so complex that I had to brood about it.

I finished dressing, and I put the .22 pistol into my belt holster where I had carried my service revolver. Then I listened to the morning news and to all the speculation about my suspension. On Channel 4, there was a short interview with Porfetto, the first, as the interviewer pointed out, on national television. I suppose that there were ample reasons why Porfetto had decided to come out of the closet, and his support of the coming Los Angeles Olympic games had created an excellent moment. As near as I can recall, the interview went like this:

Question: "Does the expansion and growth of the Hispanic population of the United States impel you to agree with those who say their education should be in Spanish?"

Answer: "Absolutely not. They are not Hispanics. I dislike the word. They are Americans."

Score for Porfetto.

Question: "And your interest in the Olympics, Mr. Porfetto. It is said that you have given more financial support to the Olympics than any other American. Do the Olympic Games occupy some special part of your heart?"

Answer: "Absolutely. What a wonderful thing it would be if we could replace war between nations with athletic games! How many lives would be saved!"

He looked benign as he offered this blessing. He was a handsome, well-tanned man with the look of a younger Ronald Reagan, except that unlike our President, he had allowed his hair to go gray over the temples. His voice was low and modulated. I felt a cold shiver come over me as I returned from the spell of the idiot box to the dismal reality of the tiny hotel room, and realized that this was the man I intended to kill a few hours from now.

I went down to the hotel dining room for breakfast, a small place that was half dining room and half coffee shop, and Bill Hoffman came and sat down across the table from me, and he mentioned that Fran had left, half as a question, but intimating the need for some explanation. He had never asked for an explanation before, but now he said, "It's just that she's such a hell of a lady, and I know it's none of my business, but I hope to God you haven't broken up, because I know that can happen."

"Oh, no. No, Bill. I don't think we'd ever break up. My kids are in Ireland. She went there to be with them for a few days. And by the way, neither of us will ever forget what you did for us."

"Nothing. My God, what did I do? I run a hotel and you

came here. So I kept my mouth shut. I see the TV, like anybody else. But if I can't trust a guy like you—I give up."

"Thanks. I'm checking out today, Bill. I'd like to leave my bag in your storage room until tomorrow, though. I'll give you a check."

"No hurry."

"And one day soon, I'll put it all together for you."

"I'd like that."

After I had paid up and written a check that approached the bottom line in our checkbook, I went back up to my room and wrote a letter to Fran:

My darling wife, I want to say first that I never doubted your assertion that you came from the blood of kings, or as Sean used to put it, in the old days, from a long line of poets and singers. Truly, I never recovered from the fact that you were willing to spend your life with me, and I saw no other woman as long as I could be with you. Well, that's how I began it, and I had written those couple of sentences when I realized I had fallen prey to the Irish compulsion to make something like this a barroom deathbed statement. It rubbed off, and when the emotion reached a certain height, there you were up on the walls of Tara. Not being Irish, I tried again and wrote: *My darling Fran. I did the only thing I knew how to do. I love you with all my heart and soul. And don't be too hard on me when you explain it to the kids.* That was better, and it laid on her a proper degree of Jewish guilt.

I gave the letter to Bill Hoffman, telling him that unless I happened to become dead in the next few days, he was to tear it to shreds after forty-eight hours. If I died, he was to hand it to Fran. But in all truth, I had no intention of dying.

It was a nice day outside. It was a nice day to live. I walked uptown to the library at 42nd and Fifth, where life on the wide steps is a better harbinger of spring than any weather service. There were two black men playing on iron bowl instruments and there was a mime imitating Mayor Koch, and there were three ballet dancers in froufrou costumes dancing on their toes without music. There were also three artists willing to do a charcoal-drawing portrait for five dollars, and I watched them for a while. They were very good indeed.

Then, right there, I ran into Swifty Goldberg, who is just about the finest pickpocket in all the five boroughs. Swifty is a small, elegant man, fastidious in his dress and manner, with the kind of poise and assurance that will admit him almost anywhere. He never works crowds and he would scorn to lift anything in a crowded subway where poor working people are packed in like sardines. His specialty is the convention, and he does very well except on those occasions when he is busted. Now he, like myself, was enjoying the spring air, and his convivial greeting must have been due to the fact that now I was a civilian.

"Nevertheless," Swifty said, "my heart goes out to you."

I thanked him and asked him how it was that at the edge of noon, when he should have been working any one of the half-dozen conventions in town, he could take the time to lounge around here on the steps of the New York Public Library and take in the entertainment as well as the spring air.

"All work and no play makes Jack a dull boy."

"True. But I had always imagined your work to be in the high-class area."

"True enough, Lieutenant. But I have antenna. You have to have antennas to survive in this jungle, and it's nervous time. The word is out."

"About what?"

"Ah-hah! That's just it. Something very large is coming down, a very big fuzz operation, and when that happens, all the fuzz get spooked and they can grab you and bust your ass for no reason at all. My word, Lieutenant, if it hadn't been for all your grief—I mean if you were still a gainfully employed cop—I would not be talking to you, because you might bust me for no reason at all. You ever hear of that dry desert wind they got out on the Coast? They call it the Santa Ana, and when it blows everyone gets as jumpy as a dog in heat. Well, it's blowing here now, and I'd just as soon have a few quiet days."

I got very impatient at that point, and I asked what the devil he was talking about and how did he know?

"It's in the air."

"Don't give me that bullshit about something being in the air. What's up?"

"I don't know what's up. All I know is that it's in the air. If you had antennas, you'd feel it. Cops don't have antenna —and I'm not trying to offend you, Lieutenant. They'll give you back your badge some day, and then you'll be on my ass. So I'd just like to have it cool between us. Okay?"

"Okay, Swifty."

He drifted away, and I wandered around the corner and into Bryant Park, where the coke dealers scattered like pigeons. Why I look like a cop, I don't know, but it's there.

But I was no longer in that line of work, so I drifted slowly over to Seventh Avenue and uptown, and it was lunchtime when I arrived at the Seventh Avenue Delicatessen. Since Fran had gone, I had become indifferent as to whether I was followed or not, and the Seventh Avenue Delicatessen was no place for me to seek for nonrecognition. Max Cronich, the top sandwich man, had served his apprenticeship at the old Sixth Avenue Delicatessen in the legendary days of corned beef and pastrami, and when that eatery beyond peer had closed down, he brought the art of sandwich making to the Madison Avenue Delicatessen, and from there he went to Seventh Avenue. As disciples follow a prophet, so did a great many of us follow Max, and today I went to the counter and ordered personally, instead of allowing a waiter to convey my desire secondhand. To a degree, I thought of it as the condemned man's last supper.

"I want hot pastrami," I told Max. "Don't cut off the fat. I want it fat and delicious."

"You got it, Lieutenant," Max said, "but they're all talking about a nice fat slice of pastrami like it's a death wish."

"So I got a death wish."

"I been reading. What did you do?"

"No politics. Thin rye and give me some extra pickles."

I took it to a table and ordered a bottle of beer. A large, overweight Italian, whom I remembered seeing around and who was in the bookmaking business, came over to my table and introduced himself as Loui Abentzi. "I'm Joey Finelli's cousin, he should rest in peace, only he never had anything

237

much to do with me because he seemed to think I wasn't honest. I don't hold that against him. Can I sit down?"

"Sure."

He eased his huge bulk into the chair and said, "He was a cop, and he was sore as hell there was a bum like me in the family. But now he's gone and we all try to help poor Paula, and she tells me that according to Joey, you're the best. All right, they bumped you, but I got something to pass on. There's a councilman I won't name who's close to the boys down at Police Plaza, and someone else I can't name hears him say they got to get rid of that pain in the ass Golding and that they should send him to Bermuda for a vacation or something."

"Someone with no name says something to someone with no name—who told you to come to me with that kind of bullshit?"

"Nobody tells me. I didn't even know you'd be here."

"Who told you to peddle that crap to me?"

Abentzi stood up. "I try to do you a favor—well, fuck you." He said it softly but intensely, and then he turned around and walked out, and I realized that he was absolutely right and that no one could have known that I would be there, and I had behaved like a horse's ass.

I sat and looked at a beautiful hot pastrami sandwich that I could not touch. My appetite fled. The very thought of food disgusted me, and my last supper was a washout. I paid the check and bought an oversize chocolate bar, which I munched as I drifted along the street. It was twenty minutes to two. A day can be as long as an eternity if you have to spend it on the streets, and at this moment, there was no place I could light without some complication that might end my existence—or at least my purpose for the day. Moving east, I paused at the Plaza Hotel, where I made use of the men's room. I'm not an urgent drinker, but it would have done my heart good to sit down in the bar and dream my way through a couple of bottles of good Pilsen beer. I didn't dare. When I used the gun in my pocket, it would have to be used with precision, and even a drop of liquor doesn't help that.

From the Plaza, I walked to Third Avenue, where I remembered that Fran and I had been trying to find a free evening to see *Terms of Endearment,* the film everyone was talking about at the moment, and which, according to our friends, promised a good cry. I decided that Fran would have to see it herself, and it killed the next two hours very nicely, even if I didn't cry. I suppose I had more important things to cry about. When I got out of the theater, I crossed Third Avenue and spent the next forty-five minutes or so in Bloomingdale's. I did a dumb, sentimental thing, and I didn't realize how dumb and sentimental it was until after it happened. Fran had been talking about needing a new purse, so I bought her one, putting it on my charge card, and having it sent to our apartment. And then I thought about the purse being delivered, and myself in jail or dead, and I had to walk back the length of the store to cancel the sale.

I decided that it was time to start downtown and get on with what I intended to do, but when I got to the Waldorf, it was still only six o'clock, and according to information in the lobby, the dinner which would honor Mr. Porfetto was scheduled for seven-thirty.

I bought a copy of the late edition of the *New York Post* and took myself down to the Waldorf coffee shop on the Lexington Avenue side. I discovered that I was hungry, having eaten almost nothing all day; and I ordered a club sandwich and coffee, thinking regretfully of the bottle of beer I had left untouched at the Seventh Avenue Delicatessen and the two bottles unpurchased at the Plaza. According to the *New York Post,* an active search was being conducted for Lieutenant Harry Golding, who had apparently disappeared the previous day. The last word from him was an incoherent telephone call to the district attorney's office, and as of today it was not known whether he was a victim of foul play or had disappeared rather than face the charges that had led to his suspension. It made interesting reading, especially as the *Post* went on to describe the curious and absolutely unexplained disappearance of Golding's wife and son and daughter. They concluded that it added up to one of the most interesting mysteries of the season, and they wondered whether it connected in any way with the murder of Lieutenant Joseph Finelli, who was known to be an old associate and good friend of Lieutenant Golding.

It was also a lesson in the likelihood of finding a person who did not choose to be found—in a place like New York City. They printed a photograph of me, but that hadn't helped during this day when I was drifting homeless around the city.

Six forty-five. I paid my check and walked over to 50th Street and turned left toward Park Avenue. The motor entrance to the Waldorf is on 50th Street, between Park Avenue and Lexington Avenue, and since Park Avenue buildings built over the train yards have no proper basements, the motor entrance was on a level with the street. It was just possible that Porfetto had already arrived, but not likely. These affairs had a sort of built-in formality, and if the time called for was seven-thirty, Porfetto would arrive a few minutes before or after that time, most likely after. I took up a position across the street. There was a broad walk beside the auto passage, about ten feet between the curb where the cars drew up and the doors leading into the hotel, and it was very well lit, allowing me to see clearly what took place.

At five minutes after seven, Toomey drove into the auto entrance. He was still driving my car, and with him were Keene, Hennesy, and Bolansky. They were met by another man who was probably one of the hotel security staff, and for a few minutes they huddled and talked. The security man made some motions toward doors, and then he shook hands with Toomey and left, going back into the hotel. Then Toomey spoke to the bell captain, who appeared to be in charge of the arrivals and departures. It was well past checkout time, so there was a very small parade of incoming and outgoing guests. This business of loading and unloading taxicabs took place beyond where the four detectives had stationed themselves.

It was twenty-minutes after seven when a stretch limousine Mercedes, one of those incredibly long, pale gray cars, came east on 50th and turned slowly into the car entrance. As it turned, I spotted a Wabash sticker, a small silver thing on the rear bumper, and I was across the street at the same moment that the Mercedes came to a stop.

What happened now happened more quickly than I can tell it, and it happened in what you might call a lump of incident which I must take apart and spell out. The Mercedes came to a stop as I entered the motor arcade. The near set of doors to the hotel elevators were up a step, which I took, placing myself a bit higher than the others and giving me a clear target. A man opened the front near door of the Mercedes and stepped around to open the back door, and I recognized him as the man who had chased me down that street where the kids' school had saved my life, the man with the cannon-like automatic, and as it turned out, the man who'd killed Finelli. The four detectives were watching the car. The man from the front seat opened the door of the car and Porfetto stepped out. A woman came out of the hotel entrance, moving past me and trailing a fragrance somehow familiar, and at that moment my gun was in my hand. But the woman blocked my shot by moving directly to Porfetto, exclaiming, "Alfred, how wonderful to see you!" The thug who had shot at me on the school street moved to block her way, but she was too quick for him. She darted past Toomey and embraced Porfetto with her left hand. He tried to pull away, but she was a tall, powerful woman, and she was firing a gun into his stomach simultaneously with her clutch. Toomey dived to grab her and Porfetto's man pulled out the huge automatic that he had used on me. Toomey would have caught the shot that was intended to kill the woman, but even as his gun came out, I flung a shot in the only place where it might be effective, into his hand which held the gun. He let out a roar of pain and I fired again, a shot that, as it turned out, smashed three bones in his wrist. As I told Fran afterward, it was the kind of shooting people write poems about, but no poems were written for me. And then Keene and Bolansky had him, and Hennesy was hanging on to the woman, and Toomey was shouting to the bell captain to get an ambulance.

From the moment Porfetto stepped out of the Mercedes to the moment he slid to the ground with two bullets in his heart and a third in his spine and his hired gun whimpering over a shattered hand and wrist, no more than a few seconds had elapsed, and at the end of those few seconds two people saw and recognized me, face-to-face. One was Toomey and the other was Deborah Alan, the woman who had just killed Porfetto, and lying on the ground, next to Toomey's foot, was the gun she had used and which he had not yet picked up. It was the .22-caliber purse gun, which I had bought for Fran. Too many things were happening at once, and after that brief glance and flicker of recognition, Toomey was shouting at the bell captain, and in that moment, I took three steps, picked up the purse gun, turned and walked out of the motor entrance. No one stopped me. It was still less than thirty seconds since it began. But everyone else was drawn to the dead man and the wounded man, whose shattered wrist was pouring blood. Their attention was totally focused at the heart of the drama, at the tall, beautiful woman who had committed the crime. No one noticed me as I picked up the purse gun or as I left.

Chapter 16

I WALKED EAST, toward the river. Two police cars raced by me as I walked. A very decent response, a matter of minutes. We were a very good police force, but if a man wants to kill someone, it's almost impossible to stop him, and I would guess that with a woman, it's even closer to impossible. And with Fran's gun. The last time I saw the little pistol, she was putting it in her purse. How did Deborah Alan come by it?

Well, all things in their time. I had two pistols in my raincoat pocket. One of them had just killed a man—although at that moment I had no way of knowing whether or not Porfetto was dead; the other gun had just smashed a man's hand and wrist beyond repair. A pocketful of trouble. I was full of elusive and scrambled thoughts as I walked toward the river. Could I have killed Porfetto, or were my two days of mental preparation an empty and fraudulent exercise? He was hatless as he bent to step out of the Mercedes, and from my position, I had a clear view of his head. I could have put two bullets into his head and still shot the gun out of the professional's hand, but there was no unraveling those few seconds. Memory doesn't work that way, and instead of being able to think back and recall what had happened in that almost instantaneous blur of action, I had to

243

piece it together and feed it into my mind. And I kept thinking that this remarkable woman had saved, if not my life, certainly my peace of mind for however long I might live. I still could not deal with a death at my hands, as strange as that might sound coming from a policeman.

Standing at the rail of the walk, with the oily surface of the East River in front of me, a rippling black blanket touched with the dancing lights of the city, I threw the two guns into the river. I was now unarmed for the first time in seventeen years—and I felt a strange sensation of light-headedness and relief. It was over. Let happen what would happen; it was over.

I walked all the distance uptown to my apartment, slowly, just ambling along with that feeling of fatigue that a man might have after a good day's work. It gave me a chance to think. If Porfetto was dead, they could not proceed against Deborah Alan. She was certain to have managed some sort of diplomatic status, which would give her immunity. As for the gun, Fran must have gone to Oscar's apartment without telling me. Well, the answers could wait. I was very tired.

Why my antennas had folded, why I had no more fear of execution, I don't know. But that was the way it was, and I turned the key in the door of my apartment and walked in with no apprehension. The apartment was empty. It was filthy, with slops of uneaten sandwiches and cold containers of coffee all over the living room. The bathrooms were used and dirty and the beds had been slept on. I called down to Fred Jones and asked him to come up, and while waiting for him, I went over the place, tearing out the bugs, the fancy and expensive listening and radio devices planted there. Somehow, with Porfetto dead or at least shot to pieces, the whole thing took on the aspect of some lunatic comic opera.

When Jones appeared, I gave him ten dollars, and together we cleaned up the place and changed the linen on the bed and scrubbed out the bathrooms.

"Some mighty funny things happening around here, Lieutenant," he said.

"That's one way of putting it."

"Going to be quiet now a while?"

"I hope so."

He left, and I drew a hot bath and sat in the water until my skin began to crinkle. Then I put on pajamas and a robe and stretched out on the couch and turned on the TV. It was almost time for the eleven o'clock news.

And there it was, the network gloating over what it termed "the most bizarre and inexplicable murder case of the year." They showed the motor entrance to the Waldorf, swarming with plainclothes and uniform cops, Mayor Koch and Chief of Detectives Crown in attendance; but, curiously enough, neither of them willing to make any comment or statement whatsoever. Inspector Max Roberts fended questions without answering any of them. He was a tall, skinny man, with a habit of raising his hands in a gesture of surrender. They wanted to know whether the cops had a motive for Mrs. Alan's action, and was she being charged with the crime, and what was all this about a disappearing gun? And who was responsible for shooting Percy Lax? Some enterprising reporter had called crime analysis, downtown at Police Plaza and had come up with information on Percy Lax before the cops could put a lid on it, and what crime analysis pulled out of their computers was a want on Lax that stretched halfway around the world, eighteen assassinations attributed to him, a connection with the PLO—and what, the media wondered, was he doing in Alfred Gomez Porfetto's pale gray Mercedes? Inspector Roberts had no comment on this or any other questions, or where Deborah Alan was being held, or where Lax was being held.

"There will be a statement forthcoming," Roberts pleaded.

But what fascinated and puzzled me most about television's coverage of this strange incident was the absence of platitudes. Here was this benefactor and philanthropist cruelly shot to death by an apparently crazed Israeli woman, and no one was telling the people what a loss this was, what a noble man had been done in. Quite to the contrary, every voice was exceedingly tentative. I know that word gets out, that no real lid can be put on anything, but still and all, it was odd.

I fell asleep in front of the television. It spewed out its mindless chatter through the night, but I slept the sleep of the dead, and it was not until nine o'clock the following morning that I was awakened by the telephone. It was Lieutenant Frawley, who was one of Chief of Detectives Crown's assistants down at Police Plaza, and he said to me, with no attempt to be even moderately polite about it, "Golding, this is Frawley at the chief's office, and he wants to see you at eleven o'clock, and you'd better get your ass down here or else."

We had evidently reached a point where nobody liked or respected Harry Golding. I shaved, put on a clean shirt, put on my striped blue and white Columbia tie, which Fran had given me as a birthday gift, and then walked over to the station house. Sergeant Laurenti was at the desk, and he looked at me thoughtfully but said nothing.

"The keys to my car," I said.

"In the ignition, outside."

"I thought I gave orders that the next time someone left the keys in the ignition, he'd get his ass reamed."

"Yes, Lieutenant. You'd better talk to Sergeant Toomey. He's upstairs."

I left the house without replying, thinking that I should be grateful that he still addressed me with some measure of respect. It's more than I can say about the chief of detectives. I was ushered into his office down at Police Plaza by Frawley, who closed the door behind me and left me standing and facing Crown, the chief of detectives, Thomas Kelley, the commissioner of police, Inspector Roberts, the zone commander, and the district attorney to complete the jury of humorless faces. No one asked me to sit down, so I simply stood and waited, calling myself all sorts of a damn fool for not asking Toomey what he had said. I had faith in Toomey, but at this moment faith did not appear to be enough.

"Lieutenant," Chief Crown said, "for the past two weeks, you have been an extraordinary pain in the ass. Your goddamn egotistical assumption that only you in this city knew the facts about Porfetto and his Wabash Protection agency almost fouled up a complex operation that we have been preparing for months. This morning, we took forty-three employees of Wabash into custody and closed up their operation. An hour ago, Captain Hallihan over at the West Side put his pistol in his mouth and blew out his brains, and right now the Massachusetts and Connecticut State Police are closing every branch of Listerman-Reed. This operation was scheduled to begin a week from now. We had to advance it and put it into play last night, right after Porfetto's death—"

Porfetto was dead, and the whole fabric had begun to crumble.

"—as a result of your goddamn penchant for doing alone what a police force was set up to do. Now what we want to know is this. Why did Deborah Alan kill him? And why did you set it up?"

Still, no one invited me to sit down. They simply sat in grim silence and waited.

"I didn't set it up," I said. "As for Mrs. Alan, I presume she killed Porfetto because Porfetto killed her husband, and since I was able to discover that fact, I presume that Israeli Intelligence was also able to dig it out, and that she learned about it and decided to rectify the matter."

"Porfetto killed her husband?" Crown said. "Would you like to tell us about that? Suppose you make a statement and we'll tape it."

"No. I'm not making any statement for tape. I'm not under arrest, and I'm goddamn egotistical enough, as you put it, Chief, to take pleasure in telling you. So if you want me to tell you, I will."

Crown looked at Kelley, who made no motion, and then at the district attorney, who nodded. The commissioner said, "Let him tell it."

I told it—the whole story, leaving nothing out of any importance until I came to the details of last night.

"That's your story?" Crown said.

"Yes, sir. I gave it to you over the phone. You know that. Now you have it again."

"We'll come back to it. Perhaps not today, but we'll come back to it. Meanwhile, you have two pistols registered in your name. One is a high-powered twenty-two special, firing special long bullets. The same bullets smashed Lax's hand and wrist. The other gun registered to you is a purse gun, also twenty-two caliber. Porfetto was killed by a small twenty-two caliber pistol. I trust you brought both guns with you."

"No, sir."

"An oversight?"

"No, sir. As I told you, my apartment was taken over by Wabash. I have ample evidence of that. In the course of that takeover, my two pistols were stolen."

"Stolen?"

Roberts grinned. The district attorney shook his head.

"And of course you reported the theft to your captain or to Inspector Roberts here?"

"No, sir. As I said before, my apartment was occupied and the first occasion I had to search for the guns was late last night, when, after hearing about Porfetto, I felt it was safe to return to my apartment. I am reporting the theft now to Inspector Roberts, my zone commander."

Kelley laughed sourly, and Crown said, "Oh, you are a lulu, Golding. You are a beauty indeed."

The district attorney said softly, "Golding, I've been studying your record, particularly your marksmanship scores. You rate highest in your zone and probably highest in the department. You are what we call an instinct shot, a man who doesn't have to aim. Very few of those. And according to the statements of Sergeants Toomey and Keene, that was the kind of shooting that happened last night. As nearly as we could piece it together, if you had shot to kill Lax, his gun would have gone off and at that close range, he couldn't miss. So you did save Sergeant Toomey's life. On the other hand, you and Mrs. Alan participated in a conspiracy to kill Porfetto."

"No, sir. I have not been in communication with Mrs. Alan, either directly or indirectly, since her first visit here before her husband died."

"You took the purse gun after she had used it. Do you also deny that?"

"I was not anywhere near the Waldorf last night, so I must deny that too."

"Golding," the chief of detectives said, "suppose Toomey or Keene or Hennesy or Bolansky put you there at the motor entrance last night?"

248

He smiled thinly and I smiled back.

"That would make it difficult for me, wouldn't it, sir? They're good, honorable men. We've worked together for years. They trust me. I trust them. A working cop puts his life in the hands of the men who back him up. I suppose that's the way it has to be."

There was a long moment of silence, and then Crown said, "That's it, Golding. You'll hear from us."

My hand was on the door when the district attorney said, "Golding!"

"Yes, sir?" I turned around.

"Golding, did you fake that Vermeer theft?"

"No, sir. I did not."

"No, I kind of thought you didn't."

I had one more bit of business at the station house. Nothing I had read or heard on television mentioned the name of Captain Courtny. I drove to the station house, double-parked as usual, and then went up to the detective room. Toomey and Keene were both there. Bolansky and Hennesy were out. I shook hands with Toomey and Keene. They asked me how it was going, and I answered that it was going well enough; but neither of them said one word about the previous night.

I went into the captain's office. He was filling in a form, his cigar in his mouth, his lined, unhappy face as lined and unhappy as ever. He looked up at me without enthusiasm.

"The night I went to my apartment with Toomey and Keene, and you were so pissed off about it," I said without preamble. "That night, someone called the apartment and those shitheads from Wabash who were in there cleared out minutes before we got there. You were the only one who knew where we were going."

"So?"

"You called my apartment."

"That's right. If you had had enough brains to tell me what you expected to find there, I might not have called. I called to tell you—" He paused and took the cigar out of his mouth. "I called," he said uncomfortably, "to try to say something nice. I got respect for you, Harry. I saw what was coming down. I wanted to tell you that maybe we should

249

work closer, trust each other more. I could help you. I knew you were in some god-awful piece of trouble. Who the hell made the California trip possible! I thought it would help. But no, sir. You wouldn't have it. You had to be a goddamn Lone Ranger and I had to be stupid enough to ask were you there yet. Oh, shit. It's over."

He held out his hand, and I took it. His grip was bone-crushing. "Harry," he said, "I know you're in deep and they're after your scalp. But if it comes out clean, I'm going to yell my damn head off for you to get the zone commander job."

I thanked him. But I knew it would never come out clean again. The net was much too tangled.

Chapter 17

THEY DROPPED the Vermeer charges and they never got to a point where they could indict me on the killing of Porfetto. They had no evidence. The guns were gone forever and they had no valid witness to put me at the Waldorf motor entrance that night. Percy Lax made a statement that he had recognized me, but since his gun fired the bullet that killed Joe Finelli, and he had been tried for murder and convicted, his word as a witness was not enough even for a preliminary before the grand jury. Nevertheless, I was finished as a cop in the city of New York. The D.A. and the commissioner and the chief of detectives all were convinced that I had been there and planned the whole thing, and nothing would ever unconvince them. Charley Murphy took my case against the department, and finally it was settled for me to resign honorably with a fifteen-year-and-better pension, no great gift but enough for Fran and me to live decently, so long as she held her job at Columbia. I have been occupied with writing this account and Fran has been on it as well, trying to make what I write read like appropriate English—or as close to that as possible.

Fran and the kids came back from Ireland and England exactly a week after Porfetto's demise. Two Wabash operatives had been arrested in Dublin by the local police. It was astonishing to me to see how powerless these men became. I had looked upon them as incarnations of the devil, but deprived of their protection, they quickly turned into sniveling defendants.

The full story of Porfetto never actually emerged. The rumor all over the place was that Deborah Alan was in cahoots with the CIA, and that Porfetto had been killed to close his mouth about connections with the White House and the Pentagon; but that was the kind of nonsense that always arises in a case of this kind.

My brother Oscar says that Deborah Alan had intimated that Israeli Intelligence had discovered Porfetto's role in Asher Alan's death, but also I recalled that Fran and Shelly let drop a good deal of what I thought and that might have helped her to put things together.

In any case, Deborah was not prosecuted but ordered to return to Israel. There a hearing took place, but she testified behind closed doors and the testimony was not released.

Gavin and Sarah returned to school with stories about their flight to Ireland and England that gave them a lot of class in the eyes of their peers. Fran went back to Columbia, and spring came, late and very wet, but here at last.

I have control. I didn't ask Fran about the gun until weeks later, when things had settled down. We were walking in Central Park, and I said, apropos of nothing at all, "I keep wondering how Deborah Alan managed to have your gun in her hand when she shot Porfetto."

"Oh? It was my gun?"

"It was, yes."

"How is it you never asked me about that before?"

"I thought some snoopy cops from downtown might come around and ask you questions. I didn't want you to lie."

"But the gun disappeared. That's what I read in all the papers. That was the great mystery of the event. What happened to the gun?"

"I can't tell you that."

"You mean you don't want to," Fran said.

"Perhaps."

"I suppose you slipped it into your pocket after you shot that monster Percy Lax."

"I never told you I shot Percy Lax."

"No, you didn't."

"But it was your gun."

"I suppose so. You know, Harry, I couldn't sit in that wretched little room in the Primrose Hotel all day. I would have gone crazy. So I took a walk and dropped into Altman's to buy some stockings, and there was Deborah buying stockings, and we had lunch together. She told me how frightened New York made her—"

"That woman? Frightened?"

"Harry, I wasn't thinking that way. I could only think that this was the city where her husband had died and she had every right to be frightened. She asked me where she could buy a gun, because she was in the army at home and she knew how to use a gun—"

"And you gave her yours."

"Of course. It was no use to me. I couldn't shoot anything."

We walked on in silence for a while, and then Fran wondered whether I should have another gun. "Since it's plain enough," she said, "that you walked over to the river and pitched both guns in."

"Did I?"

"I think so."

"No," I said. "I'm not a cop. I don't need a gun."

"Is it awful, Harry—not being a cop anymore?"

"No, I don't think so. There was a time when it was right. But times change."

"They do," she agreed.

We held hands and walked on through the park. It's pretty nice to walk in Central Park in the springtime with a woman you love.

Q: *Who wears a Smith & Wesson in his holster and his heart on his sleeve?*

A:

SPENSER
by Robert B. Parker

He's a sassy, sensitive private eye whom *Penthouse* calls "splendidly original...and never less than irresistible." Let him charm *you*—he's a master at it.

____	THE GODWULF MANUSCRIPT	12961-3-29	$3.50
____	GOD SAVE THE CHILD	12899-4-34	3.50
____	MORTAL STAKES	15758-7-29	3.50
____	PROMISED LAND	17197-0-24	3.50
____	THE JUDAS GOAT	14196-6-22	3.50
____	LOOKING FOR RACHEL WALLACE	15316-6-32	3.50
____	EARLY AUTUMN	12214-7-32	3.50
____	A SAVAGE PLACE	18095-3-25	3.50
____	CEREMONY	10993-0-25	3.50
____	VALEDICTION	19247-1-12	3.50
____	THE WIDENING GYRE	19535-7-21	3.50
____	A CATSKILL EAGLE	11132-3-25	3.95

____**YES**, please enter my order and also send me future information on other Dell Mystery paperbacks.

____**NO**, I'm not ordering now but am interested in future information on other Dell Mystery paperbacks.

 At your local bookstore or use this handy coupon for ordering:

**DELL READERS SERVICE—DEPT. B1324A
6 REGENT ST., LIVINGSTON, N.J. 07039**

Please send me the above title(s) I am enclosing $ _____ (please add 75¢ per copy to cover postage and handling) Send check or money order—no cash or CODs Please allow 3-4 weeks for shipment

Ms./Mrs./Mr _____

Address _____

City/State _____ Zip _____

Match wits with Richard Jury of Scotland Yard. And solve these cunning murders by

___	The Anodyne Necklace	10280-4	$3.50
___	The Deer Leap......	11938-3	3.50
___	The Dirty Duck......	12050-0	3.50
___	The Man With A Load Of Mischief.........	15327-1	3.50
___	The Old Fox Deceiv'd	16747-7	3.50
___	Jerusalem Inn.......	14181-8	3.50